BACK ON TOP

Also by Angela Winters

View Park

Never Enough

No More Good

A Price to Pay

Gone Too Far

Published by Dafina Books

BACK ON TOP

ANGELA WINTERS

Dafina
Books

KENSINGTON BOOKS
http://www.kensingtonbooks.com

DAFINA BOOKS are published by

Kensington Publishing Corp.
119 West 40th Street
New York, NY 10018

All Kensington Titles, Imprints, and Distributed Lines are available at special quantity discounts for bulk purchases for sales promotions, premiums, fundraising, and educational or institutional use.

Special book excerpts or customized printings can also be created to fit specific needs. For details, write or phone the office of the Kensington special sales manager: Kensington Publishing Corp., 119 West 40th Street, New York, NY 10018, attn: Special Sales Department, Phone: 1-800-221-2647.

Dafina and the Dafina logo Reg. U.S. Pat & TM Off.

ISBN-13: 978-0-7582-5933-2
ISBN-10: 0-7582-5933-6

First Printing: August 2011

10 9 8 7 6 5 4 3 2 1

Printed in the United States of America

This book is dedicated to my late father.
Daddy, I love you and I miss you every day.

1

Sherise Robinson couldn't believe she had let herself run behind today of all days. Her first day back at work from maternity leave and she was going to show up late if she didn't speed things up. That was not the message she wanted to send.

As she rushed around the master bedroom of her elegant Georgetown town house in Washington DC's Northwest side, Sherise felt panic start to set in. A lot was riding on how today went, no matter how much her husband, Justin, tried to tell her otherwise. The power-hungry, manipulative bitch, as her coworkers had secretly named her, was coming back, and if she showed any signs of softening, weakening, she was dead. The barracuda was now a mama and she could just imagine what they were all thinking: She's vulnerable.

As she stopped to look in the full-length mirror that covered her walk-in closet door, her confidence was lifted. She was going to show them they were wrong. Finally she found her missing Missoni stacked pumps and her outfit was complete. She looked sharp and sexy, and at twenty-seven, Sherise felt certain she showed no signs of having given birth six months ago. That was thanks to very expensive underwear that tucked everything in, but also to the fact that she made sure not to gain more than the twenty-five pounds her doctor told her was the minimum amount healthy during her pregnancy. While there was still a stubborn pound or two hanging around, everything was tightening up nicely.

From head to toe, Sherise checked every inch. Her shoulder-length hair, just done yesterday, was styled nicely in a sharp "don't fuck with me" bun with just a few "I might be flirting with you" dark brown tendrils falling down. She liked to keep the men confused. It gave her an advantage and Sherise was all about getting the advantage. Her makeup was flawless, highlighting her high cheekbones and dark green eyes. It was spring, so her lipstick was a soft, flirtatious pink. Her golden caramel skin was glowing and it would wow when she took off the jacket of her black and white striped Nipon wide-legged pantsuit to reveal her white sleeveless Marc Jacobs business shirt. No one who saw her at the Executive Office Building today would forget.

"I'm back," she said in that sexy, raspy voice of hers. "Bitches better step aside."

"You're late," were the first words Justin Robinson said to his wife only seconds later as she entered the contemporary European-style kitchen.

"I'm fine," Sherise answered as she rushed for the refrigerator. "I'm taking a cab."

"Ah! Ah!"

Sherise quickly closed the refrigerator door and rushed over to the little monster emitting those sounds. Her six-month-old baby girl, Cady, was the love of her life. She sat in her baby chair, her hands reaching out for her mommy with evidence of her breakfast all over her face, not to mention her bib. She was an adorable baby with soft, chocolate skin, nice and chunky with fat cheeks that Sherise couldn't get enough of.

"Sorry, baby!" Sherise leaned in for a quick kiss, but didn't trust herself for more. She knew leaving Cady today would be hard enough. "Mama has to go."

"You should eat something." Justin put down the baby spoon and leaned back in his chair. He was looking at his wife with concern. "You don't want to go in there without your fuel."

"I'm grabbing something on the way." Sherise appreciated her husband's concern, but there was a part of her that was still a little angry with him for trying to pressure her to stay home for good.

Justin, thirty, was old fashioned and his upbringing had been very different from hers. Because Sherise grew up poor as dirt on the hard streets in Southeast DC with no father to be found and a mother who couldn't give a damn, she only knew how to fight. Justin was a lover, not a fighter. From Chicago, he grew up in a traditional middle-class black family with a stay-at-home mother, a doctor for a father, and all the safety cushions that came with such an upbringing. He was stable and reliable and represented what Sherise wanted to be, which was why she decided the night she met him four years ago, when he was just a recent Georgetown Law grad, that she wanted to marry him. A reliable wage earner who was hot enough to be attractive, but not so hot that every other woman would want him too. He was the kind of guy who would come home every night. Most of all, Justin, a six-figure lobbyist on Capitol Hill, had the connections that Sherise's never-ending ambition could use to get ahead.

But Justin put a wrench in her ambitious game when he suggested Sherise be a stay-at-home mom after Cady was born. They had at first agreed to a regular twelve-week maternity leave, knowing that Sherise had plans of moving beyond her position as assistant director of communications for the White House's Domestic Policy Council. She was hungry for power and her ultimate dream was to make it from the Executive Office Building across the street to the West Wing of the White House. After endless fighting, Sherise went the route that had always served her well—refusing affection until she got her way. While she loved Justin, he did not overwhelm her, which made him a good husband candidate for her. She could control the way her body reacted to him, thus control the power he had over her.

It wasn't as if he wasn't attractive. He was six feet tall and, while he had an extra ten pounds, he wore it well. He was a sexy dark brown with beautiful light brown eyes and a sturdy face. He wore preppie boardroom glasses that made him look distinguished and was always looking sharp in his expensive business suits. The point was, while she found him perfect husband and father material, Justin had never gotten Sherise to lose control of herself. She could resist him, but he couldn't resist her. She played her games and made certain he couldn't resist, which resulted in a quick marriage proposal. This control over him was why her compromise of a six-month leave was quickly accepted and rewarded with access to affection again.

Sherise felt a pull in her gut as Cady called for her again, but she fought it and went to check her briefcase. It made her want to cry, but she wasn't a stay-at-home mom type. She was too ambitious, too greedy. Did that make her a bad mother? She didn't know. She only knew that she would be miserable without the challenge of a career. It made her feel strong, safe, and allowed her to do what she did best—power play and win.

"I filled up her bag." Sherise's back was to her husband and child as she organized the items in her briefcase on the French-villa style dining room table. "So all you have to do is grab it and walk her over to the day-care center."

Sherise almost jumped when she felt Justin's hand on her shoulder. She turned to face him and was comforted by the compassion in his eyes.

"I know this is hard for you, baby." He leaned forward and kissed her on her forehead. "You don't have to pretend."

"Please," she begged. "Don't do that. You'll make me cry. I can't walk in there with red eyes."

"You know that you'll be back in the swing of things before noon," he said. "Don't sweat it, baby. Cady will be fine at day care. I'll drop her off on my way to work and you can pick her up on your way home."

"And you don't hate me?" she asked.

Justin smiled his usual charming smile. "I couldn't if I tried."

She knew that. She could always rely on Justin to be a supportive husband and a fully involved father. Which made her feel all the worse knowing that Cady might not even be his child.

Billie Hass felt her stomach getting tighter and tighter as every second passed. Her petite fingers gripped the coffee cup in her hand as she stood at the counter and looked out the window facing the street. The building where she was starting her new job on K Street was right in front of her. She didn't look much different than any of the expensively suited lawyers who walked inside, but she knew she was different.

Growing up in Southeast DC, Billie had witnessed the injustices against the poor firsthand. A father she watched accused of a crime he didn't commit and railroaded by the legal system, and a mother who died trying to fight the corruption of health insurance companies had molded her opinion of power. Billie knew two things. She had to get out of poverty and she had to fight for those who couldn't fight for themselves. This motivated her to get through law school, always with the objective of fighting for justice.

She graduated four years ago, at age twenty-five, and began her career as a public defender in DC. She was chided for not shooting for Big Law and six-figure salaries, but was planning for something better. Billie intended to run for office one day and use her power to fight for legislation that spoke for the voiceless. The young men who were guilty until proven guilty and poor women who the system shepherded toward dependency. She had met with a lot of obstacles but was winning more than losing. That was until Porter Hass happened.

Billie met Porter at Georgetown Law School. He was four years older than her, having spent time in the navy before going to school, so she found him a bit more knowledgeable than the average brother she dealt with every day. They had so much in common. While Billie had grown up on the tough streets of Southeast DC, Porter had struggled to survive in the dangerous Highland Park neighborhood of Detroit. Seeing cops shoot and kill his brother at the age of ten and get away with it, Porter had many of the same plans to fight injustice when he started law school.

But something changed. Another thing Porter and Billie had in common was a desire to live a better life than they had known as kids, to escape the ghetto mentality of "bad is good and there is no way to succeed so why bother." They wanted to escape always being on the wrong end of . . . well, everything. But unlike Billie, who only wanted to get rid of the bad, Porter began to desire an escape from all of it. Billie didn't want to forget everything about the hood, but Porter did, and at some point during law school, he decided he wanted to *be* the power that they were supposed to want to fight.

Despite their differences, she married him because she loved him and he had a lot of good qualities. He was smart and sexy and he was a great father to his now fourteen-year-old daughter, Tara. While he was still in law school, Porter fought for custody of Tara when her mother, Shawn, got too deep into drugs to care for her. Porter and Shawn were teenagers when she got pregnant and, while Porter fought his way out of it all, Shawn never bothered. He never turned his back on Tara and for that, Billie loved him. That, and the fact that he set her body on fire every time he touched her. She had never felt the passion for a man that she had for Porter. Their sexual chemistry blew her mind.

But while it blew her mind, it wasn't enough to save their marriage. Billie could handle Porter's negative comments about the people she defended and even his digs at what he called her "ghetto tendencies," but if it wasn't clear they were moving in different directions, his affair with the blond, perky twenty-three-year-old clerk at his law firm, Claire Flannigan, was as clear as rain. The heartbreak was followed by a divorce in which Porter's expertise and connections gave him the upper hand over Billie. It all put her in a position where, financially, she could no longer afford to work for a pittance. She had six-figure student loans, new bills, and Porter had taken everything in the divorce.

Now, here she was on the corner of K Street and Eighteenth in Northwest DC, barely visible above the morning crowd with her petite five-foot-three frame. She had the skills to get a high-paying job in Big Law white-collar criminal defense. Her money problems were taken care of, but starting her life over, divorced and single at twenty-nine, was not what she had imagined.

Feeling her phone vibrate in her pants pocket gave Billie an excuse to wait just a few more minutes before entering the building and leaving the career she loved behind. The fact that it was Tara was just icing on the cake.

"Hey, sweetheart," Billie said, holding her finger to her free ear to drown out the crowd noise. "What's up?"

"I hate that bitch!"

"Whoa, Tara. What is going on?" Billie knew her stepdaughter had a short temper just like her father; she angered easily. "What's wrong?"

"Claire," Tara said with a voice that sounded a lot younger than fourteen. "Billie, you just don't know what I deal with."

"What did she do now?" While Claire was the last person Billie wanted to talk about, she would never turn Tara away. Porter was making it hard enough for her to spend time with the girl now that they were divorced. She loved Tara and missed her terribly, which Porter knew.

"She's moving in," Tara answered.

Billie felt her chest tighten at the words. She tried to control her emotions. Their divorce had only been final three months. "Well, she is your father's girlfriend."

"She's his jump-off," Tara corrected. "You don't marry the side piece."

"He's not marrying her." Billie shuddered at the thought. "At least not yet."

"He married you after you moved in," she countered. "Only I liked you. This stuck-up Barbie is not going to be my new stepmother."

Billie sighed. "Tara, I can't really tell you how to be with her. You know I'm compromised on this."

"You hate her," Tara said. "Just like me. She's selfish and stupid and had the nerve to try and tell me what to do this morning."

"You really need to talk to your father about this." Billie's instinct was to advise Tara to tell Claire to go fuck herself, but she knew that wasn't right. Tara didn't need to be put in the middle of this more than she already was. "You're gonna have to sit down and . . ."

"Billie?"

Billie didn't even need a second to recognize the voice of her ex-husband. Porter had a deep, mesmerizing voice that pulled at something inside her even when he was mad, like now.

"Billie," he repeated. "Is that you?"

"Yes it is." Billie could hear Tara complaining in the background. "Look, Porter, I was just—"

"You're not allowed to talk to my daughter without my permission!"

"Since when?" Billie asked.

"Since I said." His voice was cold and short. "You're not her stepmother anymore."

"But you know I love her and she loves me," Billie said. "We were just talking."

"You're trying to turn her against Claire," Porter accused. "And I'm not gonna let you do it."

He hung up before Billie could defend herself. Not that it would have made a difference. While he had promised to give Claire up once Billie found out, she knew he never had. And when she made it clear a divorce was what she wanted, he made it clear that Claire was what he wanted. Ever since, Billie saw only the ugly side of the man she used to love. He had humiliated her and betrayed her and now he was going to try to keep her from Tara, the closest thing she'd ever had to a child of her own.

Which made it all the more insane to Billie that she was still sleeping with him.

Perfect timing!

Erica Kent had both hands on her curvy hips and a "don't-even-try-lying-to-me" look on her face as the front door to her Adams Morgan apartment slowly opened. In walked her boyfriend of four years, Terrell Nicolli, looking guilty as hell. She wasn't about to fall for that puppy-dog look in his dark eyes as he came toward her. He was looking good in blue jeans and a short-sleeve T-shirt that fit tight enough to show off the muscles under his light brown skin. He always looked good, but Erica was so mad, nothing was going to distract her.

"Baby." Terrell held his arms out as he approached but was stopped in his tracks as she held her hand up.

"Don't try that shit with me, Terrell." Erica could deceive many with her girl-next-door cuteness but she was not one to be trifled with. "It's eight in the morning. Where in the hell have you been?"

"You know I'm working the night shift," Terrell said as he bypassed her and went for the kitchen of their tiny two-bedroom apartment. He had hoped she would have left for work by now. "You leave me some breakfast or did that asshole brother of yours eat it all?"

"Your shift ended at six," Erica said, following him to the kitchen. "Why are you walking up in here two hours later?"

Terrell took a gulp of orange juice right out of the container before answering. "Why don't you just ask me what you want to ask me?"

"I already did!" Erica knew what he was talking about and she wasn't going to let him take it there. Yes, there was a part of her that suspected he was out hustling, but he had promised that was no longer a part of his life and she chose to believe him.

"I was making some extra money," Terrell said before adding, "and not hustling. It was honest money."

"Doing what?"

"One of my clients needed me to take him all the way to his house in Bethesda and then out to Dulles airport." Terrell approached Erica and leaned in to kiss her, but she backed away. That line wasn't exactly true, but baby girl didn't need to hear that it was his client's mistress instead of him. "He paid me two hundred fifty dollars, baby. Under the table."

Erica rolled her eyes at him, not sure what to say. She was supposed to believe him. She knew Terrell loved her, but she also knew Terrell lied to her. When they met, they were both only twenty-one, and while Terrell was hustling to get by, Erica had to work two jobs to support herself and her younger brother, Nate. Their father had never been in the picture and when their mother died of cancer, Erica was only nineteen and Nate was twelve. Erica was young and easily impressed by the money Terrell flashed in front of her. He was cute and charming and treated her better than any man ever had.

But like a lot of women, as you mature, you can grow less impressed by what used to turn you on. It wasn't okay anymore that he was hustling. She needed Terrell to get his life together and that meant an honest job and helping her look after Nate. Terrell loved her enough to make that change, but he slipped up now and then. However, for a few years he'd had a job as a driver for Destin, a local limo company, and looked to be on the straight and narrow. With her secretarial position at the Defense Department, they were making a respectable living. She shouldn't complain.

"Why you gotta be so suspicious all the time?" Terrell asked. "I just paid our cable and electric bill in less than two hours."

"Is that the truth?" Erica asked. She couldn't help herself.

"Baby." Terrell slid close, this time wrapping his arms around her. He leaned in and kissed her on her full lips. "You know I would never do anything to lose you."

Erica felt herself soften and heat up at the same time. Even after all these years, she loved how it felt to have her body pressed against his. He was strong and powerful and when he kissed her, he could really get her going. She had to be more trusting in him. He was her man, the only man for her. Even though her friends disapproved and said he was too "street," Erica knew that Terrell was good and, more important, he was good to her.

"I'm taking you out tonight," Terrell said as his mouth lowered to her neck, kissing her softly, loving the taste of her and the smell of her, so sweet and soft.

Erica's eyes closed as she soaked it in. "You have to work."

"My shift don't start till ten." He tugged at her shirt until it was out of her skirt. His strong hands slid up her waist. He was already getting hard. "I'm taking you somewhere nice."

"We can't afford . . ."

He covered her mouth with his as his hands cupped her

large breast. Erica had real curves and that was what he loved
about her. She never showed it off, but her body was crazy and
Terrell couldn't get enough of it.

"Where is Nate?" he asked in a whisper.

"I have to go to work." Erica didn't even know why she
said that. She knew she was going to make love to Terrell.
They hardly ever saw each other, both of them working so
hard. With only a few minutes alone, she knew what was about
to happen and she couldn't wait.

He was caressing her breast aggressively now because he
knew she liked it like that. Sometimes Erica wanted the soft
romantic stuff, but most of the time she liked it a little rough
and that was just another one of the things he loved about her.
They could break some furniture if given half a chance.

"Where is he?" he asked.

"He spent the night at his girlfriend's place." Erica was tugging at Terrell's shirt, pulling him toward the sofa. "I . . . We
should . . ."

His mouth took over hers again, and as their bodies fell to
the sofa, they were furiously pulling at each other's clothes.
Removing her bra, he was calling her baby as his mouth trailed
from her neck down to her full breasts. He kissed them, licked
them, and opened his mouth softly to take one in. Her body
was wriggling beneath his as he tasted her and his tongue
played with her belly button.

Her nails dug into his shoulders as he went lower. He
tugged at her panties with his teeth, pulling them down as she
lifted her hips up. He finished pulling her panties off and positioned himself between her legs. Their lips connected again
and Erica could feel how hard he was against the inside of her
thighs. She reached down and took hold of him, stroking him
gently at first, but harder and faster as she went along while he
continued to kiss her face, lick her neck, and tug at her ear-
lobe.

"You good, baby?" he whispered into her hair.

"Yes, baby."

She let out a moan as he entered her slowly and she took him all in. He was large and her body had to adjust to his size every time, but the pain was sweet and enticing. She loved him and wanted every piece of him.

The Executive Office Building, the famous French Empire–styled building located next to the White House, was occupied by most of the employees of the West Wing, the executive offices of the president. Sherise had worked there as assistant director of communications for the Domestic Policy Council for a year before taking her maternity leave. Her journey leading to this position was untraditional and defied most logic. Positions at this level were rare, sought by people with long-held connections and ties.

Sherise had been working her way toward the West Wing as long as she could remember. As a young girl, the only time she would see powerful people in suits anywhere near her neighborhood was when Capitol Hill, White House, or other government-related executives would venture in groups in search of some good soul food. She wanted to know where they'd come from. Her mother told her "Northwest" was where they came from. It was the other side of town and from the looks of those people, Sherise thought it was where she was supposed to be.

Always with her focus on getting to the other side of town, Sherise used her shrewd skills and smarts to spend as much time as possible over there. In high school, she found out about internship opportunities for Southeast kids and got herself one making copies at the Department of Agriculture. Making sure she outshined all the other students, even when she had to secretly sabotage them, she got a scholarship at the University of Maryland, interning every summer on Capitol Hill, referred to as The Hill. By the time she graduated from college, Sherise had made an impression on more than a few powerful people on both sides of the political spectrum so her fate wouldn't change even when administrations did. She had to sleep with one or two and blackmail was always a last resort, but she was well on her way.

Justin was the icing on the cake. As a former legislative assistant to two senators, Justin transitioned into lobbying and made a living by knowing everyone with decision-making power on The Hill. Sherise was always sure to make it seem as if she wasn't using him to get access, but he was smart and knew better. With every door that opened, Sherise was looking for the next door. Now at twenty-seven, she had maneuvered into a good position, in charge of a small team of people and making sure that her boss gave her credit for everything that went well, even if it wasn't her work.

But the power game of politics was brutal and while it was sort of a revolving door, if you stepped away, you might have a hard time coming back. That was if you weren't Sherise Robinson. She'd only been back at the office for a few hours but was already feeling her groove. She was barking orders to her staff, the women were looking envious, and the men were intrigued and intimidated—just as she liked it.

She was positioning pictures of Cady on her desk, just about ready to dig in to the new project file her boss had given her, when she heard a knock on the door.

"Come in." Sherise made sure to sound annoyed. That way anyone she didn't want to stay would already feel pressured to leave even before walking in.

Jessica Colvin, administrative assistant to the director of communications, and Sherise's boss, Walter Nappano, stepped inside. Jessica was one of the people Sherise walked a fine line with. She was the boss's admin, so she had to get in good with her, but she also had to assert her authority when it came to getting access to Walter, which was not easy considering Walter spent most of his time out of the office.

"A warning." Jessica helped herself to the seat across from Sherise's desk. She was a fifty-something plump woman with fiery red hair who wore a dress or a skirt every day because of her religion. She was easy to manipulate. Sherise had figured out that by just asking about Jessica's favorite grandchild, a girl named Peppa, she could get anything she needed out of Jessica.

"A warning for what?" Sherise sat up straight. Warnings were not what she wanted on her first day back.

"Your welcome back party was postponed till Wednesday."

"I didn't even know there was one," Sherise lied. She was not happy to hear this.

"Yeah, right." Jessica wasn't buying. "It was supposed to be today—a surprise. But Walter has news."

Sherise leaned forward with a wicked grin. "That you're going to tell me before he tells everyone else . . . ?"

"Consider it my welcome back present." Jessica smiled with accomplishment. "He's about to announce he's retiring."

Sherise gasped before managing to ask, "What for?" even though she didn't really care. She was already thinking about what this meant for her.

"He's taking a position with a private company," Jessica answered. "Money and all that. I'm going with him."

"Are you now?" Sherise asked, wondering why Walter had never even hinted at a new job during their conversations while she was on leave. "How nice for you."

"He's not going to be leaving for three months," Jessica said. "So you'll have that much time."

"I'm sorry?" Sherise feigned confusion.

"I know you, Sherise. You've been eyeing his position since the first day you started your job."

Actually it was before that, but Sherise didn't need to share that bit. "Well, I *am* next in line."

"Technically."

Sherise knew what she was talking about. "I know this Toni person has been interloping in the department, but there is no way she—"

"There is a way for everything," Jessica interrupted. "And Toni Williams has been working Walter like crazy since you left. It's been six months, Sherise."

"I told you to let me know who was sidling up to him."

Sherise's staff had handled most of her work and Walter had taken on what was above their levels. Sherise wasn't at all worried about anyone on her staff outperforming her. But she had found out that, less than a month after she left, another department had half its budget cut and was loaning out its people who had a lot of time on their hands. Toni Williams, deputy communications director for that department, had stepped in, but Sherise had made sure to find out if she was doing too good a job. No one seemed particularly impressed. Sherise felt her job was safe.

"And I did," Jessica said, "but things have kind of changed."

"Like how?" Sherise asked. "Is she sleeping with him?"

"Oh God, no," Jessica said. "But in the last month, he seems to think the world of her. All I know is that same file Walter put on your desk this morning is also on hers."

Sherise had to admit that she hadn't been on top of things in the last month. She was dealing with weaning Cady off breast milk and the emotional strain of accepting she would be separated from her baby for most of the day. She took her eye off the ball.

"What has changed?"

"That I can't say," Jessica added. "He's not giving any reasons. I've tried to hint at it and it's not happening. He never takes the bait."

"Well, I'll get it out of him." Sherise could play Walter pretty well. He was a sucker for a pretty face and based on his reaction today, he was very happy to see her back. She would stroke his ego a bit and play the awed protégée and he would tell her anything she wanted to know.

This was an unexpected turn and Sherise was not happy about it. Her glee at an opportunity to take a step up was dampened by the surprise of some real competition. She'd been gone for six months and in a what-have-you-done-for-me-lately industry, Sherise could see where she had a disadvantage. However, her advantages were abundant and as soon as she could get little Miss Toni Williams out of her way, Sherise was going to be one step closer to an office in the West Wing.

"You gonna be okay?" Justin asked.

Billie turned to him with a smile. "This is my office?" Looking around the small, dark, cherrywood office with badly decorated shelves and dark rose red furniture, she noted that the only light seemed to be the single small window that offered a view of the back of another building.

After spending the morning with paperwork and other administrative annoyances, Justin had made his way from the lobbying division just one floor below within the same firm, retrieved Billie, and walked her to her office.

"*Your* office?" Justin laughed. "Used to be three to an office. You're actually lucky. You only share it with one other associate. Layoffs and all."

Billie shrugged. "I only had half a desk at the public defender's office. So I guess it's a step up."

"Hey, Billie." Justin stood in the doorway. "Give it a chance. You'd be surprised at how much you could like this."

"I intend to give it the best chance I can." Billie smiled appreciatively. "I know you put yourself out there to get me this job."

"It wasn't that hard," he said. "You're good. Besides, Sherise would've divorced me if I didn't help you out. She loves you like a sister."

"She is my sister," Billie said, meaning every word of it.

Justin sighed heavily. "Billie, can I just give you a warning?"

"Why do I feel like I'm gonna get a lot of those today?"

He smiled. "Porter."

"What about him?"

"They love him here."

Billie let out a sarcastic laugh. "Yes, I figured as much when they kept asking me about him during the interview process."

"He just got named one of the up-and-coming in commercial transaction law."

"But he works for the competition," Billie said. "I thought that made him evil."

Justin nodded. "Yes, but it also makes him a . . . possibility."

Billie felt ill in her stomach. "Porter would never consider coming here if I was here."

"And I'm sure they'd never try to hire him now that you're here," Justin said. "But you should know that you'll probably get questions about him even though everyone knows you're separated."

"Divorced," she corrected.

"You're here!"

Justin quickly stepped aside as a young brunette woman with large eyes, a friendly smile, who was dressed in a sharp gray suit shot into the office with her hand held out.

"I'm Callie Brewer," she said. "I'm the head paralegal on your team."

"Yes." Billie shook her hand. "I was told you would show me the ropes today."

"We have a pretty tight schedule," Callie said, turning to Justin. "So if you don't mind, Mr. Robinson."

"I'm way ahead of you," Justin said. "I've got to get back to my side of the house."

"Okay." Callie waved for Billie to follow her on her way out of the office.

Callie was already reading off the day's schedule when Billie, after waving good-bye to Justin, caught up with her. She named off all the people Billie was going to have to meet and the work they would be assigning to her. About seven people into the list, Billie had to cut her off.

"Wait a second," she said. "I'm meeting all these people today?"

"Absolutely," Callie answered.

"I'm meeting everyone at the firm on day one?"

Callie laughed. "You're so silly. Those are just the people in the White Collar Crime practice you didn't meet with during the interview process."

"This place is huge," Billie said. "It's easy to be intimidated."

Billie was surprised when Callie swung around to face her with a very serious, almost warning look on her face.

"But never, ever show it."

"What?" Billie asked.

"I'm gonna give you some advice," Callie said. "You didn't earn your ropes here, so the natives are gonna be watching you, waiting to pounce on any weakness. You're an outsider. They usually don't last long here."

"Is there anyone in particular out to get me?"

"They all are," Callie said nonchalantly all of sudden. "They think you're easy prey 'cause you came from a bleeding heart liberal public defender's office. This is cut-throat and they eat softies alive. Just so you know."

"Duly warned," Billie said. As disheartening as that news was, she had heard worse things about Big Law. She decided to see it as a challenge. As a black woman in the legal industry, she was already rare and knew that there were odds stacked against her, but there were plenty of people here who believed in her and she would pull on their support. As for those who didn't believe in her, they didn't know where she came from. She'd fought worse demons before the age of twelve.

2

After a very busy morning so far, Erica was able to take a second to get online and check out the restaurant that Terrell had texted her about, where he planned to take her for dinner tonight. Pesce was a seafood restaurant in the Dupont Circle neighborhood of DC. The online menu items looked delicious but not an appetizer under $15 and not an entrée under $40. This was certainly not in their budget, but Terrell had $250 more than expected. As long as they didn't spend it all on dinner, it should be okay.

Erica leaned back in her chair, trying to think of what she might wear to a place like that. Her closet was not the classiest and she didn't think she had enough time to steal something from anyone else's. Besides, Billie was too tiny and Sherise was too thin. She'd have to make do. Her baby wanted to treat her and she was gonna let him do it.

"Erica?"

Erica swung around to see her boss, Darleen Lee, approach her desk. Erica's desk was in the open area along with other assistant administrative assistants, which they all called triple As. She and a few other women all worked under the women who were the administrative assistants to directors within the Defense Department. Every division had its pool of triple As.

Erica had been moved around a couple of times during the three years she'd worked there. The AAs they worked under were not their bosses. Their boss was the triple A head, Darleen Lee, a middle-aged black woman who had been with the Defense Department for almost forty years. Although Darleen could be a hard boss at times, Erica got along well with her and she could tell from the smile on Darleen's face as she approached that she was about to get some good news.

A raise maybe?

"Come with me," Darleen said just above a whisper as she passed Erica's desk without stopping.

Her curiosity piqued, Erica hopped up from her desk and followed Darleen down the hallway near the break room. When she stopped, Erica did too, waiting patiently to hear what Darleen had to say.

"It's time for you to go," Darleen said.

Erica's mouth opened but nothing came out. She hadn't just heard what she thought she heard. She couldn't have.

Darleen smiled widely. "Girl, you know I'm playing with you."

"Not funny," Erica said. All she could think of was what would they do without her salary—her, Terrell, and Nate?

"I think you need to move up," Darleen said. "And I have just the position for you."

"I'm listening."

"Now, it is a triple A job," Darleen said, "but this is different. You'll be the triple A working for Jonah Dolan."

Erica gasped. "Are you kidding me? Jonah Dolan? As in Deputy Assistant Secretary of Defense Jonah Dolan?"

"This will be a great position for you," Darleen said. "You'll be able to make more—"

"Wait a second." Erica held her hand up to stop Darleen. "First of all, there is no position listed for him. I check all triple A positions that come out. Secondly, that is an advanced position. How can I be first in line to get it? Third—"

"Why are you putting up barriers for yourself?" Darleen asked. "The third most powerful person in the Defense Department needs a triple A and I'm recommending you."

Erica couldn't help but get excited even though she was full of doubts. "But why?"

"Because," Darleen answered, "I've talked to Jonah. I know what he and his assistant Jenna are looking for. It's you. You're ready."

"Okay, I'm ready," Erica said. "But there is a process in place for jobs and it takes forever to . . ."

"Not this job," Darleen said. "It's yours."

Erica was full-on suspicion now. "What's the catch? I'm not saying I won't take it if it's more money, but I need to know."

Darleen rolled her eyes impatiently. "The catch is you and I meet with Assistant Secretary Dolan for lunch in forty-five minutes. I'm sure he'll win you over."

Erica was speechless. She was both stunned and full of doubt, but no matter what didn't sound right about this, and nothing sounded right, she knew she wasn't going to turn down the opportunity. While she might be a fool to think this was as simple as Darleen was making it seem, she would be an even bigger fool to pass it up.

The second they stepped into Fyve, Erica knew this wasn't like the other work lunches she had been to. Pentagon City was an area of residential housing and shopping just across Interstate 395 from the Pentagon in Arlington, Virginia. She had been to the many restaurants in the area for various lunches, but Fyve was very different. Located in the posh Ritz-Carlton, with an impressive red and orange contemporary yet classic design, Fyve was more than a few notches above the average eatery. Not a uniform in the place. All suits and pretty much all men.

"Stop stressing," Darleen said as if reading her mind. "You look fine."

Erica looked down at her Jessica London separates. She could say at least she matched, but that was about it.

"I just feel a little . . . you know."

"You're more impressive than you think," Darleen said.

Erica smiled, feeling a little confidence boost, but before she could thank Darleen, they had reached their table.

"Ladies."

When Jonah Dolan stood up, his presence engulfed the room. He was an incredibly powerful man. He looked to be in his forties even though he was in his fifties. He was about six four with a conservative haircut, a throwback from military days. His dark brown hair had distinguished graying at the temples, and his white skin had a nice hue to it, almost a light tan. His face was commanding and very handsome in a traditional way. He had a firm jawline with thin lips giving him a harsher look, but still attractive. He was very fit in his navy blue designer suit.

"I thought all you top brass were always late to lunch," Darleen said, shaking Jonah's hand.

"We keep a tight schedule," the woman standing next to Jonah said as she offered Erica a stern look. "You should know that."

Erica didn't need any introduction. She knew this was Jenna, Jonah's AA. Her attitude wasn't a surprise; they were typically super-protective mother types who guarded their directors like Fort Knox and demanded unwavering perfection from all the triple As.

"And you're Ms. Kent." Jonah offered her his hand with a warm, welcoming smile.

Assessing someone immediately was a survival tool that Erica had grown up with and she had used it to her advantage. She could see why Jonah Dolan was not an unknown. Not only was he incredibly powerful, but also very popular, on a trajectory as high as he wanted to go. And he appeared very comfortable with this position. Might he even be president one day?

"It's very nice to meet you, sir." Erica was trying hard not to smile or laugh, which she did often when she was nervous. This man had been in two Gulf wars and dealt with heads of state daily. He would not be impressed with a giggling girl.

"The pleasure is mine." After shaking her hand, Jonah took his seat and motioned for her to sit next to him. "Please sit down. We only have a short time. We have to . . ." He looked at Jenna.

"An appointment at the White House," Jenna answered for him.

"That's fine," Darleen said as she sat next to Jenna. "I know Jonah just wanted to meet Erica. She's very excited about the opportunity, aren't you?"

Erica nodded, focusing her attention on Jonah since she had already deduced that Jenna was not going to be a fan of hers. "I was just curious as to how you knew of me."

Jonah smiled warmly and leaned back in his seat. "You used to work for Undersecretary Nez's team. He spoke highly of you."

Erica couldn't hide her surprise. She had been on his team for only a year before being reassigned when the undersecretary left the Defense Department. She had performed her best as usual, but hadn't felt noticed in the least.

"So when Jenna contacted Darleen about potential triple As," Jonah continued, "your name was on the list and I remembered him saying that you were young, energetic, and very sharp."

"Do you think you're up for the position?" Jenna asked. "It is more demanding than the average triple-A. The schedule is very challenging and you'll be constantly mobile."

"We can get to that part in a second," Jonah said as he waved the waiter over. "First let's get our order in."

Erica knew how to stand her own with Defense Department brass. They were very aggressive types, almost always men who had developed careers in the military that lead to powerful positions in defense of the country. They had a very patriarchal view of the rest of the world, felt responsible for the entire nation. Erica admired that about them, but found they could be a little too black and white at times and somewhat condescending.

But Jonah was different. He was definitely order and color like a military man, but he came across to Erica as warmer than the stereotype. As the lunch continued, he asked her questions about her career and seemed genuinely interested. He had a way about him that made Erica want to open up. He rarely asked any questions about her actual skills; that seemed to be Jenna's job. She never cracked a smile or made a joke as she grilled Erica. Every now and then, Darleen would interfere to speak on Erica's behalf, but Jenna clearly wanted answers from Erica.

Erica was caught off guard by a few questions. She was well aware of what she could do and what she had to offer, but she had literally found out about this opportunity a few hours ago. She stuttered nervously a few times and could see Jenna was disappointed. Erica had already decided she didn't like this woman and was not sure she could work under her. The only reason she continued to put a good face forward was because Jonah would interject with comments about how great this position could be for her upward trajectory.

After all, wasn't that what it was all about? Wasn't this the plan? She had been bogged down in getting by for so long, she was forgetting the ultimate goal. She hadn't had the advantage of college like her friends Billie and Sherise and the results showed. She was not as upwardly mobile as them, but she had still come very far from where she had been, and the goal was to continue to go farther.

Erica had a feeling that this position was going to be her chance to cover some ground in her lifelong quest to get "there"—the place that Sherise and Billie seemed to already be. She could get there with Terrell at her side and dragging Nate with her. But was Jenna going to let her?

Jonah seemed to sense Erica's apprehension toward the end of the lunch. Just as Darleen and Jenna began checking their BlackBerries to confirm schedules, he leaned in to Erica and with a soothing voice said, "Don't worry about Jenna. She's just a little cautious. Our last triple A didn't work out. It's what I want that matters."

By the time Erica and Darleen were in the car on the way back to the Pentagon, Darleen had already scheduled a visit for her to Jonah's office. Erica was excited about the chance to go, but she couldn't stop the nagging questions in her mind. Why was someone so important interested in her? She wasn't an expert at this thing, but she felt certain a man as busy and powerful as Jonah Dolan generally took no part in something as simple as filling a triple-A position. So why was he so involved and why was he so interested in her? She hadn't gotten a perverted vibe from him. He hadn't seemed to be coming on to her, so what was the deal? And what had he meant when he said the last triple A didn't work out?

"Darleen?" Erica turned to her.

"Yeah, hon?"

"When did this position open up?"

Darleen shrugged her shoulders, continuing to look ahead as she drove. "Just last week, I think."

"What happened to the woman who was in it?" Erica could see Darleen was suddenly uncomfortable and this made her wonder.

"Not important," Darleen finally answered.

"No one ever gets fired from the government," Erica said.

"That is not true, but it's not appropriate for me to discuss that. Let's just say she wasn't up for the job."

"How many potential people did you discuss with Jenna?"

"You know, that's what is sort of odd," Darleen said. "He

said that your name came up, but you're the only person Jenna spoke to me about. She asked about you."

"That didn't strike you as weird?"

They had reached the pass check booth in the Pentagon parking lot. Darleen stepped on the brakes and turned to Erica. "Erica, this can open countless doors for you."

"And I believe that," Erica said. "But what am I really stepping into?"

"I wouldn't just offer you up for something shady or inappropriate," Darleen said. "Jonah has political intentions and he is looking to build a team of people he can use when his aspirations grow. He wants fresh and new blood instead of old government veterans. This can pay great dividends for you."

Erica didn't doubt that. She just wondered what else it could do to her.

When she heard the knock on her office door, Sherise cringed. This was the Executive Building. Unlike other government offices, there wasn't any nine-to-five here unless you were administrative support. Not when your responsibilities depended on whatever was happening in the White House and Congress. Today was her first day and it had been a busy one, but Sherise ached to get her hands on her baby. She and Walter had agreed that her first few weeks back, her hours might be sporadic. What she couldn't get done in the office, she could take home, but that was before Toni Williams. Now, with competition for Walter's position, Sherise didn't feel like she had the option of working from home. She had to be here, in the mix and ready for the fight.

So she called the day-care center and told them she would be picking Cady up at six-thirty instead of five-thirty, but just as she gathered her things to head out, she feared the someone at her door would likely expect her to drop everything and get some additional work done.

"Come in." Sherise tossed her briefcase on the floor behind her desk and sat down, looking as if she was still working.

"I'm so glad you're still here," the woman said, opening the door.

Sherise didn't need an introduction. She had done her research; it had been most of what she'd spent her first day back doing. Toni Williams had just stepped into her office.

About thirty years old, Toni was a political veteran. She had been working on campaigns since college and been in and out of Capitol Hill offices for a long time. The black and Asian in her heritage mixed together to make a beautiful young woman with exotic features. She liked to dress sharply and wore her hair natural, with large, jet black waves that turned to wild curls at the end and went to the middle of her back. She wore very little makeup, allowing her natural beauty to shine through.

"I'm glad I caught you before you left." Toni leaned against the door after she closed it behind her.

"Left?" Sherise asked, wanting to smack that smug look off Toni's face.

"You told Jessica you were on your way out." Toni waved a dismissive hand. "It's okay. We all understand the demands of a new baby."

Sherise mumbled at Toni's sarcastic tone. "That has nothing to do with it. I worked from home all the time, even before I had Cady. It doesn't change anything."

"It does," Toni said. "If you're doing a good job."

Sherise shot up from her chair. "I beg your pardon?"

"Don't worry about it," she answered, trying to feign some southern politeness that was too saccharine to be believed. "We can pick up the slack just as we did while you were gone."

"I'm back now," Sherise said. "I appreciate your help while I was gone. You did incredibly well, but of course you would have. You seem to specialize in being in positions for a very short period of time."

Toni's smile faded just long enough to let Sherise know she got the dig. "I go where the opportunity is and I'm seeing a lot of opportunity here."

"I'm not going anywhere, Toni." Sherise placed her hands on her hips, hoping to send the message. "I think your opportunities are best found elsewhere."

"We'll see what Jonah has to say about it," she responded. "Based on what I know of him—which is a considerable amount—I'm exactly what he needs on this project. I have more experience than you and there is no babysitter calling me to come home."

"While I'm not surprised there is no one at your home waiting for you to get there," Sherise added, "don't think that puts me at a disadvantage. I've had greater obstacles, and quantity of experience doesn't indicate quality. Advantage . . . me."

Toni's finely trimmed eyebrows raised inquisitively. "We'll see what Jonah says at dinner on Wednesday."

"Dinner?" Sherise asked, regretting that she did the second the word came out of her mouth. She knew it was a big mistake to show surprise at anything.

Toni smiled wickedly. "Didn't Walter tell you? Our meeting was rescheduled from the Pentagon to dinner at Acadiana. I picked the restaurant because I know what Jonah likes."

"I'll bet you do." Sherise was trying her best to hide her frustration. Walter hadn't told her anything.

Toni opened the door and, just before walking through, let out an "Advantage . . . me."

After Toni was gone, Sherise sat back in her seat and began cracking her knuckles, a knee-jerk reaction to stress. She had just learned a few things and none of them good. Toni was going to force her to go the direct competition route. Sherise was more the underhanded, veiled contempt specialist, but she could do the bold-faced hardcore game as well. It was just harder to get away with unscathed. She also discovered that Toni was getting information she wasn't. That was a problem. Sherise had to get Walter back in line.

Worst of all, Toni had a relationship with Jonah Dolan, a man well known for getting what he wanted at the Pentagon. He had the president's ear and was the kind of man who could pick whomever he wanted to work on his projects. Was it a friendship? Was it just a professional acquaintance? Or was it a sexual relationship?

Either way, Toni was right. It was an advantage she had over Sherise and Sherise knew she had to do something about it. She had to get on Jonah's good side. This was something she was good at. Very good at.

Billie had just reached the door to her office when she heard Callie's chipper voice call her name from behind. Her entire body sighed. It was almost seven o'clock and she was dead tired. After a full day of meeting with other members of her practice group, she was grateful for the last meeting to end early due to an urgent call from a client. She needed just a few minutes to take it all in and breathe, maybe even call her girls, Erica and Sherise, and get a little pep talk. But it looked like that wasn't meant to happen.

"There you are!" Callie smiled, pointing a finger as if Billie had been hiding from her. "You're a sneaky one, but I found you. It's time for dinner."

"Callie, can you . . ." Billie held in her arms the reams of binders given to her by her coworkers, which reached up to her neck.

"Oh, of course." Callie jumped ahead of her and opened the door to the office, stepping aside. "You can just toss those on your desk. You can get to them after dinner."

"After dinner?" she asked. "We're coming back here?"

"Well, I'm not. I'm a paralegal. They don't pay me to work into the night, but the associates do."

"Maybe I'll just take them home and . . ." Just as Billie put the binders in a chair, she noticed a bouquet of flowers placed on the folders on her desk. Was this supposed to make up for working her like a slave?

"Nice," Callie said. "Who are they from?"

Billie reached for the card on top of the tulips and roses. "I thought it was from the firm, like a welcome thing."

"I doubt it," Callie said. "The firm welcomes new associates with signing bonuses."

When Billie read the card, she realized that she should have known better. Tulips and roses were a trademark apology from her ex-husband.

GOOD LUCK IN THE NEW JOB. LET'S TALK ABOUT TARA.
PORTER

"Someone you know?" Callie asked.

"Someone I know is up to something," Billie responded.

She tossed the card in the garbage near her desk, but couldn't help it . . . She picked up the bouquet and brought it to her nose. He knew all the things she loved and had no shame in using them to get to her. She doubted this was about Tara. What did he want now and how was she going to be strong enough to finally resist him?

"How are my ladies?" Justin entered the kitchen with his arms open wide.

Cady, sitting in her baby chair, began wiggling around, moving her arms wildly as she screamed for her daddy.

Sherise put the baby food dish down and watched as Justin leaned in and gave Cady several kisses. He loved her so much and it warmed Sherise's heart to know her daughter would get the fatherly love she herself never had. Cady was just as much Justin's world as she was Sherise's.

"You're gonna get baby food on your face," Sherise said.

"Don't care." Justin sat down. "How'd she do?"

"She's got a clock," Sherise said. "She cried when I should have been there."

To prepare for this day, Sherise had been taking Cady to the day-care center for two weeks in ever-increasing hours. Both she and Cady needed to get used to not being with each other all day. Today was the longest she'd been at day care and she seemed to sense it, having cried for the final half hour until Sherise showed up.

"How'd you do?" Justin reached across the table and placed his hand on his wife's shoulder.

"I need your help."

Justin's eyes squinted as he saw a familiar gleam in his wife's eyes. "What are you up to already?"

Sherise told him everything that had gone down that day, except she left out Toni's curious relationship with Jonah.

"And you need me to . . ." Jonah knew what she was going to ask. Sherise had been making good use of his connections since the day they'd met, but he had never hesitated to give her what she wanted. He couldn't say no to her.

"I need to know everything about Toni Williams," Sherise said.

"I've never heard of her," Justin said as he sat back in the closest chair. "She's a nobody."

"Not to me," Sherise said. "She's a threat, but she has a shaky history and something is going on with her. She jumps around too much."

"Sexual harassment claims?" he asked. "Or maybe she's just a bounder. There are a lot of those in your business. Jumping on the bandwagon of whoever is temporarily hot."

Sherise stood up and came around the table. She positioned herself on her husband's lap and leaned in to him as he wrapped his arms around her. She kissed him once and felt a little flutter, but she knew he felt more than a flutter. He held her tighter, pulling her to him as his lips came to hers again. She kissed him longer this time, letting his tongue explore her mouth a little. She knew the taste of her pleased him and she loved to please him.

When she leaned away, she placed her finger on his mouth and slightly pushed his face away. "You guys know everything about everyone that is ten degrees from the White House and Congress. You spend a lot of money getting the information you need to position your clients before powerful people in a way most advantageous to them."

"You think she's notable enough to have information?"

"She's got the ear of Jonah Dolan," Sherise said. "And Walter. She moves around a lot but doesn't seem to suffer for it. I don't know what she's got, but it's something and I need to know what it is."

"So you can do what?" Justin worried about Sherise's ambition sometimes. While her fire was sexy, he wished she would be more focused on him and Cady and not on the White House.

"So I can do what I always do," she answered. "Win."

"How much?" was Terrell's first question.

"I'll get to that." Erica was a little annoyed. She had barely gotten through two sentences about the new job before he wanted to know about money.

In fact, Terrell had been acting a little odd ever since they arrived at Pesce for their romantic evening. He stuttered twice while ordering drinks and oyster appetizers and commented nervously on how nice Erica looked in her hunter green cocktail dress. Something was up and as the waiter bought their thirty dollars worth of appetizers to eat with their ten-dollar drinks, Erica was getting a little nervous.

"Did you run out of money?" she asked.

"What?" He seemed confused. "What you mean?"

"You're acting nervous." She pointed to the oysters in the middle of the table. "You're looking at them like you don't want to eat them. Like maybe they cost too much?"

Terrell smiled. "I'm looking at them like I'm not sure I want to eat something that looks like snot."

"I told you they taste great," Erica said. "Put some horse-radish on them and . . ."

"I got my money," Terrell said. "Don't worry about that. I want to hear about your money."

"The salary would bump me up to a Step Seven in my pay grade. It's only about three grand more a year, but . . ."

"I ain't mad at no three grand."

Erica smiled. "Me neither, but this is about so much more than just money. This is a real job, like a career."

"Oh no, wait a second." Terrell leaned forward. "I'm all for you making that money, but you ain't gonna go all Billie on me."

"What does that mean?"

"Billie let her career take over her life and she neglected her man. Now look at her."

"Don't make me pick up one of these rolls and throw it at you in this nice place." Erica rolled her eyes. "Billie didn't lose anything. She got rid of a cancer."

"Either way you look at it," he said, "her career cost her a husband."

"A cheating bastard and a Barbie look-alike ho is what cost her a husband."

Terrell laughed. "You ain't gotta worry about that. I don't do Barbies and I ain't gonna cheat on you when we're mar-ried."

"You better not, 'cause—" Erica's voice caught in her throat as she realized what Terrell had just said. "When we're *what*?"

"I gotta come clean with you, baby." Terrell took a deep

breath. There was no turning back now. "This morning wasn't the only time I did side work, you know."

"What did you mean when you said 'when we're married'?" Erica felt her heart begin to beat at a rapid speed.

"I've been doing a lot of that kind of work to make extra money," he said, ignoring her question. "It's been for a reason."

"Terrell?"

"That's the reason." Terrell pointed to the plate of oysters on the table.

Erica gasped when she realized what he was pointing to. It had been there the whole time! Right in the heart of one of the oyster shells, the one closest to her, was a beautiful diamond ring where an oyster should have been.

"Oh my God!" Erica screamed, not caring that she attracted a look or two.

Her arms began to shake and she reached for the ring, only to pull her own hand away. She looked at Terrell, who had an expression of excitement and terror on his face.

"What are you doing?" she asked.

"I think it's pretty obvious, don't you?" he answered with his own question.

Erica let out a string of incoherent words as she stared at the beautiful ring in front of her.

"You gonna get it or what?" Terrell was laughing now.

Suddenly, Erica reached out and grabbed the ring. She brought it to her, not believing this was happening. In all the years she had been with Terrell, she imagined the day they would get married, but Terrell had made it seem unlikely.

"I thought you said only punks get married," Erica said, looking down at the ring in her hand, a Heart's Desire diamond in the center, supported by two round diamonds set in a band of eighteen-carat white gold.

"Only a punk would have a woman like you and not marry her," he answered.

"Oh my God," was all she could say as she looked at him

lovingly. He didn't say it often, but she knew he loved her and now . . .

"Can I take that as a yes?" Terrell asked.

"Are you kidding?" she asked. "Why would you even need to ask me that?"

"I need to ask 'cause you ain't wearing the ring," he answered.

Without hesitation she slipped the ring on her finger and leaped across the table, falling into his lap. She kissed him nonstop while people around them clapped. In between kisses she kept saying "yes" over and over again. Today had turned out to be a very good day all around!

While she listened to her husband and daughter play in the bathroom as she sat on the bed with her computer on her lap, Sherise found her mind getting away from itself as she formed her plan for Jonah. He was quite a man. Having grown up in Austin, Texas, the liberal hotbed of a conservative state, his family moved to the Maryland suburbs of DC when he was fifteen years old. He joined the marines at seventeen. After fighting in the first Gulf war, his skills were quickly recognized and he began to move up in the ranks.

He returned as a leader in the second Gulf war only to be pulled back to the states for a position in the Defense Department six years ago. His notable skills, in addition to his charisma, were better utilized among the higher-ups. Politicos from both sides of the aisle took to him and, in a short time, he moved fast and was considered a top contender for the next secretary of defense if the position ever opened up, regardless of who the president at the time might be.

Sherise found his trajectory impressive and imagined an affinity with him because of her own ambition. While she had moved up faster than someone her age usually did, she was not as accomplished as him. This man wasn't just a mover and a shaker. He was a thinker, which was why he came up with the

idea for a program opening up a line of communication between the Defense Department and the Domestic Policy
Council. Because of the council's responsibility for domestic
policy in a post 9/11 world, defense had become an element
to consider and even a decade after the tragedy, miscommuni-
cations continued to create conflict. Jonah's idea was to create
a formal process of communication and integration that would
precede the formal proposal to the Executive Branch.

What she read about his career and his work style would
make it easy for Sherise to reach him. She was adept at mimic-
king work styles to get on the good side of her superiors. Usually it was to get them to let their guard down so she could
sabotage them unexpectedly, but all she wanted was to impress
Jonah professionally so he would prefer her to Toni regardless
of his relationship with her.

Sherise was still waiting to hear from Justin on what that
relationship actually was. Jonah was a married man, had been
for twenty-three years. His wife, a very vanilla woman of no
consequence, had given him two sons, one in an Ivy League
college and the other at West Point. He had no reputation of
womanizing but that wasn't something the Defense Department talked about. Sherise knew if he was a man, he could be
seduced—especially by someone like her.

She hadn't made a practice of seducing men, but she had
used every advantage she had in her life to get ahead. She
found men to be weak enough that actual sex was usually not
necessary. Flirtation was a lost art with most young women
today. They showed a lot of skin and shook their ass and were
still confused as to why it never got them past the bedroom.
Sherise knew that flirtation was about the promise of something, not the actual delivery, and the anticipation could make
very powerful men trip over themselves to please a woman.

But every now and then a woman could forget who she
was and might even forget that she was married. The last time
she had played close to the edge, she was the one who was se-

duced and she ended up pregnant. It was a memory she was not interested in reliving, especially considering what it could mean—that Cady wasn't Justin's natural daughter. No, she couldn't let that happen again. She was going to knock Jonah's socks off, but she had to remember to keep hers on.

Sherise looked toward the bathroom, loving the sound of her baby's laughter and not wanting her to ever be separated from the source of that laughter—her father. As she picked up her vibrating phone, she felt uncertain about what her career held for her because, despite what she'd told Toni, things had changed.

But all her concern was wiped from her mind as she saw the text on her phone.

GETTIN' MARRIED!!!!!!!

3

Erica was already pissed off. They were late. Here she was waiting, bursting at the seams to talk to her best friends for the first time after getting engaged, and they were late. Not to mention, she'd come all the way downtown from her job in Arlington, VA, to accommodate their busy schedules.

Erica was so tense as she sat in the outdoor area of Art and Soul restaurant that when her cell phone, placed on the table, began to ring, she almost jumped out of her chair. She grabbed it expecting it to be either Billie or Sherise saying they were going to be late, but it was Darleen. She wasn't sure what she was calling about, but Erica knew that she had permission to take this little lunch trip.

"Darleen?" she asked. "What's going on?"

"Are you free tonight?" her boss asked.

"I don't know," Erica answered. "I was thinking maybe my girls and I might go out and celebrate my engagement."

"You can do that this weekend. Tonight, you need to go to dinner with Jonah."

Erica's antennae went up. "Dinner with Jonah? Umm . . . Is that . . . for another interview? I thought the decision was made."

"This is a working dinner." Darleen seemed to sense Erica's

hesitation. "Would you stop it, girl? It's a business dinner to introduce the project. Other people will be there."

"Oh." Erica sighed. "Why didn't you tell me that? Here I was thinking—"

"Jonah is not like that," Darleen said. "I've been here forever and I know how all these guys operate. Jonah doesn't try to make the moves on his staff. He's a good guy."

"I'm starting to believe that." Erica still had doubts but she was trying to look at everything from a positive standpoint. "Just tell me where and when."

As Darleen gave directions, Erica noticed that Billie and Sherise had just gotten out of a cab together and were rushing toward her. She hurried off the phone to greet them.

They all screamed as Erica held out her hand, displaying her ring, before they wrapped their arms around her in a big hug. Erica was delighted to be sharing this moment with her girls, her sisters. It was a long time coming and, while she had been willing to wait for the time Terrell was ready, she had been aching to join the club. She was going to be a married woman.

"I'm so happy for you," Billie said as she planted one last kiss on Erica's cheek before sitting at the table.

"I knew you would be." Erica was giddy. "I was worried that . . . you know."

"Because I'm recently divorced?" Billie asked. "No, girl. I'm not down on marriage. My marriage didn't work, but you're my sister. I know you've wanted this for so long. I'm happy when you're happy."

"Besides," Sherise said, waiving over the waiter, "Billie ain't hanging it up. We'll get her back in the married woman's club by next year."

"Oh, please," Billie said. "Give me some time to breathe."

Sherise knew she was going to get attitude for this, but she had to ask, so when the waiter left, she just let it out. "Are you sure Terrell is the right one, though?"

"What are you talking about?" Billie asked. "They've been together for one hundred years."

"That's not what she means," Erica said mockingly. "Sherise, don't start on my man, okay?"

"You know I love Terrell," Sherise lied, "but he's soooo . . . I just thought you'd want to marry up instead of down."

"Oh, here we go." Billie sat back wishing her drink would appear immediately.

"I am not marrying down!" Erica insisted. "Terrell is a great guy. He's good to me."

"I know he is," Sherise said. "I wouldn't let him anywhere near my girl if he didn't treat her right, but . . . he's so old neighborhood. Wasn't the whole point to get away from the old neighborhood?"

That was the point. Billie, Sherise, and Erica hadn't just grown up in the same neighborhood. They'd grown up on the same block. They'd been friends as far back as they could remember. It was always the three of them, and from the day they realized there was a world outside of the dismal one they lived in, they made a pact to get to it. As very young girls they formed a bond and a promise. They would make it to the Northwest side of DC and live the good life. That meant no getting in trouble, no drugs, and no getting pregnant.

Sometimes the challenge to stay focused on the long-term goals seemed too hard to meet and every one of them thought that if they'd been on their own, they wouldn't have been able to do it. But with all of them on each other's side, despite some unavoidable setbacks, their eyes remained on the prize and they only grew closer.

"Not everything about the old neighborhood is bad," Erica said.

"I didn't say that," Sherise argued. "I just think Terrell . . . well, he seems like he'd be okay if he was still there."

"That's because Terrell is okay no matter where he is," Erica said. "He's a survivor. He learned that in the old neighborhood and so did all of us. There were good people in that neighborhood. My mother for one, and Billie's parents."

"Doesn't mean you want to go back there," Sherise said.

"I'm not." Erica grabbed the lemon wedge off her glass of water and nibbled at it. "But I'm not gonna write off anyone just because they're from there. That would mean I'd have to write you off."

"She's right," Billie said. She paused as the waiter served them drinks and placed bread on the table. "There was a lot of despair in that neighborhood, but now that I'm out of it, there are things I miss about it too."

"I don't miss anything." Sherise took a sip of her tequila sunrise.

"You sound like Porter," Billie said. "That's how he ended up where he is. Trying to escape where he came from."

"We all tried to escape where we came from," Sherise said. "He just lost his damn mind in the process."

Erica laughed. "He sure did."

Billie wasn't laughing. "She's moving in with him."

Both Erica's and Sherise's mouths flew open.

"He can't possibly be planning a future with his mistress," Sherise said, fuming.

"Men do it all the time," Billie said. "Maybe he loves her."

"Then why is he sleeping with you?" Erica asked. She wasn't intimidated by Billie's disapproving stare. "Don't look at me like that. You know no matter how he treats you, when he wants some loving, you open your legs."

"And you promise you won't do it anymore," Sherise added. "But you lie."

It was true and Billie was ashamed. After she'd found out about Claire, Billie didn't want Porter to touch her even when he had promised he ended the affair. When her mind had been made up that she couldn't trust him again, Billie was so heart-broken that the thought of sex never entered her mind. Whenever Porter would try to persuade her, it took no effort to turn him down.

But things began to change after a few months apart from him. She still hated him and felt angry and betrayed, but Billie found herself lonely for the first time in her adult life. She found her body craving Porter's particular touch. He knew how to push all her buttons and he knew how to bring her to an orgasm more than once when he made angry love to her.

How it happened, Billie was never really sure. One of them would start a fight and the next thing she knew, they were ripping each other's clothes off. She knew he was going to leave her and go back to Claire, but she didn't care. At least not at the time. After it was all over, she would be filled with regret and shame and vow it would never happen again.

"Now that she's moving in with him," Billie said, trying hard to believe her own words, "that's it. And now there's this mess with Tara."

"You can't let him give you a hard time about her," Erica said. "You're a lawyer. There has to be something you can do."

Billie shook her head. "There isn't. I have absolutely no rights at all to her."

"You can't let him use her to keep getting you in bed," Sherise said, knowing she was the last person to preach on resisting temptation.

"I don't want to talk about Porter anymore." Billie sat up straight just as their food arrived. "I want to talk about wedding plans. What have you done so far?"

"I just got engaged last night," Erica said. "Give me a second."

"That's what we're here for," Billie said. "We'll go buy all the bridal magazines and go through them tonight."

"I can't tonight," Sherise said. "I have a business dinner."

"Getting back into the swing of things?" Billie asked.

"Heading for the top," Sherise said proudly. "I'm dining with Jonah Dolan himself."

"Who is that?" Billie asked.

"What?" Erica leaned across the table. "Jonah? Tonight? Oh my God. I'm gonna be there."

"Where?"

"Acadiana," Erica said, not believing this. "You're working on Jonah's project?"

"Who are we talking about?" Billie asked. "And why are you calling him Jonah like he's a friend of yours?"

"With the engagement stuff, I forgot to tell you guys," Erica said. "I got a promotion. I work for Jonah Dolan now." Erica told them both about the quick turnaround of fortune her career had suddenly taken and how she was jumping head first into it despite her concerns about how she actually got it.

"You sell yourself short, baby girl." Billie winked at her. "You deserve it."

"Isn't this a small world," Sherise said, her mouth forming a wicked smile.

"I didn't even know I'd be working on your project," Erica said.

"They haven't told you anything?" Billie asked. She thought it was kind of weird as Erica shook her head, but she was happy for her. She knew her girl needed the money.

"It's not my project yet," Sherise said. "I might have to put a bitch in her place first."

Sherise told the girls all about Toni Williams and how she had dispatched Justin to get the goods on her. She saw the disapproving look on Erica's face.

"Don't judge me," she quickly responded. "This woman is trying to take what is mine."

"But you always play dirty," Erica said.

"You're damn right, I play dirty." Sherise wasn't at all ashamed. "It's a dirty world."

"I have to side with Sherise on this one," Billie said. "If the woman is gunning for Walter's job, she basically declared war."

"A war I'm gonna win," Sherise added. "And you're gonna help."

"Me?" Erica asked. "How can I help?"

"I need to get an advantage with Jonah and I can't do it the way I think Toni's doing it."

"You think she's sleeping with him?" Erica asked.

Sherise nodded. "But if you're on the inside, I can get to him a different way."

"You know I'll put in a good word for you," Erica said, "but I'm not going to do something that jeopardizes my opportunity to help you get the upper hand."

"Of course not," Sherise said with a sweet smile.

This coincidence was a prize that was placed in Sherise's lap through no effort of her own. God wanted her to win this. It was a sign. She had an "in" through Erica and she was going to use that to get Toni out of the way. Starting tonight.

As she darted back to her office after lunch with the girls, Billie checked her watch. She'd been gone just a few minutes less than an hour, but from the looks she was getting, an hour was an hour too long to take for lunch. She wasn't going to make a practice of it, but she wasn't going to miss a chance to hang out with her girls. There seemed to be less and less of those chances these days, and the way they worked their associates at this firm, Billie imagined her days of hanging out with the girls were over.

She intended to get right back to work, but as soon as she reached her office, she noticed someone was sitting in her seat, moving around in it. She couldn't tell who it was because the chair's back was to her, but she assumed it was Richard Nelson, the associate she shared this office with but had not yet met.

"Richard?"

When the seat swung around, Billie knew, as happy as she was to see this visitor, it wasn't a good thing that she was here.

"This is where you work?"

Tara twirled around in the seat with a satisfied smile on her face. She was a typically cute fourteen-year-old girl, with smooth, glowing, and beautiful dark brown skin. She had Porter's piercing eyes and her mother's tiny features. She was a late bloomer, just now getting her curves, but it was obvious to anyone that the curly haired beauty was going to blossom into a knockout.

"This is much nicer than the place you used to work," she added.

"What are you doing here?" Billie came around the desk.

Tara stopped, looking up at Billie and clearly disappointed. "Nice to see you too."

"I'm always happy to see you, baby." Billie leaned down and kissed her on the forehead. She was very happy to see her. It had been a couple of months. "Porter is gonna be pissed. You should be in school."

"Half day today." Tara stood up and went over to the small window with a view of the next building only ten feet away. "And I don't care what he wants."

"You have to. He's your dad." Billie had already explained to Tara how every time she acted out, it was Billie that got Porter's wrath, but she wasn't getting through. "I'm very busy, Tara."

"I won't bother you," she said. "I'll text and be quiet until it's time to go home."

"Go home?" Billie asked. "We have different homes, re-member?"

"Yeah," she answered. "And I'm going to yours. I'm not living in that house if she's living there."

"Stop being silly." Billie sat down in her chair. "You're going home. You know you can't come live with me. We've had this conversation. You have to find a way to deal with Claire."

"Fine." Tara reached into her pocket and pulled out her

tiny phone. She flipped it open. "I'll find someone I can stay with, one of my friends. Someone will take me in."

"You can't do that." Billie was getting frustrated. "This is a new job, Tara. I can't spend billable hours dealing with your problems with Porter's girlfriend. Why don't we talk later this—"

"Week?" Tara asked. "Next week? We never talk anymore. I don't understand why I have to suffer because he's a ho."

"Don't talk about your father like that." Billie wished there was more she could do for Tara. She loved the girl, but her hands were tied. "And if you want to see me at all, this is not the way to do it. You're fourteen. Your dad can decide who you can and can't see. If he finds out you're trying to come live with me, he'll make things worse for us."

"Then you have to make things better," Tara pleaded. "Billie, please. You have to do something. You don't know this woman like I do. She doesn't even want me there. She wants it to be like Dad didn't have a life before she met him. I'm . . . messy to her."

Billie hated Claire for her own reasons, but she really wanted to strangle the woman for what she was doing to Tara. "I'll talk to your father, but I know that he won't let you come live with me."

"Then can I at least come home with you tonight?" she asked. "Just for the night."

Billie nodded even though she knew she shouldn't have. She didn't want Tara running off with some friend and getting in trouble. Either way, once Porter found out, he would blame Billie. At least this way Billie could keep an eye on her. She just knew she was gonna get hell for it.

Erica rushed into her apartment and was headed straight for her bedroom to find something suitable for tonight's dinner and rush out, but she halted in her steps when she realized a full-fledged party was under way in her apartment.

"Hey, girl!"

"Congratulations, Erica!"

Others were giving their well wishes as she passed through the living room to Terrell, who was sitting in the window, talking on the phone.

"What the hell is going on here?" she asked as soon as she reached him.

He held up his hand to ask for a minute, but Erica snatched the phone out of his hand and turned it off.

"Hey! That was a possible side job you just messed up."

"What is going on here?" She pointed to the crowd playing SEGA and eating and drinking her refrigerator to empty. "Do I even know these people?"

"Yeah." Terrell stood up and glanced at the crowd behind her shoulders. "You know Mike. You met him when we went bowling at—"

"That's not the point," Erica said. She looked toward the bedroom. "We need to talk."

The second she got to the bedroom, Erica saw some girl lying on her bed talking on her phone. She was ready to have a fit.

"What are you doing?" Erica asked.

The girl looked at her as if she was about to get an attitude, but Erica could see the girl knew what was about to go down if she did. She quickly jumped off the bed and rushed out of the room just as Terrell walked in.

"Who the fuck was that?" Erica asked.

"Umm . . ." Terrell was trying hard to remember where he'd seen that girl. "I think she's Big Boy's girl."

"Some strange ho in my bed with her tacky ass shoes on?" Erica slammed the door behind Terrell and locked it.

"Come on, Erica." Terrell reached out to her but she slapped his hand away. "These are our friends. I thought I'd just call a few of them over here and—"

"These are *your* friends," she corrected. "Hustlers and their sidekicks. I told you how I feel about those guys. I don't want them here. What if Nate was here?"

"Nate is nineteen years old, Erica." Terrell was tired of her constant dig on his friends. They weren't all bad. "He's not an impressionable kid."

"Yes, he is, and it's hard enough keeping him in line as it is. And whatever happened to not inviting people over without discussing it with each other first?"

"An attempt at a surprise is what happened." Terrell followed her to the closet. "What are you doing?"

Erica was tossing clothes from her closet onto the floor. "I have to find my purple dress for dinner tonight."

"We're ordering pizza."

Erica turned around and pointed toward the living room. "They are leaving! You can do whatever you want. I have a business dinner."

"Business dinner." Terrell threw his arms in the air. "And so it begins. The making of Billie Junior."

Erica ignored that comment. She didn't have time for it.

"Terrell, get rid of them. I'm gonna be dressed in five minutes and when I come out of that bathroom, I want my living room hustler and ho free."

She slammed the bathroom door behind her and tried to focus on getting herself together and not thinking about what Sherise had said to her earlier that day at lunch. She had a big night ahead of her. She would have to deal with Terrell later.

Within a second of walking into the apartment, Tara darted for Billie's transitional-styled kitchen.

"Don't get comfortable," Billie called to her as she tossed her suitcase on the sofa. "Your dad is coming over."

"Why?" Tara looked up from the refrigerator.

"I called him and he's on his way over to get you."

"That's your idea of talking to him? Having him come retrieve me?"

"You have to go home." Billie felt bad about it, but she re-sented Tara's drama causing her to leave work early in her first week. This was not making a good impression. "Regardless of when Porter and I talk. You don't realize it, but you're making things worse."

"So it's my fault?" Tara asked. "Dad cheats, you leave, but I'm the one who ends up being the problem?"

"Tara." Billie started toward her, but the doorbell rang. That was fast. "Okay, he's here. Let's just not make this worse than it is. I promise you I will talk to him."

Billie took a deep breath before opening the front door, planning to be as civil as possible, but when she saw that flaxen-haired bitch standing next to Porter in front of her, Bil-lie knew civility was out the window. How dare he bring her?

"Where is she?" Porter asked, making his way in without any hesitation.

Billie and Claire held eyes for a second and Billie didn't bother to hide her hate. Claire had a smirk on her face. It seemed like an eternal smirk to Billie, who had tried to smack it off once or twice. She had only come face to face with Claire three times before this, and twice, the encounter ended in a shouting match and once with Billie grabbing a chunk of Claire's hair and stuffing it in her face.

But those days are gone, Billie told herself as she stepped aside so Claire could walk in. Despite the role this woman had played in destroying her marriage, Billie was beyond it all. At least that is what she told herself.

"Get in the car!" Porter yelled as soon as he saw Tara.

"I'm staying here," Tara yelled back.

"Tara." Billie turned to her with a warning stare.

"How could you let this happen?" Porter asked Billie.

Porter looked like a handsome model one might find on the cover of a men's magazine. He was always sharply dressed, and his hair was always trimmed tightly to his head. He was six feet tall, but his deep voice gave him a presence that made him seem taller. He had milk chocolate skin and a finely shaven goatee surrounding his full lips. His dark, mesmerizing eyes bore into Tara at the moment like daggers.

"We discussed this on the phone," Billie said, unwilling to get into an argument with Porter in front of Claire. She wasn't going to give the bitch the satisfaction. "This was not my doing."

"Stop blaming her for everything," Tara interjected. "It's Claire. It's her fault. I can't live with her. She's a fucking troll and she only wants to get rid of me."

"Tara!" Porter slammed his fist on the kitchen counter. "How many times do I have to tell you not to talk to her like that? You're just a kid. You can't—"

"It's not her fault." Claire stepped forward.

Claire wasn't particularly beautiful, but she was very cute in a Southern California natural surfer girl kind of way. She was very fair, with shiny blond hair that went halfway down her back. Her most interesting feature was her eyes, which were ocean blue with yellow flecks.

"She's just a kid," Claire added, her voice holding a hint of a southern drawl from her Richmond, Virginia, upbringing.

"She isn't making this stuff up," Billie said.

"No, but someone is," Claire said. "You're trying to poison her against me, Billie. It's so obvious."

"Claire." Porter held up a hand to his girlfriend with a warning tone.

Billie could have told him not to waste his time. "Are you accusing me of using Tara, who is like a daughter to me? How dare you?"

"Easily," Claire said. "Because it's true. You hate that I'm with Porter and you're trying to make me miserable by getting her to make things hard on me."

"I'm making things hard on you?" Tara laughed out loud. "This bitch."

"Enough, Tara!" Porter yelled. "Now, Claire . . ."

"It's true, Porter," Claire said. "Tara is nothing to Billie but a way to stay in your life and make me pay because you chose me over her."

"You simple bitch." Billie stepped to her, stopping a few inches away. "First of all, he didn't choose you over me. He chose you after I made it clear I was no longer a choice."

"Oh, please." Claire tried to laugh, but she had a nervous look on her face. "Porter, can you tell her—"

"Claire," Porter warned again. "Billie, just calm down."

"Second!" Billie yelled, her face just inches from Claire. "I love Tara. I love her like a daughter. I would *never* use her! And if she says you're making life miserable for her, I believe her."

"You need to back off," Claire said, her voice skipping a bit.

"You need to get the fuck out of my home before I make you wish you were never born."

"Exactly what I mean," Claire said. "Tara doesn't need to be around anyone with such a gutter mouth."

The palm of Billie's hand made contact with Claire's face and pushed, sending her screaming back several feet. She almost fell on the sofa, but bounced back and started for Billie. Billie was waiting for her. As Claire's arms flailed, Billie reached out and came back up with a clump of blond hair in her hand. She pulled it back with Claire gripping her hand, trying to pull her off.

"Get out of my house, bitch!"

"Billie!" Porter was trying to stand between the women and pull them apart. "Let her go. Dammit, Billie. Tara is watching."

Billie quickly let go of Claire's hair and turned around to see Tara staring at them with her eyes and mouth wide open. It made her sick to her stomach to think of how she acted in front of the girl. She was only fourteen. Billie tried to get a hold of herself as she walked over to Tara.

"I am so sorry, Tara."

"You're sorry?" Tara asked. "She was asking for it."

"That wasn't right," Billie said. "You have to know that. Sometimes things just get—"

"Get in the car, Tara." Porter approached his daughter and took the can of pop she had been drinking out of her hand. "Now!"

"I hate you!" Tara yelled before grabbing her purse and storming out of the apartment.

"What in the hell is wrong with you?" Porter asked Billie.

Billie pointed to Claire, who was still standing, looking stunned as she held her hand to the part of her head where Billie had almost pulled her hair out. "I'm not gonna let her get away with accusing me of using Tara."

"You just need to calm the fuck down." Porter ran his hand anxiously over his head.

"She's crazy!" Claire screamed.

"Get out of my house!"

"Claire, please leave." Porter stood in front Billie, blocking her view of Claire. "Wait for me in the car."

As soon as Claire was gone, Billie felt herself begin to calm down. She pointed a warning finger at Porter. "Don't you ever bring her to my home again."

"We were on our way to dinner."

"She should have waited in the car," Billie said. "And going out to dinner? Do you really think that's the best move when your daughter is practically running away?"

"Don't tell me how to raise my daughter."

"I'm just . . ." Billie sighed. "Porter, this is your job. You keep telling me that Tara is yours and not mine, so it is your job to help her out with this. She's clearly not adjusting."

"With no help from you," he accused.

"Is that your plan?" she asked. "To just blame it on me? No matter how much you try, you know I love Tara and I would never use her to get to you."

Porter came over to her in a conciliatory gesture. He looked at her tenderly. "You don't need her to get to me."

Just as he reached his hand to her face, Billie moved away from him, hating that part of her that wanted to stay right where she was.

"You bring your whore to my home, accuse me of using Tara, and think you can make the moves on me?"

"I wasn't trying to make the moves on you." Porter straightened his demeanor and stepped away. "I'm doing you a favor by even agreeing to talk to you. Tara is really none of your business."

"If you claim to want to do what is best for her, you'll want to figure out how to let me be a part of her life."

"I can't deal with this now," Porter said.

"I promised her we would talk."

"You're not in a position to make promises to my daughter." Porter reached into his pocket to pick up his vibrating phone.

"Barbie calling?" Billie teased.

"We can talk over dinner tomorrow night." He shoved the phone back in his pocket.

"I'm not having dinner with you." Billie knew what that could lead to.

"Then we don't need to talk at all." Porter headed for the door.

"Wait," Billie called after him. "I already left work before anyone else today. I can't afford another—"

"That's not my problem." At the door, Porter turned to her. "I'll be at City Zen at eight."

When he closed the door behind him, Billie already knew she would show up for dinner. She had made a promise to Tara, and especially after that ridiculous display in front of her, trying to work out something with Porter was the least of what she owed the girl. He just better not show up with that bitch or they would all end up getting thrown out.

* * *

Erica rushed from the Gallery Place metro stop to Acadiana, the Louisiana-themed restaurant on New York Avenue, wishing she had chosen to drive instead. The dinner was set for 8:00 and it was 7:55. She didn't want to be late to her first business dinner with Jonah. She knew it didn't look good.

To her surprise, the host led her to the private table reserved for the Dolan party and all she found was one woman talking on her cell phone. She was an attractive middle-aged white woman who, although dressed in a simple white cocktail dress, was clearly awash in money. Everything about her look, from head to toe, showed meticulous care, and her jewelry was shiny enough to be seen from the other end of the restaurant.

Erica sat a couple of seats away from the woman at the circular table and waited for the woman to look her way. When she finally did, Erica smiled, but the woman didn't bother to smile back. This was getting off to a great start.

"Erica." Jonah finally appeared at the table with a bright smile on his face. He was wearing a pair of khaki-colored cotton pants and a white oxford shirt and looked even better in his casual gear than in his suit.

"I thought I was late," Erica said, "but . . ."

"Traffic is hell out there." Jonah tapped the shoulder of the seated woman as he stood at the chair next to her. "Have you met my wife, Juliette?"

"Not yet. She seems busy."

Juliette placed her phone on the table and looked at Erica with a pasted smile that Erica, or any other woman, could tell was completely fake. "So this is Erica," she said. "Jonah talks about how happy he is you're joining his team. It's nice to meet you."

Erica began to lift her hand for a shake but, realizing quickly that the woman had no intention of shaking her hand, sat it back down on her lap. "Nice to meet you too."

Jonah sat down next to his wife with a look of discomfort on his face. Erica wasn't sure what was going on but her delight at not being the last to show up was officially replaced with unease. Her usually suspicious mind was racing miles a minute, recalling the dismissal of the previous triple A and Sherise's suspicions about Jonah and the woman who had taken her place while she was away, Toni Williams. Did Juliette suspect that Erica was onboard because of a personal relationship?

Stop trying to psych yourself out, she told herself. She'd let her pessimism get in the way too many times. If only Sherise would get here, she might feel more comfortable, because this little three-way was not going to work in her favor. She was starting to get a little suspicious again when Sherise's boss, Walter, and her current competition, Toni, showed up only seconds later. Erica was very used to Sherise's signature late entrance.

Right on cue, just as everyone sat down, Sherise showed up with Justin on her arm. She looked amazing in a multicolored sleeveless drape silk dress that stopped just above her knees, and she knew it.

Sherise fought every bone in her body to avoid focusing on Jonah because she wanted to see his reaction. She didn't need to. She knew he was entranced; any man would be and that was the point. Wait until everyone was seated, make an entrance and wow them all. She knew Jonah would be impressed, but Sherise had the real prize. Toni Williams looked livid. She wasn't even attempting to hide her envy. And the night was only beginning.

Erica watched in amusement as Jonah, a man who was known for his composure and poise, almost tripped over himself to stand up and greet Sherise.

"It's nice to finally meet you," Jonah said as he held his hand out. "Walter has been speaking very highly of you."

"Assistant Secretary Dolan," Sherise said, liking the firm, powerful grip of his handshake. "It's great to meet you too."

Sherise immediately found him attractive, but that was no surprise. He was an alpha male and that was clear. It meant nothing to Sherise, but she didn't need to pretend she didn't notice how good he looked for an older man.

Hearing his wife clear her throat seemed to be the only thing that distracted Jonah from Sherise and when he introduced her she could tell this woman was very protective of her husband. That was fine. Despite her attraction to him, Sherise had no intention of getting involved with Jonah. He was a means to get Walter's position and get Toni out of the way.

A means that included Justin, who had found out that Toni had made a few enemies on The Hill for shifting loyalties at the worst possible times. Sherise had convinced Justin to be the bad guy. He would do his job inquiring about Toni's past in a way that seemed innocently curious but in actuality hinted at her lack of trustworthiness. Meanwhile, Sherise would stay completely professional and focused on impressing Jonah. And she did. She took over the table within seconds. Everyone, especially Jonah, was focused on Sherise.

And Justin wasn't happy about it. He knew the woman he married. She was a flirt, a seductress, and although he trusted her, Sherise loved male attention and that bothered him at times. Especially when a man as commanding as Jonah was her target, it could be intimidating. He knew coming into tonight that she was trying to wow, something she did very well, and he was eager to be the supportive husband and play the bad guy with Toni, but if his wife leaned across the table showing her cleavage in Jonah's direction one more time, it could be a problem.

"Take it easy," he whispered into her ear halfway through the dinner.

"I'm fine," she reassured. "Do your job and I'll do mine."

"You're walking a fine line," he said. "Do you want to be the sex object or the alpha female?"

"Alpha all the way." She turned to him, placing her hand on his thigh. She squeezed it reassuringly. Justin's jealousy was cute. She leaned in and pecked him on the nose. "I'm so glad I have you to keep me in line."

"Always." He winked at her.

Sherise leaned toward Erica, who was sitting on the other side of her. "I'm working it, right?"

Erica whispered, "You don't want my opinion."

Sherise leaned back, noticing Erica's judgmental tone. She needed some perspective because she didn't want to take what was obviously a winning night too far. She grabbed Erica's arm, squeezing tight. "Ladies' room, now."

Inside the ladies' room, Sherise waited patiently for Erica to answer her.

"I wouldn't say you were being slutty," Erica said. "But you're being way too flirty."

Sherise placed her hands on her hips and rolled her eyes. "Fine, I'll lay off the flirting a little bit, but you have to admit I'm working the hell out of that table."

Erica laughed. "You don't need me to tell you. Just remember, I don't want to get involved in any games you're playing."

"You're already involved," Sherise said. "Jonah only takes his eyes off me to look at you. What's going on with that?"

"I don't know." Erica had noticed Jonah's attention. Even when he was talking to someone else, he seemed eager to look at her and smile. She was especially aware of how often his wife noticed. "But I wish he would stop. It's making me uncomfortable."

"Fuck that," Sherise said. "Work it, girl."

"I've already got the job."

"For me," Sherise said. "Work it for me."

Suddenly, Toni Williams entered the ladies' room with a

look of pure hate on her face. She headed right for Sherise. "Call off your dog," she ordered, without any of the manufactured perfection she attempted to display at the table tonight.

"My dog?" Sherise asked with a bitchy smile. "The only dog I saw at that table was—"

"Sherise." Erica elbowed her in the arm.

"Do you think I'm stupid?" Toni asked.

"Yes," Sherise answered, "but now is really not the time to—"

"I know you sicced your husband on me," Toni accused. "Tonight was supposed to be a business dinner, but every time I try to put in a word edgewise, your husband interrupts me with stupid questions."

"That's just Justin." Sherise waved a dismissive hand. "He's curious. You know it's his job to know everything about everyone."

"You put him up to it and you know it."

"Is that true?" Erica asked.

"Of course not." Sherise straightened her shoulders, holding her head high. "Toni's just a little paranoid when anyone brings up any of those bridges she's burned."

"It's not the time or place," Toni said.

"I disagree," Sherise responded. "Jonah should know who may or may not be on his next big project."

"And that's going to be me," Toni said. "And none of your underhanded tricks are gonna change that."

"You're the only trick I'm aware of," Sherise said.

"Whoa!" Erica reached up and grabbed Toni's hand just as it was about to make contact with Sherise's face. She pushed Toni back. "You don't want to do that."

"No surprise," Sherise said with a victorious smile. "She's a little hood rat. That's how they settle arguments."

"Fuck you, bitch!" Toni tried to compose herself.

"In the world of civilized people," Sherise continued, "we prefer to use our brains to kick ass."

"No one is kicking anyone's ass," Erica said, "physically or otherwise. You're both insane."

"You should stay out of this," Toni warned Erica. "It's got nothing to do with you."

"Oh," Sherise added. "I didn't tell you? Erica isn't just Jonah's new assistant. She's also one of my best friends."

Sherise reveled in Toni's expression as she realized what she was up against, and as Toni stormed out of the ladies' room, a triumphant smile formed at Sherise's lips.

Erica turned to her. "I will give you that she is a crazy bitch, but so are you."

"You're damn right I am," Sherise said. "And it's time she figured that out."

Erica didn't know exactly how this would turn out, but she had a feeling she was in the middle of a bloody war and she wasn't going to be the only casualty.

4

"Hello."

Her head deep in the documents on her laptop, Billie looked up from her desk to see a young Latino man standing in the doorway. He was wearing an expensive gray striped suit, a crisp pink shirt, and a wide, generous smile. He didn't look a day over twenty-five years old, with a thin build and dark hair that framed an appealing olive-skinned face.

"Can I help you?" Billie asked as he stepped inside.

"Not really." He tossed his suitcase on the desk at the other end of the small office. "I'm Ricardo Nelson, but everyone here calls me Richard."

"My roommate." Billie stood up and met him halfway. They shook hands. "I'm Billie Hass. Nice to finally meet you."

"I thought I was going to be the first in," Richard said as he followed Billie back to her desk.

Billie sat down. "I kind of left early last night so I felt like I needed to come in."

"By early," he said, "I take it you mean seven."

Billie smiled. "Seven at night is like a half day around here."

He nodded. "I felt the same. Just back from vacation, I feel like everyone hates me."

"Getting used to this law firm culture is not going to be easy."

"You'll be fine," Richard said. "This is one of the better firms you can work for. At least they pay you for your bother."

Billie felt it was sad that this is what it had all become about.

"Morning!" Callie knocked on the door as she practically hopped in with a chipper look on her face. "You two finally meet? Good, that's out of the way."

She walked over to Billie's desk and offered her a folder. "This is for you, Billie. Richard, you need to meet with Alvin at . . ."

"I have my schedule," Richard said as he made his way to his desk. "I'm getting ready now."

Billie opened the folder in front of her. "Can you explain this to me? Grady Pharmaceuticals?"

"That's a new client." Callie sounded and looked as if she was personally excited by the news. "Not that big a client, so only one associate needs to work on it, and that's you. Read it. You have a meeting with Jerry and Marcos at ten."

"I'm supposed to go through all this by ten?" Billie sifted through the very thick folder of affidavits, articles, notes, and more.

"Also bring your notes." Callie headed for the door. "There's doughnuts and stuff in the kitchen. Might want to get some before everyone gets here."

"I don't have the time it would take to go all the way to the kitchen," Billie said. "I can't spare the ten seconds."

"They're starting you on Big Pharm." Richard laughed. "Baptism by fire."

Billie suddenly remembered something. "I know this company. They were accused of environmental racism."

"There is no such crime last I checked the books," Richard said.

"No, not officially," Billie said. "But they targeted minority communities throughout rural Virginia to illegally dump their waste."

Richard looked at her, confused. "Is this going in your notes?"

"I'm supposed to be defending Grady?"

"Supposed to be?" Richard asked. "You are."

Billie felt a brick in her stomach. So much for fighting for the voiceless, fighting the man. Now she was defending the big, bad guy.

Seeming to sense her dread, Richard offered advice. "Remember, you're defending the law. Whether or not you like your client is irrelevant."

"Whether or not they're actually guilty isn't," she said.

"No," Richard corrected. "It's not whether or not they're guilty that matters. It's whether or not they can be proven guilty. It's a valid principle and it applies to Big Pharm just as it does to the little guys you used to defend."

"There are poor people throughout Virginia who have filed civil claims against Grady. If I get them off in criminal court, what chance do those fines have?"

"That's not your business," Richard said. "And it's not your problem."

Billie got up and headed for the kitchen. She was depressed enough to eat twenty doughnuts.

Sherise was delighted, but not the least bit surprised when she stepped into her office the next morning and saw a bouquet of flowers on her desk. It was a beautiful selection of red orchids and purple flowers she wasn't familiar with.

She rushed to her desk and grabbed the bouquet, smelling it once before opening the card.

IT WAS A PLEASURE. JONAH

Of course it was. Sherise was more pleased with herself than she should be as she brought the bouquet to her nose again. The smell of victory was sweet indeed.

"Who are those from?"

Sherise swung around to find Walter standing in the doorway looking curiously and somewhat cautiously at the flowers in her hand. Sherise knew Walter to be generally oblivious to matters of a sexual nature, but he wasn't an idiot and Sherise didn't want to concern him.

"My husband," she answered. Until she was clear whose side Walter was on, she was going to play it safe. "Sweet, isn't he?"

Walter nodded with that fatherly approval he always displayed. "You did great last night. You wowed them as usual."

"I'm looking forward to working on this project." Sherise placed the flowers down. "I just don't see the need for Toni to be involved anymore. Wasn't she here to pick up the slack while I was out?"

"You said yourself that your hours might be a little sporadic when you first came back."

"Maybe my hours." Sherise regretted saying that, but it happened before she knew about Toni's intentions. "But not my commitment."

"I've never doubted your commitment," Walter said. "You know things have changed while you were gone."

"Clearly. You used to tell me everything."

"I'm sorry you had to hear about the dinner from Toni. She just beat me to it."

"Maybe she beat you to it," Sherise said, "but she isn't going to beat me to anything. Not unless you give her an advantage."

Walter frowned. "Sherise, you're so competitive—something I've always liked about you. I know you want my job and being lead on this project is the best way to get there."

"I don't just want your job, Walter," Sherise said. "I think I have a right to be first in line for it."

"You are," he answered. "You're just not the only person in line. You're very young and there is so much politicking here."

"Toni doesn't have the savvy to deal with these government types and you know it."

"Toni has more talent than you give her credit for." Walter seemed to notice the reaction his words had on Sherise. "No, I don't mean that. I mean that Toni is the reason I have this new job in the private sector making twice what I'm making here."

"So you're paying her for a job with a job?" Sherise asked. "Doesn't seem like you. You're a believer in people earning what they get."

"I promised her a chance," Walter said. "I owed her that just based on the work she's done while you've been gone."

"But I'm back, Walter."

Walter seemed to sense what Sherise was saying and she felt good about that. She admired Walter immensely and he knew that. He also knew that she wouldn't let even him get in her way.

"It's yours to lose," he answered, before heading out.

Yours to lose. The words offered some sense of assurance to Sherise, knowing that the power was in her hands. After last night, she felt certain that if Jonah had any say, he would recommend her. She just wanted one last chance to remind him of how good she was, and she needed a chance to do this without competition from Toni and without raising Justin's suspicions.

As much as things change, they tend to stay the same. That is what was on Erica's mind the second she sat down at her new desk, which was already piled high with work. It wasn't as if she was in a position to ask for a little time off between jobs. Besides, she was eager to get to work to find out exactly what was going on. She wanted to dismiss all her suspicions, but doubted she would be able to.

"Good morning." Jenna darted out of Jonah's office over to her desk. She was picking up the phone. "Get your notepad."

"Morning." Erica dropped her stuff in the chair and searched for a notepad and pen. "Do you want me to . . . ?"

As she started talking on the phone, Jenna had her hand up to silence Erica. Not sure what she should do, Erica started toward Jenna's desk, which was about ten feet away. But Jenna grabbed a stack of folders and started for her. She seemed to be handing them to her, so Erica held her hand out, but Jenna passed her and placed them on Erica's desk. Awkwardly, Erica started back for her desk, but Jenna snapped her fingers and waved for her to go into Jonah's office, which was behind her desk.

Erica hesitated and she could tell that Jenna noticed as she hung up the phone and let out an impatient sigh. She flew past Erica and into Jonah's office. Erica followed her as quickly as she could.

Taking a cue from Jenna, Erica sat down in one of the old leather chairs on the opposite side of Jonah's desk as he spoke on the phone to someone in a foreign language she vaguely identified as Russian. When he saw them, he nodded at Jenna and winked at Erica.

"Welcome, Erica," Jonah said as soon as he hung up the phone. "Jumping into the fire?"

"Thanks, I . . ."

"Let's get it started." Jonah gestured toward Jenna.

Erica was caught off guard as Jenna began reciting the day's schedule. Was she supposed to have a copy of the sheet Jenna was reading from? Was she supposed to be writing this down? Erica was on her way to freaking out when she heard her name spoken.

"I'm sorry?" she had to ask as both Jonah and Jenna looked at her.

"Are you paying attention?" Jenna asked, annoyed.

"I'm trying to keep up." Erica smiled nervously.

Jonah laughed. "We go real fast around here. Probably a little different than most government offices."

Jenna wasn't as understanding as Jonah. "I asked if you can do all the invitations by the end of today."

"You want me to write invitations?"

"You have to listen," Jenna said. "There's a stack of invites for Jonah and his wife to social events. On each of them I've indicated accept or decline. You need to follow through and RSVP or decline with a card. Have Jonah sign them."

"Of course," Erica answered. That was her task? To reply to a few invitations?

"Okay." Jenna shot up. "I'm off. Jonah, I'll see you outside the briefing in one hour."

Erica stood up and turned to rush out behind her until Jonah called her name. She turned around, certain she looked like a fool. "Am I supposed to follow . . . ?"

"Sit down, Erica." Jonah gestured toward the chair.

"I'm sorry I wasn't paying attention earlier." Erica began to rattle on as she sat back down, but Jonah silenced her.

"It's okay," he said. "You'll be fine. It just takes a few days to get used to Jenna's style. I know you have what it takes."

"Thank you."

Jonah reached down and opened the top drawer of his desk. He pulled out a small, oval, mahogany box with tiny brass handles and offered it to Erica. "This is a welcome to the team gift," he said, seeming to sense her hesitation. "Take it."

Erica cautiously accepted the gift with a nervous smile. The box was beautiful. She could only imagine what was inside. She lifted the top of the box and found a wooden world time dial clock trimmed in gold. It was new and shiny but fashioned to look antique and expensive.

"This is . . . this is nice," she said. "Thank you."

"You're welcome." Jonah's response was quick and unemotional. "I was hoping you and I could find a few moments to get to know each other."

Erica wasn't sure how to react. Was this where the weirdness started? "Umm . . . I . . . Well . . ."

"Let's be clear." He leaned forward and looked directly at her. "You're wise to be suspicious, but I assure you I have no inappropriate interest in you. If we're going to work with each other, I have to be able to trust and know you, that's all. So calm down."

"I'm fine." She laughed nervously again.

"Okay." He wasn't buying it. "I just want you to know that you don't have to worry about my intentions. I'm looking for a professional friendship with you."

Erica used that encouraging statement to help muster the courage to ask a question that was nagging at her. "Can I ask a question?"

"Anything." He leaned back in his chair.

"What happened to the last triple A? The one I replaced?"

"Grace Kim was dismissed because information was discovered during the follow-up process to her security clearance that made it . . . unwise to keep her on."

Erica's eyes widened. This was much more interesting than she thought. There were various levels of security clearance a person needed to pass to work in certain positions within the Defense Department. The government delved into absolutely every area of your life to determine how vulnerable you could be to an enemy. Even after you passed, periodic follow-ups were made to make sure one hadn't been further compromised.

"What did they find out?"

Jonah laughed. "I admire your curiosity, but I can't tell you that. It's no matter. Jenna didn't like her anyway."

"She doesn't seem to like me very much."

"I like you," Jonah said. "And Jenna will come around if you do a good job."

"That I can do," Erica said, feeling much better now.

"Can I ask some questions?"

Erica nodded.

"Do you have family?"

"Yes, but it's just me and my nineteen-year-old brother, Nate."

"Is he in college?"

"He's not . . . the college type. He's a repairman at Metzer Medical Center."

He smiled as if that pleased him. "Do you have plans to go to college?"

Erica guessed that was his way of telling her he knew she hadn't. "I think it's a little late for me."

"It's never too late," he said. "You should really consider it, Erica. You're a smart young woman. I was your age when I started college because I'd been in the marines. I was already married."

"I have someone to take care of."

"I thought you said he was nineteen?"

Erica was getting uncomfortable. "Yes, but . . ."

"He's old enough to make it on his own. You need to start thinking about your future."

"Well . . . right now, I'm just focusing on this job and my wedding."

"Wedding?" Jonah looked surprised. "You're getting married? Since . . . since when?"

She proudly showed him her ring. "No date or anything yet. You don't have to worry about me taking a leave from my job or anything. I—"

"Who is he?"

Erica thought that was rather abrupt. "His name is Terrell Nicolli. He's a driver for a small limo company and we've been together for a long time."

"A driver?" Jonah clearly wasn't impressed.

Erica was a little offended by the way he looked. "He's a great guy."

"I'm sure he is," Jonah said. "You said both of your parents are dead? Were you close to them?"

"Of course." Erica was very uncomfortable now.

She wasn't a trusting soul naturally. It took her a while to open up to people and even longer when they gave her a snotty reaction when she told them her boyfriend was a limo driver. Now he wanted to know the details of her relationship with her parents?

"Well, I was close to my mother," she said. "I didn't know my father. . . . Why are you asking me again?"

"I don't mean to make you uncomfortable," Jonah said. "I'm just curious as to—"

There was a knock on the door before Jenna poked her head in. "Briefing, Jonah. Now!"

"Of course!" Jonah stood up from his chair. "I have to head to my morning briefing. We'll talk more when I get back."

"Sounds good." Erica smiled as he darted past her.

She followed him out of the office and rushed past Jenna to her desk. She wasn't at all inclined to get more into her personal life later, but at least she felt confident that Jonah didn't want something from her she was not willing to give. It left her free to focus on her job and try to figure out how to keep up with Jenna.

Justin was moaning his pleasure as Sherise moved on top of him. Her movements, which started slowly, were now picking up pace, and the noises she made when they made love, the noises that drove Justin insane, were picking up. He knew she was about to orgasm.

Moving up and down, Sherise felt her body start to take control away from her. She was straddling Justin and leaned over, grabbing at the headboard in front of her. She felt Justin stroking her hips and the side of her body as she moved to a rhythm.

She screamed his name as frantic sensation rushed through her body all the way to the tips of her fingers and toes, sending pleasure to every inch of her. She shuddered all over as little aftershocks teased her body.

As always, her orgasm turned him on immensely. Taking hold of her body, he kept her connected to him as he rolled over and positioned himself on top of her. He began moving inside her again, thrusting harder and harder. She was grabbing his arms as if urging him to come closer to her even though he could move no closer. When he exploded, his groan was deep and shattering as it rushed through him.

He pulled out of her and fell on the bed beside her, completely spent.

Sherise felt completely relaxed and in that state of euphoria that she loved so much as he wrapped his arm around her and she leaned into him.

"I'm very happy I turned down an invitation to happy hour," Justin said, lowering his head just enough to kiss her on the lips slowly and passionately. "This was much, much better after-work entertainment."

"We have to take our chances when we get them." Smiling widely, Sherise leaned away so she could look up at him.

They hadn't had very many opportunities to have sex since Cady was born. It wasn't that they didn't want to, but usually by the time they made it to bed at night, which was never before midnight, at least one of them was too tired. In an unusual series of events they had gotten home from work at the same time and Cady was sound asleep. After putting her down, Sherise initiated the lovemaking and Justin was more than eager to comply.

"It's getting better," he said. "She's sleeping pretty much through the night now."

"That is a blessing." Sherise reached out and ran her fingers along the side of Justin's face. He was good in bed and always patient. She adored him.

"The question is," Justin said, "how long do we wait before we have another one?"

"Way to kill the mood," Sherise said. They agreed before they were married on two children, but she couldn't even think about that right now.

"I was thinking we wait another year and get pregnant."

"*We* get pregnant?" she asked. "Remember, I'm the one who actually gets pregnant and with everything going on with my career, I don't know if another year is a feasible time plan."

"You said Walter's job was yours to lose."

"I'm not sure I can trust him." She moved away, lying on her back and looking at the ceiling. "Do you have anything more on Toni?"

Justin shrugged, not too happy with the way this conversation was going, but he wasn't able to deny Sherise anything, especially not after sex. "I think something might have gone down when she was with the White House Economic Policy team a couple of years ago. She was just an underling, but she lasted three months."

"That's par for the course for her, right?"

Justin nodded. "But this time I can't find out why she was . . . moved out. Usually it's pretty easy. Things are so incestuous on White House staff teams. Everyone assumes it was another personality clash or her jumping ship the first chance she got to get on someone else's bandwagon."

"But not this time?"

"And no one who worked on the council at that time will talk to me." Justin noticed Sherise's wide smile. "What are you thinking?"

"I'm thinking I need to find out what happened and when I do, I'll have one less problem to deal with."

"I'm not so sure about this one, baby. I got some weird

looks when I asked for more info from people." Justin placed his hands behind his head on the pillow. "I get a feeling anyone who pushes on this one could be bringing some trouble onto themselves."

"I'm not afraid of a little trouble." Sherise slid over and cuddled next to him, her breast pressing against his chest. She leaned in and kissed him on his neck. "You should know that by now."

Sherise tried to drown her thoughts into her husband, thinking only of him, but in the back of her mind was this little nagging thought. Those flowers that Jonah had sent her had been red orchids and a type she couldn't identify. She couldn't wait for the next time she would see him so she could have the chance to ask him what they were.

Erica would never underestimate the task of RSVPing ever again. She soon found out why she had only one task for the day. RSVPing for Jonah Dolan and his wife was a huge project. There were over two hundred invitations to social, commemorative, and other occasions and there was a code on each of them indicating the particular reply requested. For those he had agreed to attend, there was an RSVP letter that he would sign and it must include a security clearance inquiry the host had to follow up on. For those he would have to decline, there were a variety of note cards that were appropriate based on the occasion. Purely social events such as weddings had one card and public events such as memorials or official events had another.

After complying with each of the invites' individual requirements, Erica placed the stack on Jonah's desk for a signature and went to work on the envelopes. It was almost seven when Jonah completed all the signings and called her into his office to retrieve them.

"Sorry to keep you so late," he said.

"I don't mind," Erica replied. "I'm just surprised you sign them all individually. I thought all the bigwigs had their assistants place a signature stamp."

"It's an old habit." He handed her the box full of signed invitations. "My wife was brought up in social circles that taught it was tacky and classless to reply without a genuine signature. Everything must be personalized."

"It makes sense." Erica noticed that he looked very tired. For once, he looked closer to his age, but was still handsome. "I'll get these out right away."

"You can do that tomorrow," he said. "Don't let Jenna intimidate you. She stays here until I stay here. It's just a thing for her. You're not expected to. As long as they're ready by mail pickup tomorrow, you'll be fine."

"Thanks, but I know I need to win Jenna over if I have a chance here."

Jonah smiled, his eyes waking up a little. "That's really nice to hear, but I know you have someone at home waiting for you."

Erica was eager to get home to Terrell. Since she kicked his friends out last night, they hadn't really spoken and it upset her. They had just gotten engaged and they were already fighting.

"Well, good . . ."

"Your boyfriend, Terrell?"

"My fiancé," she corrected.

Jonah nodded. "I would like to meet him. I might have an opportunity for him. I know someone in our official driving service and since there are so many contractors out there trying to bid on our projects, there are a lot of people coming to and from the Pentagon. They could use some help."

While Erica thought it would be great for Terrell to get more work, she wasn't really sure why Jonah would do this for him. Or was he doing it for her? It was all a little confusing, but from the earnest look on Jonah's face, she had to say something.

"I'll definitely tell him." And with that she was out the door.

"I think it's a good deal," Porter said as he placed his napkin on the table.

Billie looked at him from across the small table where they had just finished dinner and an entire bottle of wine in the intimate setting of City Zen inside the luxurious Mandarin Oriental Hotel in DC. She knew he was right, but didn't want to admit it.

"Once a month?" she asked. "What if I have my day and two weeks later, Tara needs me for something?"

Porter sighed. "I'm not preventing you from talking to her on the phone, as long as you don't try to talk against me or Claire."

"I've never done that," Billie insisted angrily. "How many times do I have to tell you that? I've bitten my tongue a million times because I don't want to do that with her."

"What about yesterday?" he asked.

Billie looked down at her lap, ashamed. "I shouldn't have attacked Claire, but she took it there and you shouldn't have brought her to my home. She was your mistress when you were married to me."

"This isn't about Claire."

Billie nodded. "Fine. One day a month I can have Tara to myself and I can talk on the phone to her anytime I want."

"No," Porter said. "You can talk to her anytime she wants and as long as it isn't a conversation against me or Claire. Also, I need you to work with me to back out of her life."

Billie was getting very emotional at the thought. She loved Tara, but knew there was nothing that she could do to force herself into Tara's life. "Maybe it is better if she gets used to me not being there, but that doesn't mean I don't love her."

"I know you love her." Porter's deep voice softened.

His voice caused a reaction in Billie as she looked back up at him. There was a sincerity to his tone that touched at something in her, pulled at her.

"You're the only real mother she's ever had, Billie." Porter shook his head. "You're the only woman to put her first, to be a good example for her. Despite any of our differences, you were a great mother to her."

Billie didn't realize until his last word that Porter had been working his hand across the table toward hers. When she felt his fingers brush against her own, she felt a sharp jolt of electricity run through her and all her warning signs began to blare.

She pulled her hand away. "How do I know you won't change your mind next week when you're mad at me for something?"

"You don't," Porter answered. "But I won't do that. I love Tara and I've reached an impasse with her. I want her happy. I can't be happy unless my baby girl is happy."

Billie noted the emotion in his voice, remembering that he used to say that about her. How much of that wine had she drunk? She should probably get going. She looked around for the waiter.

"I've already paid the bill," Porter said. "While you were in the ladies' room."

"How much do I owe you?" She reached for her purse.

"Please, Billie." Porter stood up. "While our income gap has tightened significantly with your new job, I still make a crapload more money than you."

"But I'm not going to owe you anything." Billie stood up, but realizing he was too close, she took a step back. She felt one of the stone pillars that decorated the modern restaurant stop her.

"Who said anything about owing?" he asked, moving closer. His hand went to her waist as he looked into her eyes.

"Stop it." She couldn't move back any farther because of the pillar, but he certainly wasn't going to try to kiss her in this full restaurant. "There are people here."

"I know that." Leaning away, Porter lifted his hand and dangled a white card in his fingers. "I got a room here. Let's finish this upstairs."

"You son of a bitch." Billie wanted to slap him, but she only pushed him back. "Did you think I was going to fuck you because you gave me access to Tara once a month? You are some kind of asshole."

"I'm the kind of asshole that satisfies you," he said, undaunted by her resistance. "And you satisfy me like no one ever has or ever will. We've reached a new stage in our relationship. We've agreed on Tara. We should celebrate."

Her expression revealed her fury. "You can go upstairs, use that key card and fuck yourself."

She turned to leave, but he grabbed her by the arm and pulled her back to him. He grabbed her by the other arm and pulled her even closer, pressing his lips hard against hers. She struggled at first, trying to break free, but she was too tiny and small to even make a dent. Despite the screaming inside her, Billie's body began to respond to him immediately, and within a few seconds, she felt her lips begin to give in. They opened just an inch as she stopped pushing against him. His tongue entered her mouth as his lips pressed harder and she felt a quiet sound escape her.

"Let's go," he said as he finally removed his lips from hers and leaned away from her.

He had taken her hand and was leading her out of the restaurant, where they were getting stares from other diners who had witnessed the display. She was humiliated and excited and not once did she think of pulling away as he led her through the lobby. Once they were in the elevator, they did everything short of tear each other's clothes off as Billie felt her body getting hotter and hotter.

She could hear her brain yelling for her to stop as it had so many times before, but her body was in control and it wanted Porter inside her. Billie's body ached to be devoured, and when he finally got her to the hotel room, Porter did just that. Twice.

When Erica finally got home, she was starving and exhausted. She warmed at the sight of Terrell and Nate sitting next to each other on the sofa eating and watching TV. She was finally home.

"I'm sorry I'm so late," she said as they both turned to greet her. "First days are always hard."

"We ordered pizza." Terrell jumped up from the sofa and headed for her. "Don't worry about it, baby."

He kissed her quickly on the lips and winked at her, making Erica feel much better than she had when they'd left this morning without speaking. Before she could respond, he turned and headed back for the TV.

Nineteen-year-old Nate Kent looked younger than he was, a sort of poster boy for the brooding teenager. He was a nut brown with thick black eyebrows that framed his handsome young face. He had a large nose and full lips and was currently sporting the bald look. He liked to goof around and waste his time. Girls chased him constantly, but he had a real girlfriend for the first time in his life, was holding down the same job for a little over two years, and seemed to Erica as if he was beginning to finally grow up.

When Erica joined them, grabbing a slice of pizza and falling into the closest chair, Nate turned to her. "So, sis." He smiled wide, showing bright, white teeth. "How many people did you help get killed today?"

Erica almost choked on her first bite of pizza. "What?"

"You're working under Jonah Dolan," he said. "He's part of the group to blame for all these wars we're in."

"Boy, shut it," Terrell said, laughing.

"Stop being stupid," Erica said. "It's just another job at the Pentagon."

"But the higher up you get, the more you become part of the problem." Nate stuffed a handful of cookies in his mouth and spoke as he chewed. "Come on, girl. How can you sell out like that?"

"Don't be disgusting," she said. "And I don't need one of your self-righteous rants."

The boy always thought he knew so much when he barely knew enough to even take care of himself. She had taken care of him herself since their mother died and it had been a constant struggle to keep him on the straight and narrow. In the old neighborhood she'd had to fight gangs who preyed on fatherless boys. Even after they left, it seemed like a constant struggle to fight the outside elements that tried to pull him down the wrong path. So far, so good, but lately he'd been on a rage-against-the-man phase and that was a precursor to excusing a hustle.

"Why can't you get a job someplace respectable instead of the headquarters for imperialism and oppression?"

Terrell laughed out loud this time. "Now, you're pushing it. You need to do a better job of manufacturing your outrage."

"I'm not outraged." Nate shrugged. "I'm just making a statement."

"Are you?" Erica asked sarcastically. "Or are you just talking shit without any real point?"

Nate didn't like that. "Hey, Jonah Dolan has been bred and brought up through the ranks by the war-mongering crowd that has always dominated the Pentagon."

"Aw, shucks," Terrell said. "Somebody done gone and read a book."

Erica laughed but Nate was getting angrier.

"Fine." He shot up from the sofa. "I'm going to Kelly's."

"Run to your little girlfriend," Terrell yelled back at him.

"And remember, you have a warm bed to come back to courtesy of your sis, who has been saving your ass for a long time."

"Whatever!" He slammed the door behind him.

Erica hopped over to the sofa and snuggled up to Terrell, kissing him on the lips. "Thank you."

"I always got your back, girl. You should know that by now."

"I do know," she said, smiling from the inside out. "I'm sorry about yesterday. I just . . ."

"Don't trust me."

"I trust you," she corrected. "Just not all your friends, and I don't want them around Nate."

"You talk about that boy like he's a baby, Erica. He's not. He's a grown-ass man. He has to choose his own path now."

Erica shook her head. "He's all I have left. I just don't want to lose him."

"Hey." Terrell took her by the arms and turned her to him. "What are you talking about? You got me and we're going to have our own kids. Nate isn't all there is."

Erica smiled, warming at the thought. She was really going to get married and start a family with the man she loved. "If I haven't said it recently, I love you sooooo much."

"You're damn right you do." He kissed her on her nose. "Now, why don't you just show me how much?"

Just as his mouth went to her neck, Erica suddenly remembered what Jonah had said.

"I can show you in an even better way."

"There is no better way than this."

"It could mean more money in your pocket." She leaned up and kissed him on the chin. "More money for our wedding."

"Money?" he asked with a curious grin. "I'm listening."

Billie sat up in bed next to Porter. After two sessions of vigorous sex, they were both sweaty and breathing heavy, but very satisfied. Billie was basking in the afterglow of great sex as long as she could. In a second, her senses would come to her and she would again realize how horrible a mistake it was.

"We're good together," Porter said. "We should do this . . ."

"Stop." Porter opening his mouth was always the catalyst to her senses returning. "We aren't good together. Not anymore. This was just sex. Regrettable sex."

"You always say that." He leaned into her.

Billie slid away, grabbing as much of the sheets as she could to cover herself. "And I mean it. I'm under a lot of stress and I needed that, but it's over."

"You'll get used to the new job." Porter reluctantly got out of bed and started gathering his clothes. "Just suck it up."

"Suck it up?" Billie grabbed a pillow and threw it at him. "I'm in this position because of you."

"Now we get the blame game," Porter said in an annoyed tone.

"Fuck off."

"You should be thanking me," he said. "You needed a release and I provided it for you."

"You provided sex," she said. "I need a whole man, not a working dick. I need someone to listen to me."

"Get a dog."

This time she pulled the bedside lamp cord out of the socket and threw the entire lamp at him, but he ducked out just in time.

"Get out!"

5

Aching to see how her baby was doing, Sherise had just grabbed the phone and was ready to dial the number to day care when she heard a knock on her office door. It was a good thing. She had to be tougher than this. She had to get back into warrior shape and warriors don't nag the babysitter.

"Come in," she said, placing the phone back down.

When Jonah Dolan appeared in her doorway, Sherise caught her breath. Her first thought was what did she look like? She always looked fierce at work, but it was late afternoon and things could slack a bit.

"Jonah." Sherise casually got up from her chair.

Although she was nervous, she never let it show. She made her way around the desk as he stepped inside, closing the door behind him.

"I hope you don't mind my stopping by," he said. He looked attractive and in command as usual in a dark gray suit. "You look . . . lovely."

"Thank you." Sherise was sure she did, but was a little too distracted by how good he looked.

She held her hand out and smiled as he shook it. His shake was not as vigorous as before. It was softer, gentler, and more personal this time.

"Please sit down." She gestured toward the two chairs on the other side of her desk.

He obliged, sitting down, but said, "I can't stay very long."

"That's too bad." She sat across from him and watched his eyes lower to her legs as she crossed them. It was only for a second, but she knew he liked what he saw. "What brings you here?"

"Lunch meeting with the president."

"Sounds exciting." She flipped her hair flirtatiously.

"You'd think." He laughed.

"I'm glad you thought to stop by on your way back to Virginia," she said. "Walter has been hoping to update you on our ideas for the project and he prefers to communicate in person. He's old school."

"I didn't come here to see Walter."

There was a short silence as their eyes connected and no one said a word. Sherise wasn't sure how long it lasted, but she quickly reminded herself that she had to stay in control of this.

"Jenna informed me of your invitation on Sunday," he said.

The invitation had been sent out yesterday afternoon for an intimate dinner at her Georgetown home. It was just another chance for Sherise to put the nail in Toni's coffin.

"I know it's short notice," she said, "but I certainly hope you can come. Feel free to bring—"

"Juliette," Jonah said. "We wouldn't miss it. We usually don't go out on Sunday, so it will be a nice change for us. I assume Walter and Toni will be there."

"Of course." Sherise had already concocted an elaborate story on how Toni's invite must have been misplaced. But she didn't want to talk about Toni. "Your flowers were lovely."

"I received your thank you card." A thoughtful smiled curved his mouth. "I'm glad you liked them."

"I was curious though." She leaned forward in the chair. "Red orchids I get, but what were the other ones?"

"Purple calla lilies. Do you like them?"

"They're lovely." She gestured toward the shelf behind her desk where the flowers still sat in a trumpet-shaped glass vase. "But you really didn't have to."

"I disagree," Jonah noted. "It was just an acknowledgment that you're an extremely talented young woman. I hope you know people talk about you."

"I hope they're kind."

"They're impressed," he said. "That's better than kind. And I agree with them. I felt compelled to acknowledge your mastery the previous night."

Sherise smiled, trying her best to feign humility. "Well, I love them, so thank you."

"While red orchids represent sophistication and sincerity, calla lilies are often used in paintings to represent womanhood and power. They symbolize resurrection and birth."

Sherise wondered if he was referring to the recent birth of Cady. Even if he wasn't, it made her think of Cady and the world of trouble Sherise would be bringing on herself if she didn't get control over the feelings that his presence and attention were causing inside her. Powerful, magnetic men were nothing but trouble and she had a family to think of.

"So," she said, standing up, "I look forward to seeing you and your wife Sunday night."

Jonah looked up at her, confused. "Did I say something wrong?"

"Of course not." She smiled kindly. "You say things . . . just a little too right."

He smiled, getting her notion. He stood up before adding, "A man has to stay on his toes around you."

And a woman needs to stay on her guard around you, she said to herself.

After he left, Sherise felt her body sigh a little bit. She had been tense just being close to him. It was insane how certain men could affect a woman a certain way. Going back behind her desk, Sherise reached for the picture of Justin holding

Cady in his arms. This was her life, her baby and her wonderful husband. So why were her eyes veering to the left to look
at those damn flowers?

Erica didn't like the look on Sherise's face as they walked
through Tysons Galleria, an upscale boutique shopping mall in
Tysons Corner, Virginia. Things had been going fine as the
three women spent their Saturday shopping with the main objective being finding a new outfit for Sherise to host her Sunday dinner in. That was until Erica mentioned that she would
be bringing Terrell and Sherise made a face.

"Sherise, you make me sick," Erica said with a smack of
her lips.

"What?" Sherise replied.

"That look." Erica nudged Billie, who was walking in between them. "You saw it."

Billie shrugged. "I didn't see it, but I know it was there."

"Oh, get out." Sherise smacked her lips. "I just don't want
any hood on display at my dinner."

"For your information," Erica said as she followed Sherise
into a store, "Jonah wants to meet Terrell."

"Why?" Sherise asked.

"Why are we in here?" Erica asked, noticing they were in
Jacadi, a children's clothing store.

"I want to get something for my baby," Sherise said. "And
why does he want to meet your boyfriend?"

"Fiancé," Erica corrected. "He might have some work for
him."

"Like what?" Sherise found it odd enough that Jonah was
so interested in Erica, but it was even odder that he wanted to
get to know Terrell more.

"Driving, of course," Erica said.

"More driving?" Sherise rolled her eyes. "He should be
hooking him up with some kind of an office job. Would have
more promise for him."

"Terrell is going to own his own limo company one day," Erica said, although she knew her words were falling on deaf ears with Sherise.

"I guess it's a good thing in the long run," Sherise said. "Terrell can only be improved by Jonah's interest no matter what type of work it leads to. He's a remarkable man."

"So is your husband," Erica said with a sly smile. "Remember him?"

"Why would you say that?" Sherise asked. "I just mentioned that Jonah could be a good influence on Terrell."

"You've been talking about him all day." Erica nudged Billie again as they stopped at a rack of tiny dresses. "Hasn't she?"

Billie nodded. "You've been talking about him like a schoolgirl with a crush."

"Don't be silly." Sherise nervously sifted through the dresses, not really paying attention to any of them. "This man is nothing but a means to an end for me. My only crush is on Walter's office."

"Remember what happened the last time a man was just a means to an end," Erica said. "You almost got in trouble then."

If they only knew, Sherise thought. Eighteen months ago, Sherise met Ryan Hodgkins, a forty-year-old self-made millionaire playboy, at a fund-raiser for the Rails, a social group Sherise would give her life to be a member of. Its members were mostly upper-class professional black women or women who had been born into money or married into it. She had become friends with a couple of members through her professional connections and attended some of their events.

When one of her friends invited her to help plan a Rails fund-raiser for local public schools, Sherise saw it as her ticket to a membership. Her task was to get sponsors, and Ryan, the owner of a government-contracting architecture firm, was a primary target. Intending to use her charm and beauty to get him to open his checkbook, Sherise ended up being the one who was impressed. She was very attracted to him and he pursued her relentlessly. This was despite his knowledge of her marital status.

Sherise hadn't been married long, but she was already wondering if she had made the right choice in picking the "safe" husband as opposed to going after a more complicated man like Ryan. Despite that, she had no intention of taking things beyond flirtation. But Ryan was compelling and convincing. He was seductive and enchanting and one thing led to another.

It was only one night, after which Sherise came to her senses and cut Ryan out of her life for good. Two months later she found out she was pregnant. It was a textbook case for her to go to her girlfriends for advice, but she couldn't. Despite their promise, and follow through, to tell each other everything no matter what, Sherise was too ashamed and kept the night she spent with Ryan from Billie and Erica. They'd known about the flirting, the phone calls, the flowers, the secret lunches, and the stolen kisses. Both of them urged her to stop before she made a mistake she would regret forever and she promised them she would. She promised them she did.

Sherise was too ashamed to tell them what she'd done and when she found out she was pregnant, she resolved to take this to the grave. Too many lives could be destroyed from a stupid mistake she made without thought. She would break Justin's heart and could cost Cady a relationship with a father that Sherise never had the chance to have. She would destroy what she had worked to get through a union with Justin. So as far as the girls knew, Ryan was a dangerous flirtation that was over and done with and it would be all anyone would ever know.

"There is nothing to be worried about," Sherise said. "I may make a lot of mistakes, but I learn from them."

"We're gonna keep an eye on you Sunday," Erica said. "Aren't we, Billie?"

Noticing Billie had completely zoned out, Sherise snapped her fingers in front of her face to bring her back. "What is wrong with you?"

"Nothing." Billie blinked. "What?"

"You've been acting weird all day," Erica said. "Like you're a step behind. Are you okay?"

"I'm fine." Billie turned to leave, but Sherise jumped in front of her.

"Oh my God!" Sherise knew that look of shame on Billie's face. "You did it again, didn't you?"

"Did what?" Erica asked, confused.

"Shut up, Sherise." Billie wanted to get out of that store. She could barely breathe. She pushed Sherise aside and headed out.

"She slept with Porter," Sherise told Erica as they darted after her.

"Please say you didn't," Erica begged once they reached her outside.

Billie was ready to argue her defense, but didn't have the strength. Her shoulders slumped and she lowered her head. She started crying the second Erica placed her arms around her.

"It's okay, baby." Erica held her tight.

"No, it's not." Sherise was disgusted. "What dirty trick did he play this time?"

"That's just it," Billie said. "It took nothing really. We were talking about Tara and—"

"That's it," Sherise said. "He keeps using your affection for Tara to get to you."

"Did he ply you with drinks?" Erica asked. "Why were you even alone with him?"

Billie felt overwhelmed, unable to relay the true course of events. "To make a long story short, it was so obvious what he was doing, but I let him. I wanted it and . . . Why can't I say no to him?"

"You did say no to him," Erica said. "You divorced his ass. You just need to find the strength it took you to do that, and use it the next time he . . ."

"Swings his dick in your direction," Sherise finished. "Or maybe we just need to cut his dick off."

Billie wiped her face with a tissue Erica gave her. "We were negotiating my time with Tara and he started to compliment me on how good a mother I was to her."

"Oh, the good mom card," Erica said. "That's not a new one."

Billie threw her arms in the air and let them fall to her sides in defeat. "Next thing I know, he's moving in on me and he already had a hotel room key. He'd been planning to seduce me, made that clear, and I still went upstairs with him."

"I told you not to be alone with him anymore," Erica said.

"We were in a restaurant full of people!" Billie had to laugh at that fact.

"Then you don't get to be around him without one of us nearby," Erica said.

"That's not a real solution," Billie said.

"But I know what is," Sherise said.

"I'm afraid to hear this," Billie said.

"You need some dick!" Sherise was adamant. "The reason that boy has got you lit up is because he's the only one stoking your fire."

"I don't have time for a relationship right now," Billie said. "I just got divorced!"

"Who's talking about a relationship?" Sherise asked. "Sex has nothing to do with relationships. It's a release. You need to tear one off before you meet with him. Then you'll be all sexed out and nothing he can do will turn you on."

"So just call some guy up and ask him to have sex with me real quick before I meet my ex-husband?"

"Exactly," Sherise said without a hint of sarcasm in her voice.

"Are you hearing her?" Billie asked Erica.

Erica laughed. "Sherise is crazy, but you gotta do something to get the edge off before you see him."

"Fine," Billie said, exasperated. "My best friends are suggesting I ho it up. Do you have any men in mind?"

"Billie?"

Billie swung around at the sound of her name. She composed herself just as he approached her, appearing to be alone, and she recognized him from work.

"Hey, Richard!" She smiled wide. "Fancy meeting you here."

Billie waited patiently on the phone for Porter to respond. She knew every second he took could mean bad things. After getting home from the mall, trying her best to thwart Sherise's attempts to hook her up with her coworker, Richard, Billie worked up the courage to call Porter and ask for her one day a month with Tara to be Sunday, so she could spend the day with her and bring her to Sherise's dinner party.

She felt relatively safe over the phone, but still felt the shame of their last encounter just at the sound of his enticing voice. While Sherise's suggestion was not one she was taking seriously, Billie was going to do everything she could to not come face to face with Porter until she could figure out how to resist him. She'd had enough of this.

"You can have Tara on Sunday," Porter finally said. "If I can see you some time next week."

Billie sighed. She knew that last week's agreement was too good to be true. "We didn't agree to that."

"I'm adding an addendum to our oral contract," Porter said. "I want to see you and you know you want to see me again."

"Why are you whispering?" she asked. "Claire nearby?"

"Leave her out of this," he said.

"Is that what you told her when you were cheating on me?"

"I want to see you, Billie."

"I'll be over to pick up Tara tomorrow at noon," she stated, "and I don't want to see you then or any other time."

"I won't agree to this until you agree to see me."

Billie hung the phone up and screamed at it, hating Porter and hating herself for believing that he meant anything he'd said. Maybe it was better if she let Tara go out of her life. She was the only thing keeping Porter around and Porter was nothing but trouble for her.

When the phone rang, she hesitated to pick it up, knowing that Porter was on the other line. When she did, she spoke before giving him a chance.

"The answer is no," she said. "No and no. Stop fucking with me Porter. Can I have Tara tomorrow or not?"

"Fine," he said angrily. "Hanging up is childish shit."

"Using your daughter as a tool to get your ex-wife back in bed is bullshit."

"I'll tell her to be ready at noon, so you don't have to have a fit on—"

"Who is this?"

Billie immediately recognized Claire's voice and without even thinking, she started to laugh.

"Claire?" Porter said. "I'm on the phone."

"Who are you talking to?" Claire asked. "Is this Billie? Who is this?"

Billie continued laughing as Porter yelled at Claire to hang up, but she herself was the one who finally hung up.

There was one upside to all of this. Knowing that she was doing to Claire what Claire had done to her offered some sort of sick sense of revenge, but Billie knew that, ultimately, the consequences weren't worth the temporary sense of satisfaction. Claire wasn't her problem anymore. Billie was her own worst enemy and she had to figure out how to defeat the hold that Porter had on her.

"Where have you been?" Sherise asked Justin the second he entered the kitchen.

"I've been making calls in my office."

She looked him over, glad she never had to be worried about how he would dress. Justin knew what looked good on him and he had a very classic, casual style. "You look good, baby."

He smiled and kissed her on the cheek. "You look a little too good."

"How can anyone look too good?"

"This is an informal Sunday dinner in our backyard," he said. "Look at you."

Sherise knew she looked amazing in an eye-catching yellow, black, and gray silk BCBG Maxazria pleated one-shoulder dress that went just above her knees.

"It's too much?" Sherise asked. "Because I bought it with the girls and they both thought I looked incredible."

"Of course you look incredible, but . . ." Justin glanced around the kitchen. "Check out this spread." The spread was a catered order from Dean and Deluca, a famous eatery in the Georgetown area. Sherise spared no expense in getting their best platters. "I think you're trying too hard," Justin said.

"You know what I think?" Sherise's hands went to her curvy hips. "I think you don't want me to have Walter's job."

"You're being ridiculous."

"I thought I was at first," she said, "because you've always been so supportive of me, but it seems like ever since Cady was born, you want me to dial down my dreams."

Justin's jaw tightened and his lips thinned with displeasure. "I'm not going to get into this with you right now, but clearly we need to clear some things up, because if you think I don't support you, then this is all fucked up."

"I need to be the only one Jonah can see heading his project and the only one Walter can see replacing him." She filled up the sterling silver ice bucket. "Why can't you get that?"

"What have I been doing for you this past week and a half?" he asked. "Bending over backward to help you try and ruin some woman's life so you don't have to compete with her for a job. Hosting some military brass while you flirt your ass off with him. What the fuck else would I be doing if I actually supported you?"

"Justin!" Sherise called after her husband as he stormed out of the kitchen, passing Billie as she entered. "Come back!"

"What is going on?" Billie asked.

Sherise leaned against the refrigerator, angry with herself for snapping at him and worried that it might carry out into the party. She didn't need Jonah or Walter seeing her home as anything but happy, which it was most of the time.

"He's just jealous of Jonah."

"Does he have reason to be?" Billie asked.

"Don't you start with me." Sherise pointed to the appetizer platters at the end of the granite counter. "Please take those outside. I'm gonna get the wine."

Just then Erica entered. "What's wrong with Justin?"

"What is he doing?" Sherise asked nervously.

"I just said hi as he passed and he grumbled something," she answered. "He didn't seem too happy."

"He thinks I'm overdoing it," Sherise said.

"You are," Billie and Erica said in unison.

"Look," Sherise asserted, "both you bitches just smile and serve, okay? Save the judgment for later. I have to go placate my husband so he's in a good mood by the time our guests arrive."

"Too late," Erica said. "That's what I came to tell you. Jonah and his wife are here."

When Jonah and Juliette entered the home, Erica felt a notable tension. Most of it was created by his wife's apparent coldness. While she pasted on a fake smile and offered Juliette a glass of expensive wine, Erica could tell that she didn't want to be there. She made eye contact with the woman for only a second, but saw nothing but ice behind those eyes. Erica was certain that this woman either felt she had a reason to dislike her or was just a cold bitch in general.

It was just a flash, but Erica noticed Jonah and Sherise exchange quick, awkward glances and she wondered if Sherise really knew what she was doing.

Sherise ushered everyone through the living room into the finely landscaped backyard where Walter, Terrell, Tara, and Cady were already sitting. The second they were out there, Sherise pulled Erica aside.

"You have one task," she ordered. "If there is any mention of Toni, you change the subject immediately."

"I'm not getting involved in—"

"Just do it!" Sherise ordered. "I have to go round up my husband."

"Fine," Erica agreed reluctantly.

She was going for something to eat until she saw Jonah walk toward Terrell, who was sitting comfortably in a chair near the pebble fountain. Erica made a beeline for the two men and positioned herself next to Terrell, standing beside his chair.

"So this is Terrell. . . ." Jonah held his hand out to the young man.

"Nicolli," Erica said as she tapped Terrell on the shoulder.

Terrell leaned up and firmly shook Jonah's hand. Terrell knew from the second he saw Jonah that he was one of those types who thought the world belonged to him, and his stuck-up wife was a clone of those women who held their purse tighter whenever he stepped into an elevator.

"Terrell," Erica added, "this is Deputy Assistant Secretary of Defense Jonah Dolan."

"It's nice to meet you, young man," Jonah said.

"You too, sir." Terrell hated the condescending tone of the man's voice.

"Erica says you're planning to get married." Jonah took a seat across from Terrell.

Terrell nodded. "She's right."

Erica looked down at Terrell and could tell he was being short on purpose. "We just got engaged, so nothing is really planned yet."

"So how long have you been driving for Destin?" Jonah asked.

Erica blinked, curious as to where Jonah found out the name of the company, because she knew she never told him.

"A few years." Terrell shifted in his seat, feeling judged. "Well, I've been driving for a few years. I started out cleaning the cars."

"Are you allowed to take on additional work?" Jonah asked.

"Work is actually very good right now."

"But you only work about thirty hours a week." Jonah looked up at Erica and seemed to catch the curious look on her face. He smiled at her before turning his attention back to Terrell. "You could use some more money to pay for the kind of wedding Erica would want."

"How would you know that?" Terrell asked. "You've only known her, what, a week?"

"Terrell." Erica squeezed his shoulder. "You were mentioning that you wanted to do some more drives to make extra money."

"Don't you have to get contracted with the government and all that to drive around Pentagon brass?" Terrell asked.

Jonah shook his head. "It's a private company that drives around the lobbyists and contractors. They aren't government employees. They'll do a security check on you because you'll be on Pentagon property, but that's it."

"Well," Terrell said, "I'm getting some extra work already. I think I'm doing fine."

"You would pass a security check, wouldn't you?"

"What the hell kind of question is that?" Terrell leaned forward.

Erica was thinking the same thing, but didn't want any trouble. "Do you want something to drink, Jonah? I can get you a glass of—"

"Because if you can pass it," Jonah continued as if Erica hadn't even spoken, "there could be a lot of opportunity in it for you. What kind of future does Erica want with you? Has she discussed this—"

"You're not in a position to know what Erica does or doesn't want." Terrell turned to Juliette, sitting only a few chairs away engaged in conversation with Walter. "I don't think she'd be happy to hear you asking all these questions about another woman and I know I'm not."

Erica felt her chest begin to tighten.

"I'm sorry," Jonah said. "I didn't mean to push. I can be very aggressive. Of course I don't know Erica very well, but she's part of my team now and—"

"*She* is," Terrell said, "not me. So you can leave me out of it." Terrell shot up from his chair and darted for the house.

"What was that?" Erica asked Jonah, knowing that everyone, although previously engaged in their own conversations, was looking at them now.

Jonah seemed unfazed by the abrupt exit. "Are you sure you want to marry someone who gets so defensive at the suggestion of a simple background check even though it could make him a lot of money?"

"How did you know all that about him?" Erica asked. "I didn't tell you even though you said I did."

"Erica, did you really think your background was the only one that mattered when I decided you could come work for me?"

Erica wasn't so sure what to make of the look on Jonah's face at that moment, but it bothered her and fed her suspicious soul. He was looking at her like he was disappointed in her. It made her angry, but she didn't have time to try to figure it out. She had to find Terrell and calm him down before Sherise killed her for making a mess of the dinner.

Billie was on her way back to the kitchen when the doorbell rang. She rushed to the door, wondering who it was because everyone had already sat down to eat. She should have checked through the half-circle window at the top of the door before opening it because, if she had, she would have never opened it.

"What are you doing here?" she asked.

"You have two options," Porter said as he leaned against the doorway with his trademark smug superior grin. "You can invite me to the dinner or you can tell Tara it's time to go and I'll leave with her."

"You son of a bitch," Billie said. "I have her all day."

"It's not day anymore," he answered. "Come on and let me in."

"You can't take her," Billie said. "She's watching Cady. She's enjoying herself."

"So your day with my daughter is spent with her babysitting your friend's baby?" A frown set into his features. "Real quality time, Billie."

"Your games aren't going to work," Billie said. "This is Sherise's house and she's gonna rip you a new one if you mess with her party."

"I have no intention of doing that." Porter inclined his head to look inside the house. "I'm looking forward to meeting Dolan and I will be on my best behavior."

"What is going on?"

Billie turned to Sherise, who was quickly approaching. "Just calm down."

"Why?" Sherise grabbed the door and opened it to see Porter standing on the threshold. "What are you doing here?"

"Came for dinner." Porter smiled wide and attempted to step inside, but Sherise pushed him back.

"You are not welcome anywhere near my house. What do you think you're doing?"

"He's trying to cause me problems," Billie said. "You are such an ass."

"I was actually just trying to spend some time with you, Billie," Porter said in a cool tone. "You and Tara. It's been a long time and . . ."

"Bullshit," Sherise stated. "Billie may fall for your crap, but I'm not going to. And honestly, Billie, if you find this sort of display convincing, you're as stupid as he is."

"What did I do?" Billie asked.

"Fine." Porter crossed his arms over his chest. "Then just tell Tara I'm here and we'll be gone."

"Sherise." Billie turned to Sherise, knowing that the host would rather have Tara leave than Porter come in. "Just let him in. Tara is gonna be upset if she has to leave."

"Tara isn't going anywhere," Sherise said, "and Porter can go to hell."

"Sherise!" Billie knew that Porter had stepped into the house when she moved aside to hold Sherise back. "I can handle this."

Sherise rolled her eyes. *This girl is pitiful*, she thought.

Billie turned back to Porter. "This is more childish than I'm used to from you."

"I know," he muttered, "but you don't give me a lot of choices when you won't let me see you."

Billie took a look outside. "Where is Claire? She waiting in the car again?"

"This isn't about Claire." His voice held a hint of sincerity. "This is about me watching Tara get so excited this morning because she was going to see you. You should have seen her, Billie. She was smiling and . . . it was like old times."

Billie couldn't help but smile at the thought because she

knew Tara loved her, but she wasn't going to go weak. The smacking sound Sherise made with her mouth was also a reminder for her to stay strong.

"Daddy!" Tara rushed into the living room with Cady in her arms. "I thought I saw you. What are you doing here?"

"Didn't have anything to do." Porter marched farther into the house to greet his daughter. "Thought I would drop by."

"Not to get me?" Tara looked concerned.

"No," Porter said. "To join you. If it's okay with Billie."

"It's not Billie's house," Sherise said.

"Oh, can he stay?" Tara held Cady up. "Look at her, Daddy. Isn't she just the cutest thing? She's like a little perfect doll."

"Reminds me of you," Porter said.

"You have got to be kidding me," Sherise added.

"I knew you'd be a good babysitter," he added. "You should do this more often."

Billie sighed, closing the front door. She looked at Sherise with a pleading expression on her face. She didn't want any more drama and she didn't want to upset Tara. "It's only a couple more hours," she said.

"Christ on a cracker." Sherise pointed to Billie. "You and I are gonna talk later. I'll go get an extra setting."

"Can I hold her?" Porter asked after Sherise left.

"She's not a football," Tara said. "You have to be gentle."

"I know that." Porter slowly, carefully took hold of Cady, who was half asleep and didn't seem to really care who was holding her.

Billie softened at the sight. She had imagined the day when she would be watching Porter hold their baby. It broke her heart to think that just before she found out Porter was cheating on her she was considering going off the pill and getting pregnant, since he had been asking her to for the previous four months. All while he was sleeping with Claire.

Porter smiled, turned to Billie and whispered, "I think she likes me."

"That's because she doesn't know you," Billie whispered back.

Sherise was not happy with the way the night was going so far. She had finally gotten Justin to come out of his office and act right. Then she had to go in search of Erica and Terrell, who had been arguing upstairs. Now, Porter the asshole had invited himself to the party and she hadn't had one second to get Jonah's attention. At least she could say that her story that Toni had not responded to the phantom invitation she was sent didn't seem to raise any suspicions. As she hurried to get an extra place setting ready for Porter, she only hoped that Billie and Erica could control their men long enough to keep the dinner attention on her.

"Need some help?"

Sherise looked over her shoulder to see Jonah standing in the kitchen doorway. She almost dropped the plate in her hand from the intense stare on his face, but quickly recovered.

"Jonah! Do you need something?"

"My wife thinks she might have been bit by something." He entered the kitchen. "It seems a little early in the season for mosquitoes, but she was wondering if you had some . . ."

"Bug repellant candles." Sherise hated that she had forgotten that. She imagined the snotty little Mrs. Dolan, who had completely ignored her since greeting her at the door, complaining. "I certainly do. I think they're . . . down here." She opened a cabinet door.

"I'll get them." Jonah held up a hand to stop her before she bent down.

"You're a guest," Sherise said. "You shouldn't have to."

"I don't mind." He came back up with a couple of candles in his hand. "Lighter?"

With the setting in one hand, Sherise reached for the lighter that was on the counter. When she handed it to him, their fingers accidentally touched, and Sherise felt a bolt of electricity race up her arm.

Their eyes caught each other's and Sherise felt her body react to the look on his face. It wasn't dirty or intimidating, but his eyes seemed to sear into her, making her feel flush all over. There was no need for their fingers to keep touching as he had the lighter in his hand, but Sherise didn't move her fingers away until she saw something shift behind him out of the corner of her eye.

Jonah seemed to notice the distraction and turned around, giving them both a full view of who was standing in the dining room looking into the kitchen. It was Terrell and he did not hide the fact that he had been watching them for some time. They were both looking at him now and were going to try to play it like nothing was happening, but Terrell was no fool. He could feel the tension between them all the way from where he was. He played it right and just smiled before turning and walking toward the bathroom, his intended destination, but he wasn't going to forget what he saw.

Erica didn't want to push the subject, but she was too curious. After having gone after Terrell earlier that evening, she had to listen to him talk about how much he wanted to leave because he felt disrespected by Jonah. She begged him to stay and give Jonah another chance. She agreed that it probably wasn't a good idea that he work with Jonah, so she promised to never bring the topic up again. She promised they would leave as soon as the meal was done. He agreed to sit down for dinner and behave.

Everything seemed to be going fine, but Erica noticed that during the entire meal Jonah and Terrell seemed to be exchanging weird glances. She didn't know what was going on and was reluctant to bring up the topic again, but that look on Terrell's face was too familiar. It was that I-got-an-idea look and it usually meant Terrell was trying to get into something that was none of his business.

"What is going on with you?" she whispered in his ear as Sherise entertained the rest of the table with her stories of her and Justin's trip to Greece in 2008.

"Nothing." He smiled and winked at her, taking a bite of his soft-shell crab roll. "This is fucking delicious. We gotta get some of these, baby."

"They're out of our price range," she said, and added, "but why are you staring at Jonah like that?"

"I'm looking at you right now." He leaned in to kiss her on the cheek. "Did I tell you how hot you look in that little sundress? You look all innocent and sweet."

"Stop it." She slapped him on the arm. "I know you, Terrell. What are you up to?"

Terrell wasn't about to tell Erica all the things that were going through his mind right now. "I'm just trying to make a better life for you and me, baby girl."

"How is staring at Jonah Dolan going to do that?"

"I'm not staring at anyone. You're being paranoid, as usual."

Erica was about to respond to the accusation when Terrell abruptly raised his voice to steal Jonah's attention away from Sherise. Jonah turned to him, not seeming pleased to have his adoration of Sherise interrupted, but Terrell didn't care.

"You know what, sir?" He leaned forward over the table, looking at the man across and two seats away. "I think I'll take you up on that offer. You know, for some extra driving money. Sounds like a good deal."

Erica's eyes widened as she turned to Jonah, who seemed to have no reaction. When he reluctantly smiled and agreed that it was a good idea, before turning his attention back to Sherise, Erica was more curious than ever.

She tugged at Terrell's shirt. "Now you want to do it?"

Terrell shrugged. "I wouldn't say I want to, but I love you, baby. I'll do anything to give you the wedding you deserve and that's gonna cost money."

When he kissed her on her lips, Erica warmed inside, wanting so badly to believe him. She knew he loved her, but she also knew Terrell, and something was up with him. However, the idea that he was sacrificing his own comfort to work with Jonah so she could have the wedding of her dreams only made her even more convinced that she made the right choice. Things were going to work out as long as she and Terrell believed in each other.

As Billie looked in on Tara, who was lying on Sherise and Justin's bed with Cady sleeping next to her, she felt someone coming up behind her. She knew it was Porter. She could feel him, smell his scent, and hated how much she loved it. He came only inches behind her and she clenched her hands in fists at her sides to try to keep her body from wanting to lean back into him.

"She really likes that baby," Porter whispered.

"It's like a doll to her," Billie said. "An adorable little doll."

"I can't say I'm too happy about this."

Billie turned to face him, uncomfortable with how the softness of his expression touched her. "Why not?"

"Look at her, Billie." His voice was soft and soothing. "She's not a little girl anymore. She's getting . . . she keeps talking about this boy. I overhear her on the phone with her friends."

"Jesse." Billie had already been talking to Tara about her latest crush.

Porter looked disappointed. "She talks to you about him, but she won't talk to me?"

"It's not something you talk to your dad about."

"Can you tell me what she says?"

Billie didn't want to be in this position. "I don't want to . . ."

"I'm her father," he said. "If she's sexually active, I need—"

"She's not," Billie assured. "And she isn't interested in any of that any time soon."

Porter sighed. "You see, Billie. I need you to help me with her."

"I'll always be here for her."

"But not for me," Porter said.

She turned around and looked at him, seeing the tenderness in his eyes that always did it for her. No matter how cold and hard Porter could be, any mention of his little princess and he was a soft little teddy bear.

"That's not my job anymore." Billie turned her back to him again, hoping he couldn't tell from her voice how emotional she was about to get.

"Maybe it should be again." He placed his hand on her shoulder, slowly turning her back to him. "Billie, I . . ."

"You're still here?"

Porter turned to Sherise, who was quickly approaching. Without any shame, Sherise practically pushed Billie out of the way to stand in between them.

"I didn't know I had to leave," Porter said.

"Dinner is over." Sherise ignored Billie, who was tugging at her arm. "That's your cue."

"I behaved, didn't I?"

"And I expect you to keep behaving," Sherise said, "and leave."

"Sherise . . ."

"Porter." Billie stopped him. "It's time to go."

Porter sighed, annoyed. "I had to park four blocks from here. I'm gonna go get the car. Please wake Tara up and tell her to be ready to come out when I get back."

"I will," Billie promised.

Sherise gave Porter one last glare before he turned and headed away. A second later, she turned to Billie and grabbed her as she headed into the room. She pulled her back.

"What is the matter with you?" Billie jerked free.

"What were you doing?" Sherise asked. "Can I not leave you alone with that fool for five seconds?"

"We were just talking."

"I have eyes," Sherise said. "You were five seconds away from kissing him. Damn, girl. He ain't that fine."

"It's not about that," Billie said. "And I wasn't going to kiss him."

"I've been thinking about you tonight."

"Really?" Billie asked. "I'm surprised you had time. You seemed so busy talking about yourself all night. You put on quite a show for Jonah. His wife wasn't impressed."

"Do you want Porter to leave you alone or not?" Sherise waited for a response, but not getting one, she answered her own question. "Bitch, you do."

"I'm dealing with it."

"Your way," Sherise said. "And you suck at it. It's time you do it my way."

"What exactly is your way?" Billie couldn't be picky. She was desperate to get rid of Porter's hold on her, but always suspicious of Sherise's suggestions. "And remember, I have Tara's feelings to think about."

"What about Claire's feelings?"

"I don't give a damn about that bitch," Billie said. "In fact, knowing Porter is doing to her what he did to me is the only good thing to come out of all this."

"The one thing that is better than you knowing what he's doing," Sherise said, "is *her* knowing. Porter needs to know that you'll tell her."

"Oh, God." Billie noted the twisted smile on Sherise's face. "I don't need more drama from that bitch. I get enough as it is."

"She's living with him now," Sherise said. "He's got a lot invested and if she finds out that he's sleeping with you, the grief she could give him might not be worth it to him."

Billie didn't like the sound of that. She wanted to believe

that being with her was worth the grief Claire might give Porter, but Sherise had a point. Porter was getting away with this because neither of them wanted anyone to know about what they were doing. Claire was on her high and mighty thinking that she had Porter all to herself. She was the victor. Porter wanted her enough to have her move in; maybe he would want her enough to keep her if she threatened to leave him over Billie. Maybe fear of that could get Porter to leave Billie alone and she could stop giving in to him.

It was worth a shot.

6

Rachel Ford made no effort to hide her discomfort as she sat across from Sherise in B. Smith's restaurant in Union Station. Sherise didn't give a damn. The girl owed her. They both had worked together as interns for the same senator, and one night Sherise returned to the office after the whole staff had left and ran into Rachel grinding underneath the married senator on top of his desk. She promised to keep her mouth shut for a promotion in return, which she promptly received. Rachel, on the other hand, was transferred to another senator's office, where she worked, it pleased Sherise to find out, at the same time as Toni.

Rachel was a Jersey girl at heart, as anyone could tell from her accent. She was a pretty brunette who had gained about fifteen pounds since their internship days but was still attractive. She wore drab clothes that made her look more invisible than anything.

"I don't remember all that," Rachel said.

"Liar." Sherise sipped her glass of iced tea with a sweet as saccharine smile on her face. "Something that secretive in a place like that . . . you knew something about Toni."

"I heard things," Rachel said, lowering her head, "but nothing was ever confirmed."

"I don't believe you." Sherise could tell she was lying. "What things did you hear?"

Rachel looked around as if she could find someone to save her from this. She shook her head before saying, "She might have participated in something that could have . . . she might have facilitated a bribe."

"What kind of bribe?" Sherise leaned forward, excited.

"I'm not sure."

"Well, how can you get sure?"

"What do you expect me to do?" she asked.

"Whatever you have to, I assume. Use your connections, whatever. Threaten, blackmail if that's what it takes. Get proof of what she did."

"Isn't the rumor enough?"

"No," Sherise said. "I need enough proof to make Walter want to investigate and then have him face the brick walls I have. That will be enough."

"What if I can't find anything?" Rachel asked. "You just call me up out of the blue and threaten me if I don't help you destroy someone else's career. I don't really even know who is working over there now."

"I'm not destroying her career," Sherise said. "I'm just getting her out of my way. And I'm not threatening you. I'm just . . . motivating you."

"You're a bitch, Sherise," Rachel pouted. "You know damn well what exposing my relationship with the senator could do."

"I know that it could cause trouble for your husband, John. Not only is he an aide to the president now, but he was your boyfriend when you were sleeping with our boss. Though with you being the spokesperson for that Christian family values political action committee, I'm sure your family believes in forgiveness."

Sherise didn't expect a response, but she waited a few seconds anyway. After a while, she continued. "You have three days to—"

"Three days?" Rachel asked loudly. She lowered her head as people around them turned to look at her. "Are you crazy?"

"No," Sherise said. "Just in a rush. As I was saying, you have three days to find proof. You find a way to get that proof to Walter Nappano in a way that absolutely leaves me out of it. If he in any way thinks I had something to do with it, I'm going to become a problem for you."

"I'll try my best," Rachel said after a while in a defeated tone.

"I know you will," Sherise said. "Also, your hair is beautiful. Where do you get it done?"

"Go fuck yourself," Rachel said as she grabbed her purse, stood up and stormed off.

"Bye," Sherise said politely as she reached for her vibrating phone. She opened the phone to read the text.

Free For Lunch? Jonah

He was texting her now? Sherise felt an immediate knot in her stomach. She couldn't believe the way she'd reacted to his touch on Sunday. She'd felt the hair on the back of her neck go up every time he looked at her for the rest of the night. She had intended to flirt with him and be just attentive enough to not offend Justin or Juliette, but barely made eye contact with him after that. She didn't trust herself.

She had been thinking about him ever since and knew that wasn't a good thing. Now he was texting her asking her to lunch. She was walking a fine line and had already crossed it enough times. This was about Walter's job, not Jonah, she told herself as she placed her phone back in her jacket pocket.

As she left the money for the bill and got up to head back to work, she felt the phone vibrate again. It was Jonah and this message seemed to show he had a sense why she hadn't responded.

ERICA WILL JOIN US. BUSINESS ONLY. PROMISE.

Sherise smiled, grateful to have not only someone else there, but someone who would be honest with her if she was crossing the line, something she seemed to do whether she wanted to or not. She typed back:

SOUNDS GOOD. TIME & PLACE?

Billie looked down at her watch to see how long she had been waiting in this lunch line. It had been fifteen minutes since she left the office and she was getting a little anxious.

"Stop doing that," Richard said.

The two had decided to take a quick break and pick up Mexican, but neither had time to stay for lunch. Too much work to do.

"The bosses know we have to eat," he said.

"I know," Billie responded, "but sometimes it just feels like they expect us to strap feeding tubes to our arms and hunker down."

"At least you're getting the hang of it."

"Some things more than others."

Richard shook his head. "Still feeling sorry for yourself because you have the big bad pharm client?"

"Leave me alone." Billie laughed. "My job is to defend my lying, racist client to the best of my ability. I can do that. I'm doing that."

Richard feigned wiping tears from his cheeks. "Stop whining. Billie, you've defended rapists and murderers, haven't you?"

"Alleged rapists and murderers," she corrected. "And yes, I have. I get it, Richard. I'm not complaining."

"No, you just pout."

"You don't have to look at me," she said, stepping ahead as the line moved on.

"You're too easy on the eyes not to," he answered.

His words made her uncomfortable, so Billie didn't look at him. She glanced away toward the counter and said, "Is this line always this long?"

"It's twelve-thirty, Billie. I'm gonna go out on a limb and say . . . yes."

Billie was grateful that he didn't push the issue any further. It could have been a simple compliment, but she had looked up more than once to find Richard watching her . . . admiringly. He was a handsome man, but the last thing on Billie's mind was a relationship and she would never get involved with a coworker. She was already dealing with a handful.

There was an awkward silence before Richard spoke again. "I might be able to help you."

"Richard, I'm fine," she said. "I know what my duty to my client is and I'm going—"

"But it might make you feel better if you can work on some pro bono stuff."

Billie wished she could. One of the reasons she'd wanted to work at this firm was because of its emphasis on pro bono work, work the lawyers conducted at no charge to the poor and indigent. The firm had won awards and placed in the top ten in the country among law firms of its size in public interest commitment. Billie's problem was that you had to be at the firm for at least six months before you could get to work on a pro bono assignment.

"It's too early," she said.

"Too early for an official assignment," Richard said, "but I could use a little help on my case."

Billie turned quickly around with an excited gleam in her eyes. "The housing case?"

Earlier that week, Richard told Billie about the case of an

elderly woman who was threatened with eviction from her apartment after her grandson—who had been arrested and charged, but not convicted, for possession of narcotics a year earlier—stayed with her for three months during the holidays. The apartment community had a rule that any resident involved in drug-related charges would face immediate eviction. They were claiming that allowing him to stay there placed her grandson in the position of a resident. Richard was defending her and fighting the eviction. It was the kind of case Billie loved—a little old woman who hadn't done a bad thing in her life against an apartment management company that owned more than five hundred units in the city.

"Now," Richard added, "you won't get any credit for your work, but if you want to, you can spend a few hours a week helping me out."

"Are you kidding?" Without thinking, she reached out and wrapped her arms around him tight. "I would love it! Thank you. Thank you."

"Okay," Richard said, laughing. He pointed ahead to the gap in the line in front of her. "You better get moving or the people behind us are gonna get violent."

Erica was busy completing folders for a briefing when Jonah came out of his office to give some papers to Jenna. Jenna immediately pointed him to Erica.

"Give them to her," she said. "I'm swamped."

Erica was already overwhelmed with work, but she wasn't going to let on. Jenna was starting to warm to her and she had to be ready for anything. "Sure I'll do it."

"You don't even know what it is," Jonah said. He placed the papers on her desk.

"Doesn't matter," Erica said confidently.

"That's what I want to hear," Jonah said. "Make sure copies of that are given to everyone on that list. These are personal memos from me so I don't want them going to the assistants."

"But mail always goes to—"

"Not if you deliver it personally," Jenna said. "Where are the folders?"

Grateful she had just finished them, Erica grabbed the folders for the briefing and handed them to her.

"Look them up on the address book," Jenna said, "and deliver them yourself so the admins know it's for the recipients' eyes only. I'm off to the briefing."

"I'll be there in ten minutes," Jonah said.

"Make it five!" Jenna yelled back on her way out.

"Okay, five!" Jonah reached into his pocket. "I got you something."

"More work?" Erica asked, laughing.

She stopped laughing when Jonah offered her a tiny white envelope. "What is this?" she asked as she took it and started opening it up.

"My wife gets a bunch of those due to her charity work."

Erica pulled the card in the envelope out and saw it was a gift certificate to Bloomingdale's. She looked at the back for the amount.

She gasped. "It's two hundred and fifty dollars!"

"Not bad," Jonah said. "She gets so many and sometimes they expire before she uses them."

Erica imagined that Juliette wasn't the type of woman who needed gift cards to shop. Her gold American Express would probably do.

"This is really too much," she said, placing the card back in the envelope. She offered it back to him.

"It's really not," Jonah said. "And I won't take it back. Besides, I'm not sure if two hundred and fifty dollars will get you very far at Bloomingdale's."

"It can if you shop the right way," Erica said. She smiled and placed the envelope in her purse on the desk.

"Good," Jonah said. "It's in capable hands then. Are you clear on everything you have to do?"

"Deliver memos to the whole Pentagon," Erica said jokingly as she reached for her directory.

"It won't be that hard," Jonah said. "Everyone you need to
reach is in the E-Ring. It takes Jenna just a few seconds."

"Jenna's got twice the energy I have."

"She's a dynamo. She always . . ." Jonah reached for the
picture on Erica's desk and held it up so he could see it better.
"Who is this?"

"That's me, my mom, and my little brother, Nate." It was
Erica's favorite picture of her family because she remembered
the day it had been taken—the day before they found out her
mother had cancer. It would be five years before she passed
away.

"Good-looking family," he said, placing the picture down.
"Must have been hard on you, being so young when your
mother died."

Erica placed the directory down and looked up at Jonah.
"How much do you know about me, exactly?"

"I'm sorry," he said. "I know it seems intrusive, but in my
position I have to know everything and I respect you too
much to insult your intelligence by pretending like I don't
know."

Erica had to give him credit for being honest at least. "It
was hard. I was only nineteen."

"I was seventeen when my mother died," he said. "It wasn't
cancer. It was a car accident, but I know how it feels. I was the
oldest too, but we still had a dad around to take care of things."

"I didn't," Erica said. She was touched by the compassion
in his eyes. "But we figured it out."

"You were responsible for your brother, but I was able to
leave. I had to leave. My father and I . . . we hated each other."

Erica was surprised he would say such a thing. "I hope
you're exaggerating."

He looked at her without a hint of doubt on his face. "We
never got along, but my mother's death just made everything

worse. That's why I went into the military. To get away from him."

"Turned out to be a good decision." She gestured to all of the plaques on the wall distinguishing him for his service.

"I'm sure Nate is a good kid."

Erica laughed. "He's doing okay. I've been able to keep him out of trouble. He's got a lot of potential."

"I know I tend to get too personal," Jonah said, "but I think knowing about a person's family tells you a lot about them. I hope one day you'll feel comfortable talking to me about your brother and your mom."

"And Terrell," she added. "He's my family too."

Jonah pasted an unconvincing smile on his face. "Well, we're getting him going now. He'll be driving people by the end of the week, I expect."

"He's very proud," Erica said. "Just remember that."

"He seems like a good enough guy," Jonah offered, "but I'm not gonna pretend like I think he's good enough for you. However, it's none of my business."

"No, it's not," Erica said quickly. "And he *is* good enough for me."

Jonah hesitated before nodding and turning to leave.

Erica didn't know what to make of him. He was a focused man and barely spoke to her, but when he did, he always managed to make her uncomfortable. In her second week of this, she was starting to believe that maybe there wasn't any reason to be suspicious of him anymore. Besides, she was so busy working and trying to put together ideas for her wedding that she had little time to wonder what Jonah Dolan was all about.

When Sherise arrived at the Capitol Hill Club, a favorite lunch spot of politicos, she knew everyone was looking at her. She looked extremely sharp in her lavender pants suit with a peach silk blouse and high white Jimmy Choo heels. Walking confidently as the host led her to Jonah's table, she smiled and waved to those she knew, trying to convince herself that she was excited to get some work done with Jonah and not just excited to see the look on his face when he saw her.

When she reached the table, Sherise was very pleased with the look on Jonah's face. He didn't attempt to hide his pleasure at seeing her. She was not pleased, however, to see that he was alone.

"Where is Erica?" she asked.

Jonah stood up, a gentleman's gesture that Sherise loved. "She'll be here."

Sherise sat down two seats away from him at the half-circle table. She already knew everyone was looking at her, and Jonah was way too high profile to go unnoticed. While Sherise had crossed some lines in her relationships, she was always careful to keep things discreet in public to protect her professional reputation.

"When will she be here?"

Jonah laughed. "Sherise, don't worry. This is way too out in the open for anyone to be suspicious. Now, if I had asked for a booth in the corner people might think things, but we're practically in the middle of the room."

"You know how people love to gossip in this town."

"Well, we won't give them anything to gossip about." Jonah waved the waiter over. "I hope you like red Cabernet. I already ordered a bottle."

Sherise felt herself begin to relax. "It's my favorite, but there is no way I'm drinking wine around you."

"Why not?"

"I need to be on my guard with you, Jonah," she said flirtatiously. "I can see that now."

"You have no idea," he offered, and leaned back in his chair.

"Shouldn't we wait for Erica?" Sherise asked, wondering if Erica was even coming. She should have texted her about this.

"I don't like waiting," Jonah said defiantly. "You don't look like a woman who likes to wait either."

They ordered and Jonah excused the waiter to pour the wine himself.

"I discovered this brand while I was in Nice over the summer," he said. "Its taste is very smooth and not too fruity."

"Nice?" Sherise asked. "Did you vacation there with your wife?"

Jonah smiled with a little hesitation as he seemed to assess why Sherise mentioned his wife. Sherise felt she was very clear about her meaning. At least she hoped she was, despite what other voices in her head were trying to say to her.

"Yes, Sherise, I am a married man," he said.

"And I'm a married woman," she added.

"Justin is a very lucky man." After pouring her glass, he poured his own. "I hope he knows that."

"He does."

"I doubt it."

The look he gave her sent her pulse racing and Sherise glanced away, certain that everyone in the room could see what was going on. She couldn't let him take control of this lunch.

"You know nothing about Justin," she said, pretending to smooth out the napkin on her lap.

"No," he agreed, "but I'm a good reader of people. I felt an attraction to you from the first moment I saw you in that restaurant."

"Don't be silly." Sherise laughed nervously, wishing Erica would get her ass here now.

"I'm never silly," he said seriously. "Foolish at times, but never silly."

"You're being very foolish now. I love my husband."

"And I love my wife, but—"

"But?" Sherise cursed herself for even asking that. "There should never be a 'but' after that statement."

"There is definitely something between us," Jonah said. "Attraction to a woman is not uncommon, but very rarely is it something I can't ignore. With you, it's different. Like a bolt of electricity."

Sherise couldn't deny the attraction between them but she had to think of Justin. She had to think of Cady. "I prefer we keep things professional."

"So would I," Jonah said, "but I'm curious as to how that can happen. You're not the kind of woman a man can ignore, especially if you'll be heading the project."

Sherise's eyes lit up. "Do you know something I don't?"

"I know that the head of this project needs to be someone who can take over a room of bureaucrats and get them to change the way they communicate. Walter and I both agreed that it has to be you. That's what this lunch is for."

Sherise couldn't stop the smile that formed at her lips. Another battle won. *Take that Toni.* "That is certainly good news."

"Come on, Sherise," Jonah said. "You knew all along this was yours. You get what you want. You always do."

"Is there anything wrong with that?" Sherise felt silly for letting Toni get to her. It was just jitters after being gone so long.

"Coming from a man who gets whatever he wants," Jonah said, "absolutely not."

Sherise responded to his mischievous expression with one of her own, not thinking about the consequences. *Damn those powerful men*, she thought.

"You can't have everything you want," she added with a cautious tone.

"Bullshit," he answered unequivocally. "You just can't give up. And I don't, Sherise. I never give up."

Sherise felt a chill run down her spine from the way he looked at her. It was as if he had her already and it sparked a fire inside her, a defiant one. How dare this man assume so much?

"It's a good thing Erica isn't here," Sherise said. "There would be nowhere for her to sit. Your ego is big enough to fill the chair between us."

"My ego is big enough to fill this room." Jonah took a sip of his wine. "But I assume you wouldn't have it any other way."

"I don't care either way," Sherise said.

"You can't fool me, Sherise. Though it's puzzling that you married a man like Justin."

"Justin is a wonderful man," she proclaimed argumentatively.

"Of course he is. He's wonderful, reliable, stable, successful, all that. But he's not you."

"I could never marry myself," she said. "I'm far too difficult."

"I don't imagine you being happy in the long run without a difficult relationship." He took a sip of his wine, never taking his eyes off her. "You're fire, Sherise. I can see it across the room. You need ice, not a cool glass of water."

"Your metaphors are a little tired," Sherise said, feeling a second wind as he continued to challenge her marriage. "I suppose you think you're ice."

"Is there any question?" he asked haughtily.

"This is an interesting side of you, Jonah. All the charm goes out the window."

"I'm sorry if I'm being too forward," he said.

"No you're not," Sherise snapped back. "You like displaying your dominance, especially to a woman who doesn't fawn over you or a man who doesn't cower to you immediately. I've known men like you all my life."

"You've never known anyone like me, Sherise."

Sherise didn't doubt that and as every second passed she was finding herself more attracted to his ego, his arrogance and pure manliness. It sickened her and excited her at the same time.

"What is going on?" Erica asked as soon as she reached the table.

"Erica." The disappointment in Jonah's face at her arrival was obvious to both women. "Nice of you to join us."

"What took you so long?" Sherise asked, grateful one of her watchdogs was here.

"What took me so long?" Erica repeated as she sat between them. "I'm early and you two look like you've been here a while."

"We've already ordered," Jonah said, gesturing for a waiter. "I'll get them to give you a menu."

Erica wasn't stupid and when she turned to Jonah, she gave him a look that told him she knew exactly what he was up to. He'd told her to show up at 1:00 PM for the lunch, but imagined he told Sherise to meet him there earlier than that. It was 12:45 now. Looking at Sherise, Erica had the feeling she wasn't in on it. Jonah had tricked them both.

"So what exactly have we been talking about?" Erica asked Jonah.

"The project," he answered. "And other things."

Sherise turned away as she got a judgmental stare from Erica. "I'm heading the project, so I'll get to see you more often."

"How nice for all of us." Erica accepted the menu from the waiter but took her time opening it. Was this the key to it all?

Was Jonah's interest in her just a way to get to Sherise? It couldn't be that simple. Could it?

"Go away!" Billie tried to slam the front door to her apartment but Porter jumped halfway in to stop it.

"Ouch!" he yelled as the door hit him. "I'm trying to apologize to you, Billie. Why you gotta be like that?"

"I told you about coming by my place," Billie said. "You have no right or reason to be here except to try and get some."

"I'm not here to get some." Porter entered the apartment

and closed the door behind him. "I was wrong to show up at your little dinner and I know it."

"It means nothing when you apologize over and over again after the fact," Billie said. "That's your whole life, Porter. Do whatever the fuck you want, then apologize."

"I know, and I paid the ultimate price for that." He followed her into the kitchen where she was making a late dinner for one. "I lost my wife."

"Go fuck yourself," Billie responded. "Or better yet, go fuck your blond whore. I'm sure she's waiting at home for you."

"Hey," Porter said, leaning against the counter. "I feel like I've been pretty generous in the past week. I let you see Tara."

"Not being a complete asshole is not the same as being generous." Billie grabbed the spoon to stir the instant mashed potatoes. "Seriously, Porter. Just leave. I don't want you here. I don't need you here."

"I can deal with a lot," Porter said as he came around the counter, stopping just inches from her. "But I can't deal with you not wanting me."

Billie had to laugh at that even though his closeness made her nervous. "Then you lose, I guess. You can't have your cake and eat it too."

"I know that," he said. "I know this is stupid and selfish, but I can't stay away from you, Billie."

"Meanwhile, you make my life miserable."

"I acted a fool during the divorce. I know. I was hurt. I was angry. What do you want me to do? Do you want me to give you some money?"

Billie reached out and slapped him across the face as hard as she could. "You son of a bitch!"

"That's what this is about, isn't it?" Porter was holding his cheek, but otherwise seemed unfazed by the slap. "I screwed you over in the divorce. You got more debt than money. I can make that up to you."

"In exchange for what?" she asked. "You drop by and I break you off a piece every now and then?"

"I don't want to be cut out of your life," Porter said.

He reached for Billie, his hands on her waist. He tried to pull her toward him, but she pushed away.

"You should have thought about that before you fucked Claire."

"It all comes down to Claire," he said.

"What a surprise." Billie's tone was intensely sarcastic. "Who would have thought I'd hold a grudge about you cheating on me? Go figure."

"Is it because she's white?" he asked.

Billie's expression was incredulous. She didn't even know what to say.

"It is, isn't it?" he asked.

"Do you think I give a shit what color she is?" Was he that stupid that he could believe Claire's skin color could have an effect on the amount of pain and betrayal Billie felt? Just the though only made her angrier.

"I think it is," Porter said.

"Of course you do," Billie said. "Because you're an idiot. Only an idiot would think that a woman would sit back and say, 'Damn, my husband left me for another woman, but at least it's with another sistah.' "

"I didn't leave you, Billie. I wanted to stay married. You left me."

Billie looked at him in astonishment. "That is really how you see it, isn't it? That I'm the one who ended this marriage."

"You're the one who wanted the divorce."

"News flash," she offered. "You left me the second you stuck your dick in her."

Porter rolled his eyes. "So you're saying it has nothing to do with . . ."

"It has nothing to do with her color," Billie said. "It has nothing to do with her. It's about you thinking you can still be a part of my life after you've moved on. I have a right to move on too."

"It seems like you have," Porter said. "Richard what's-his-name."

Billie was caught off guard.

"I know you share an office with him," Porter said. "You two are in there laughing all day long. And you go out to lunch with him. What else are you doing with him?"

"Are you having me . . ." Billie could barely find the words. "Are you having me spied on?"

"I know a lot of people and you're pretty much carrying on with him in the open."

Billie remembered Justin's warning words about how much people at her firm liked Porter so much. Of course someone would be willing to spy a little for him. But who?

"Every time I think you might not be the biggest bastard on this planet," she said, "you up and remind me that you absolutely are."

"I'm just saying that nothing is preventing you from moving on." Porter reached out to her as she passed him by, but she slapped his hand away.

Swinging her front door wide open, Billie took a deep breath. Porter's spying was the last straw. It was at least enough to give her the courage to consider Sherise's advice.

"You're going to leave my apartment and you are never going to come back."

Porter was angry now. "Remember, Billie. I have all the cards. I have Tara and I can decide if you see her or not. I don't think you want to—"

"I have one card," Billie said. "I can make your life hell if I tell your new little roommate about us."

Porter stopped on his way toward her with a doubtful look on his face. "You're full of shit. You wouldn't—"

"I'll call that bitch right now."

Porter's eyes tightened into angry slits. "She would never

believe you. Claire believes anything I tell her. She'll just think you're trying to make trouble."

"She'll be right," Billie said. "And I will make trouble. My girls will back me up. Besides she's not a complete idiot. She has to suspect something. From the tone of her voice the last time she interrupted us on the phone, I could sense it. A woman knows these things. You're on the verge of a big problem."

Billie stepped aside as Porter seemed to be willing to give up and headed for the door.

"Unlike you," he said, "Claire is replaceable."

"You are one cold son of a bitch," Billie said.

"But I'd rather not have to do that right now," Porter said. "You want me to stay away from you?"

"That's all I want."

Without a second to react, Billie felt Porter wrap his arms around her waist and pull her to him. When his lips came down on hers, she felt a crushing heat rage through her. She fought vigorously and finally, after a few seconds, pushed him away.

"I'll give you what you want," Porter said. "Let's just see how long you can deal with it."

Billie slammed the door behind him and leaned against it. She wanted to kick something and scream. In that one second he kissed her, she wanted him. What was wrong with her? She should be happy that he agreed to stay away from her, but his last words were hanging around and she knew she wouldn't be able to get rid of him. She had convinced herself that Porter staying away from her was the solution. But what if she couldn't stay away from him?

"Terrell!" Erica yelled at the top of her lungs this time as she jumped on the sofa next to her fiancé.

"Dammit!" Terrell pressed the pause button on the video

game he was playing and turned to Erica. "Baby, I'm gonna lose this level if you keep interrupting me."

Erica didn't give a damn about a stupid game. "What happened to all that 'baby we gonna plan this wedding together'? 'You and me all the way.'"

"We figured out the date together."

He turned back to the game, but Erica snatched the joystick out of his hand.

"We have to pick a place or the date doesn't matter," she said. "I have a few ideas I want to share with you, unless you'd rather play your little game."

Terrell really knew he had no choice, so he paused his game and turned his attention to her as she placed pictures she had ripped from some magazines on the coffee table. He recognized some of the locations, but every picture just looked like a big dollar sign to him.

"Who is getting married? Us or royalty?"

"Stop it." Erica pointed to her favorite. "I want this one and they have our date open. I called them earlier today."

Terrell was shaking his head. "Baby, this is . . . who exactly are you thinking of when you plan this wedding?"

"What do you mean?"

"That place isn't us," he said. "It looks like . . . like a place someone like Jonah would get married."

"Where in the hell did that come from?" Erica snatched the picture away, offended that he wouldn't think something this beautiful wasn't right for her. "I'm not good enough for this place?"

"Not that." Terrell tried to choose his words carefully. "You're good enough for any place, but that doesn't mean the place fits who you are. We aren't all this white and frilly and stuff. Besides, who can afford this?"

"They have all types of wedding packages. Obviously this picture represents their most lavish, but we would get a scaled down version of it."

"There are a lot of places closer to us that—"

"I want to get married downtown, Terrell. And why would you even mention Jonah? He has nothing to do with this."

"Are you sure?" he asked. "It seems like ever since you've started working for him—"

"Which is less than two weeks," Erica interjected.

"Still."

"Still what? Are you saying I'm not the same girl you wanted to marry just because I've worked for Jonah for two weeks?"

"No." Terrell was getting frustrated. "Look, I don't know what I'm saying. I'm just . . . I don't like that guy."

"Just because he was a little condescending to you?" Erica asked. "Like you haven't faced that before. The money is what matters, Terrell. The opportunity."

"But at what cost?" He reached out and placed his hand gently on her cheek. "I feel like . . . I love you, baby. I just don't want to lose you."

"Why would you lose me?" Tossing all the magazine pieces aside, Erica slid toward him, wrapping her arms around him. "I love you, too, baby. We're getting married. Some new boss isn't going to change that."

She leaned in and kissed his forehead, then the tip of his nose before coming down and placing a big, fat kiss on his full lips. He kissed her back, wrapping his arms around her and pulling her to him so she was sitting in his lap.

"I get a weird vibe from him," Terrell said when their lips finally separated.

"Are you still on this idea that he's interested in me?" she asked. "I've already told you. He doesn't hit on me. He gets a little too personal sometimes and he gives me a lot of gifts and stuff, but it's never sexual."

Grabbing her at her hips, he picked her up and lowered her down on the sofa, positioning his body on top of hers.

"Are you sure he's just not leading up to it?" he asked.

She nodded. "Positive. A woman has intuition. He's not trying to get with me. Besides, if he's after anyone, it's Sherise."

"Really?" This certainly got Terrell's attention. So his suspicions after eyeing them at the dinner were true. "They gettin' it on?"

"No, but I'm certain he'd like to. It's pretty gross."

"His wife is a cold fish."

Erica wouldn't disagree with that. "Still no excuse. But Sherise won't let it go too far."

"That man could have a lot to lose if it ever did." Terrell's crafty mind was racing a mile a minute. He was right to take Jonah up on his offer. There might be more money to be made than he thought.

Erica noticed that look on Terrell's face. What was he thinking and why was he thinking of anything other than her being ready to go underneath him?

"Hey!" She grabbed his face at the chin and made him look at her. "Hot fiancée here and you're zoning out?"

Terrell smiled wickedly. "I'm just thinking of all the bad, bad things I'm 'bout ready to do to you."

Sherise jumped with a start when she stepped out of the shower. She didn't even know Justin was home, let alone in the bathroom.

"Where did you come from?" she asked, reaching for the towel.

"Work." Justin was leaning against the sink of their recently refurnished master bath. "Where else?"

"I just thought you had a dinner thing." Wrapping the towel around herself, she fluttered over to her husband and kissed him on the lips. Not feeling that enthusiastic of a response, she leaned back and studied him. "What's wrong?" she asked.

He shook his head. "How long has Cady been asleep?"

"She just fell asleep, so she'll be sleeping for hours." Sherise rubbed against her husband. "In case you were planning anything."

Justin smiled this time, but wasn't in the mood. "I'm actually pretty tired. The dinner ended early."

"Okay." After a hesitation, Sherise went over to the sink.

"How was your lunch with Jonah?"

Sherise peered at him through the mirror, but she didn't need to look to see he was upset. The cold tone in his voice told her everything.

"Yesterday?" She continued to act nonchalant as she brushed her hair, but was curious what he was up to. "I told you about it."

"No you didn't," he said.

"I told you that I got to take the lead on the project and—"

"You made it seem like . . ." Justin didn't feel like getting into details. "You didn't tell me you were having lunch with Jonah."

"I didn't know I had to." She turned to him, leaning against the sink. "Are you jealous?"

Justin was jealous, but he didn't want to be. He loved Sherise and trusted her, but she always flirted with men like Jonah and he knew she'd do anything to get ahead. "Do I have a reason to be?"

"No, silly. Besides, Erica was there. Didn't whoever told you about my lunch with Jonah tell you that?"

"No." That did make him feel a little better.

"Who exactly told you about my clandestine lunch with Mr. Dolan?" Sherise asked. "Some woman who would like you to be mad at your wife?"

"Don't try to deflect, Sherise," he said. "And it wasn't a woman who told me."

"Who was it then?" Sherise realized that using her charm to distract him wasn't going to work right now. Something had made him angry and she felt guilty, knowing all the thoughts that had been going through her mind during that lunch, and since.

"Jonah did." Justin reached out and placed Sherise's phone on the sink before turning and walking out of the bathroom.

Sherise picked up her phone and saw that Justin had left it open to a text that Jonah had sent her only a few minutes earlier.

LUNCH WAS GREAT. LET'S DO BREAKFAST TOMORROW.

"Dammit," she whispered under her breath.

She was going to have to put Jonah Dolan in his place or he could ruin everything for her.

7

"More documents for you both!"

Callie had a habit of knocking on Billie's office door after she was already inside.

"What are these for?" Billie asked as Callie dumped a stack about eight inches high on her already packed desk.

"Work shift," Callie said. "Betz Advertising is going to cut billing next month, so we have to get as much work done this month as possible."

"Exactly where am I supposed to fit this in?" Billie asked no one in particular.

"You'll figure it out." Callie placed the remainder of her stack on Richard's desk. "Do you know where he is?"

Billie shrugged her shoulders. "He left an hour ago."

"Didn't he say anything?"

"He doesn't tell me where he's going."

"But you should have some idea," she said impatiently. "We really have to get started on this."

"Why should I?" Billie asked.

There was a slight hint of sarcasm in Callie's voice as she said, "Since you two are so close."

"What do you mean, since we're so . . . ." Something just hit Billie. "It's you, isn't it?"

"Me what?" Callie was genuinely surprised.

"Why would you think I was so close to Richard?"

"I don't know." Callie began backing out of the room nervously. "You two spend all your time together and you—"

"We work in the same office, Callie. That's not the same as spending time together."

"Yeah, well . . . you always order lunch together or you go out and get it together."

Billie got up from her desk and walked over to Callie, who froze just as she reached the door. "What is it, Callie? Do you have a crush on Porter? Did he pay you? Why would you go reporting to him what I'm doing?"

"I don't know what you're talking about," Callie said. "Why are you acting so weird?"

Billie stood in place, her hands on her hips. "If you have enough free time to spy on me and report back to my ex-husband, maybe I need to talk to your boss so you can get more work."

"Hey," she exclaimed, "I was just looking for Richard."

And with that, Callie was out the door.

When Billie went to close the door to her office, feeling paranoid and suspicious now, she almost ran right into Justin.

"What did you do?" he asked.

"Why did I do anything?"

He pointed down the hallway. "Callie is running away like a scared little girl."

"Or a guilty little girl." Billie looked at her watch. She thought Justin was early for their lunch, but he was actually a few minutes late. "I can't believe it's already one."

"Guilty of what?" he asked as he stepped inside the office.

Billie told him about Callie's guilty reaction when she accused her of spying on her and reporting to Porter.

"You don't know if it's her," he said.

"Have you heard anything that might lead me to believe it's someone else?" she asked.

Justin shook his head.

"Besides," she continued, "no one else would know who I spend my time with. I'm stuck in this office all day and she's the only person who comes in here."

"What reason would she have to do that?"

"Porter can be very persuasive," Billie said. "I'm gonna report her to someone. Who should I go to?"

"Whether or not she did anything," Justin said, "—and you have no proof she did—you're not reporting it to anyone. You haven't even been here a month, Billie. You can't go around making waves, trying to get people in trouble."

"So I'm supposed to put up with her spying on me?"

"You're supposed to look like a tough, competent attorney who doesn't go crazy on the paralegals and start making accusations she can't prove. This is a jungle, Billie. You're gonna have to figure out how to deal with Callie a different way."

"You sound like your wife," Billie said.

"Speaking of my wife," Justin said, "I need to ask you a couple of questions about Jonah Nolan."

Oh great, Billie thought. Jumping out of one pot of foolishness into another.

Erica almost jumped with glee when she saw Terrell standing by the limousine as she came out of the Pentagon. She was trailing behind Jonah, carrying his briefcase as he discussed last minute details with a man who was interested in a Defense Department contract for weapons labor. This was Terrell's first job, driving the contractor to and from Ronald Reagan airport, which was only five minutes from the Pentagon.

But there was no smile on Terrell's face as he stood next to the open door to the backseat. Leaving Jonah and the contractor to their conversation toward the front of the car, Erica made her way to Terrell.

"What's wrong?"

Terrell shrugged his shoulders. "Nothing. It's easy stuff."

"And you get to see me," she said, smiling.

Terrell finally smiled. The only good part of his day was seeing his baby and the cars this new company drove, which were much nicer than those he was used to. Other than that, Terrell wasn't getting anything out of this. He knew what he needed to do in order to make the money he wanted. He needed to drive Jonah Dolan's car.

"Come on over here and give me a kiss," he said.

"Oh God, no." Erica looked over at Jonah, who didn't seem to be paying them any attention. "That's unprofessional. You see, I knew you were gonna be trouble to work with. I should have never recommended you."

Terrell laughed. "I'm glad you did now. I can keep an eye on you and make sure old Jonah keeps his hands to himself."

"Will you get off that?" Erica asked, even though she knew he was mostly kidding. At least she hoped he was. "He is not remotely interested in me."

"He better not be if he knows what's good for him."

"Watch who you threaten," she said with a teasing tone. "He has access to weapons of mass destruction."

"So do I." Terrell patted his biceps. "And if he doesn't want . . ." Noticing that Jonah and his client were walking toward them, Terrell straightened up and stepped aside.

"You're going back to the airport," Jonah told Terrell in a cold, authoritarian voice. "You're going to wait there until three. That's when Jenna Adams's plane lands. You'll bring her back here and that will be it for the day."

"Yes, sir." Terrell closed the door and winked at Erica one last time before rushing around to the front and driving off.

"You shouldn't do that," Jonah said.

Erica turned to him noting his stiff demeanor. He was angry with her. "What did I do?"

"Flirting with him," he said. "That's unprofessional."

"We weren't flirting noticeably." Erica tried to keep up with him as he was already heading back into the building.

"If you weren't flirting noticeably, I wouldn't have noticed it. What you do on your own time is fine, but you shouldn't give any indication to the passengers that you have a personal relationship with the drivers."

"That isn't true, is it?" Erica asked, her tone laced with a little attitude. "What I do on my own time seems to be your business too. You know everything."

Jonah stopped, turning to her. "I haven't interfered with your life beyond finding out if you were safe to employ."

"Finding out how many hours a week my fiancé works at his job is essential to my employment with you?"

Jonah's brow furrowed in frustration. "My point stands. It's inappropriate."

"Your clients might care if you associate with the help, but I'm help, remember? They don't care about me."

"You're not help," he said. "Erica, you are an essential member of my team. Your position will put you in very real confidence with me. And the point isn't to not appear friendly to the help. The point is not to give the contractors who are vying for billion-dollar contracts with us any additional avenues of influence."

"What influence?"

"You're someone I talk to every day," he said. "Someone I listen to. I will value your input. They know that. If they think they can get to me through you, they'll try to take advantage of your relationship with Terrell if they know one exists."

It felt good to Erica to not be regarded as a lowly staff member for once, but that didn't change Jonah's hypocrisy. The way he carried on with Sherise at that lunch and other times was a clear indication of mixing business and personal, but Erica was smart enough to know that when people were as high up as Jonah, their own rules didn't apply to them.

"It won't happen again," she assured him as they stepped into the elevators.

★　★　★

Sherise felt better. She had been working hard all day on her new project with the Defense Department, but all she could think of was Jonah. She thought of reasons she could come up with to call him and ask him a business question even though she knew all she wanted was to hear his voice. She thought about the moment their fingers touched and their eyes connected. She felt like a girl. Something about powerful men made her feel that way and she loved it.

And it was wrong.

Sherise thought if she could take a short walk outside and get some fresh air, she could get her head on straight. She brought her wallet with her so she could look at pictures of Justin and Cady and remind herself of who she was, where she was, what she had. She had something that she had wanted all her life and knew she didn't want to lose it for anything—a real family.

But the second she returned, Jessica was right on her with a very worried, concerned look on her face.

"What is it?" Sherise asked, knowing something had to be going down.

"You wanted me to tell you when Walter asked me to summon Toni to his office?" she asked.

Sherise shrugged. "Yes, but it turns out it was just about work yesterday."

"Today is different." Jessica sidled up to her. "He was very, very angry. He even . . . cursed. Walter . . . swore, and then he snapped at me to tell Toni to get in his office right away."

Sherise felt her chest tightening and her heart beginning to beat. So Rachel had finally come through. Only took her a few days too. Could Toni's reckoning be happening?

"How long has she been in there?" Sherise passed her office and headed for Walter's.

"About twenty minutes," Jessica said. "Where have you been and what is this about?"

"I don't know exactly," Sherise lied. She had already given

out too much info to Jessica, but she was on her way out and posed very little threat to her. "But you say he was really mad?"

"Walter cursed, Sherise."

Sherise smiled at her.

"You know something," she said accusingly.

"What I know are only rumors that have been going around, but I didn't think anything would ever come of it."

"So you're not the reason she's in there?"

Sherise tried her best not to gloat. "I was confident enough in what was being said to tell him, but I knew it would get around to him eventually."

"Liar," Jessica said. "What are you planning to do now?"

Sherise held her head up victoriously. "There is nothing I need to do. Everything is just going to fall into place."

At that second, Sherise wasn't sure what she was saying, but she could hear Toni yelling. Everyone could hear her yelling. Sherise could barely contain herself as other people in the office turned their heads and leaned back, looking in the direction of Walter's office.

"I should do something." Jessica was starting to look worried. "Walter doesn't know how to deal with screeching females."

"Don't you dare," Sherise ordered. "Walter should have done better due diligence before letting her get so close."

By the time Toni exited the office, in a huff, her eyes fuming with anger, a nice-sized crowd had gathered in the open area around Jessica's desk outside Walter's office. Sherise wasn't going to let this opportunity pass her by. There was a voice in the back of her head telling her to just let it go. She'd won, no need to take it any further. But she was who she was and Sherise knew she wasn't going to let this chance go by.

When Toni realized how many people had been standing outside the office, she sort of froze in place. She was there long enough for Sherise to put on a concerned and caring facade and reach out to her. She hurried to her side.

"Toni, are you okay?" she asked, looking to anyone as if she was completely concerned, but in reality hardly able to control her laughter. "What's wrong, sweetie?"

"You bitch!" Toni lashed out at her, pushing Sherise, and her open arms, away. "You did this!"

"What?" Sherise knew her injured shock was convincing. "What did I do?"

"You told him!" she yelled.

"Told him what?" Sherise asked. "I was just trying to comfort you and—"

"You're a lying bitch and you know it," Toni spat.

"Now that is enough," Jessica said. "This is an office, Toni. You can't—"

"Shut up!" Toni was clearly beyond control. "You probably helped her. You never liked me. I'm the reason you're going to that plush new job, you—"

"Toni!"

Everyone turned to Walter as he came out of his office.

"Don't you dare," he warned.

"It's true," Toni said. "If it wasn't for me, you'd still be—"

"Not wise," Sherise warned.

Sherise's advice seemed to be the final straw for Toni. Her entire body seemed to shake as she lunged for Sherise. Caught off guard, Sherise fell back onto the floor. Her instinct was to get up and start kicking Toni's ass, but when she realized what had just happened, she stayed on the ground. While Walter grabbed Toni to keep her away from Sherise and Jessica got on her phone to call security, a couple of her coworkers tried to help Sherise up.

This was more wonderful than she could have ever planned herself.

"Are you okay?" Walter finally asked after Toni was taken away and the crowd began to disperse.

Sherise, sitting in the chair behind Jessica's desk, nodded. "I just don't . . . Jesus, Walter. What happened?"

"I fired her." He patted Sherise's shoulder in a fatherly manner. "I'm sorry she took it out on you. She seems to think you're behind it."

"Behind what?"

Walter looked at her with a doubtful expression. "I'm not a fool, Sherise. You can't sit here and tell me you didn't know about the rumors of some of her earlier exploits."

Sherise shrugged her shoulders. "I'd heard she was involved in some sort of bribery thing, but no one would confirm if it was true or give me any details, so I decided not to say anything. I didn't want to make a fool of myself if it wasn't true."

"It was." Walter sighed, like a disappointed father. "She facilitated a bribe to help out her then-boyfriend who was a lobbyist for an oil and gas company. It didn't work, but she threatened the senator with exposure if he fired her."

"If it didn't work, what did she have to threaten him with?" Sherise asked, happy to finally get some details even though they didn't matter anymore.

"Nothing has to actually happen in politics, Sherise." Walter held out a hand to help her as she started to rise from the chair. "The possibility alone and the twenty-four-hour news cycle can be enough to ruin a person. Besides, the senator in question is now vice president, so he had a lot to lose."

Sherise had to hand it to Toni. She was a girl after her own heart. Hustling herself out of trouble was admirable, but every good run had to come to an end, especially if it clashed with her own good run.

Walter stuffed his hands in his pockets as if he didn't know what to do with them. "She's threatening to call my future employer and ask him to rescind the offer he made me."

Sherise wasn't sure what to say. This upset her. Part of her blamed Walter for letting Toni get so entrenched in their group while she was gone and keeping her out of the loop, but she knew that Walter was a good guy who deserved this job. She didn't want him to suffer.

"It's okay," Walter said, as he seemed to sense Sherise's concern. "I've signed an iron-clad contract. If they rescind, they'll have to pay me a year's salary and that's more than I make in three years here."

"And they would take you back here anyway," she said.

"No, I'm done here." He looked around the office. "Sherise, I'm going to recommend you replace me."

Sherise's smile broadened in approval as she tried to contain herself. "Walter, I don't know what to say."

"I know what you're thinking," he said. "You damn well better recommend me."

Sherise laughed nervously. She never knew when Walter was serious or playing with her when it came to her overactive ambition.

"Just remember," he said, "in this competitive world we're in, getting a job may seem like winning the battle, but actually being able to do the job is the real challenge. Someone will be shooting for you soon, Sherise."

Sherise knew that to be true, but Walter underestimated her. Not only was she ready to fight for what was hers, she was looking forward to it.

"You overreact to everything," Billie told Erica as they made their way down Wisconsin Avenue in DC before reaching their destination, an early lunch at Maggiano's. "Jonah has some ulterior motive for hiring you. First he was a perv and wanted to get with you. Then he showed an unusual interest in Terrell. Now, he wants to use you to get to Sherise?"

"I'm not making this up," Erica said.

"You always think the worst of every situation that turns out good for you. I'm surprised you didn't see an ulterior motive in Terrell wanting to marry you."

"I trust Terrell. I don't trust Jonah."

"Why not?" she asked. "The man has done nothing but open up opportunities for you and Terrell."

"I know. I know." Erica didn't know why she couldn't just enjoy what she had, but she couldn't ignore that voice that told her something was up. "It's just . . ."

"Is he still trying to get all up in your business?"

Erica nodded. "Although he isn't as bad as he was at first. Yesterday, he was asking me more questions about Terrell. Can you believe that? The nerve of him trying to get the info on . . ."

Erica realized that Billie was no longer walking with her. She turned around to see Billie staring through the window of a bridal shop, her mouth almost hitting the ground. When Erica walked back to her she could see that familiar expression on Billie's face. The girl was about to blow.

"What is wrong with you?" Erica said.

"There is no fucking way!" Billie ignored her and rushed into the store feeling her anger completely take over any common sense she might have had.

Confused, Erica followed Billie into the store and watched as Billie walked up to a group of young white women who were looking at a dress one of them was holding to her body. It took Erica a second to realize that the woman holding the dress was Claire, Porter's girlfriend. She'd only seen the girl once, when she went on a stalking mission with Billie, who suspected Porter was cheating on her. They found him holding her hand outside a seafood restaurant in Tenleytown.

"What in the hell is going on here?" Billie asked. She didn't know what she was doing. She wasn't thinking. She saw Claire holding that dress and the only thing she could think of was that Porter had asked Claire to marry him. Billie was about to go insane.

Claire, looking more shocked than any of the girls around her, took a second to speak. "What are you doing here?"

"We were only divorced a few months ago," Billie yelled.

"You have no shame, but I guess I shouldn't expect you to, being a home-wrecking whore."

One of the girls, a tall brunette, started laughing, but Billie gave her a look that shut her up quick.

"Billie?" Erica asked as she stayed a foot behind. If anything went off, she would have Billie's back, but she could tell her girl wasn't thinking straight right now. "Calm down."

"Oh my God." Claire suddenly realized what Billie assumed and started laughing. "Jealous much?"

"Let's go, Billie." Erica wanted to save her friend as much embarrassment as possible, but Billie didn't want to move.

"This is her?" the brunette asked.

"Her?" Billie turned to her. "You mean is this the woman whose husband your whore of a friend fucked?"

"Why don't you just leave, Billie?" Claire handed the dress to her friend. "This is none of your business."

"You mean like my marriage was none of your business?"

"Should I call somebody?" the shorter girl, who looked scared as hell, asked.

"You don't need to call anyone," Erica said. She grabbed Billie by the arm and tried to pull her back. "Come on."

"Your marriage is over," Claire said. "It's about time you get over it."

Erica jumped in front of Billie, who looked ready to lunge. "You do not want to do this, girl."

"I'm not afraid of you," Claire said, even though her voice was uneasy. "I've got my friends here and—"

"I'll take all you bitches!" Billie shoved Erica out of the way and an evil smile formed at her lips. "You think you've won something, don't you?"

Claire crossed her arms over her chest and stared haughtily at Billie. "He's mine, isn't he?"

Billie laughed. "No, he's not, and I think you know it. He's only with you because I wouldn't take him back and even though he's with you . . ."

"Billie," Erica warned.

"He's still sleeping with me," she finally said, feeling fifty pounds lift off her just at hearing the words.

"You're a fucking liar," Claire spat out, losing her composure.

"Oh please," the brunette said. "Let's just go."

"No, stay," Billie said. "You can doubt all you want, but Claire knows. Don't you? You know he's a cheater. That's how you met him. You've been suspicious all along. The phone calls, not knowing where he's been, but he comes home freshly showered. You see the clues and you try to ignore them, but you know better. And you've known better for a long time."

"You're lying," Claire responded, even though the pain and anger in her face told everyone there that she believed every word Billie had said.

Billie felt a wicked sense of victory at the look on her face. She placed her hands on her hips and began laughing hysterically. Partly it was to upset Claire even more, and partly because she knew she seemed crazy for doing this, so she thought she might as well go all the way.

When Claire lunged for her, Billie was ready and she reached out and grabbed the arm that Claire was trying to slap her with. She turned it and twisted it until Claire was screaming bloody murder.

"Oh shit," was all Erica could say as the brunette dropped the dress and went after Billie. Erica dropped her purse and went to block.

She couldn't get in between her and Billie, so Erica did the next best thing. She grabbed the brunette from behind, pulling on her cotton sundress. She could hear the dress rip in her hands as she pulled the girl back. She had pulled so hard that the girl, who was taller, but not bigger than her, crashed into her and the both of them hit the ground.

"Let me go!" Claire screamed as she tried to turn with Billie as Billie kept pulling her arm. "You're gonna break my arm."

"You came at me, bitch!" Billie felt like she was having an out of body experience and loving every minute of it.

"Leave her alone!" yelled the third girl, almost in tears, while the fourth was nowhere to be seen. "I'm calling the cops."

That got to Billie. As a lawyer, she knew getting in trouble could mean not just a legal hassle that everyone had to deal with, but also a professional one. The DC bar would not be happy if they heard of her arrest, even if it wasn't in any way related to her job.

"Just remember," Billie said, "you might want to leave that honor part out of your wedding vows, because neither of you knows what the hell that means."

Billie pushed Claire away and looked derisively at her as she cried and huddled in her friend's arms. She was ready to tell Erica it was time to go until she realized that Erica was rolling on the floor, cussing at the brunette and trying to pull her hair out at the same time.

Nothing, not even Jonah's constant glances and suggestive smiles, could ruin this moment for Sherise. Called to a meeting for the joint project in Jonah's office, Sherise was determined to make sure she wasn't left alone with Jonah for even a second. With Toni gone, it was just Walter and her. When they showed up at the Pentagon, not only was Sherise happy to know there were two other people there, but when she met them, she could barely maintain her calm.

Most people couldn't pick out the power brokers in DC if you gave them forever to do it. They knew the president, vice president, maybe the Speaker of the House and a boisterous, insane senator or two, but most members of Congress and major decision-makers were a mystery to them. Unless you lived in DC, in which case, these people were celebrities and knowing them meant you were "in." Sherise had been reading *Washington Life* magazine since she was a young girl. As the official local social diary, it was a primer in the powerful, rich, and beautiful in DC. It followed the cultured set, the people with names that were displayed on buildings, streets, and major charities.

Elena Morgan and Derrick Robins were two of those people. A girl from the Southside of Chicago, Elena married money and her union to Alexander Morgan, heir to an Atlantic coast real estate empire, made her a major socialite on the scene. She was known for hosting some of the biggest parties in DC for Morgan House, the charity her husband's family created thirty years ago, but she made great in the last ten years. Derrick Robins, a senior counsel to the president, was recently nominated to be director of operations for the Office of Homeland Security. Not sexy, but a powerful position and someone to know.

It wasn't obvious how giddy Sherise felt to meet these two because she knew very well how to act when encountering the hot shots. You acted as if you met a hot shot every day. Nothing turned them off more than being impressed with them.

Jonah wanted the launching of the program to be accompanied by a party with the White House, Pentagon, and Homeland Security all celebrating new and improved communications. Elena was there to turn the event into a fundraiser to pay for school supplies for DC school children. Sherise was going to be part of the planning.

It would have been a perfect meeting if it hadn't been for Jonah, who made her shift and turn in her seat the entire hour under the piercing glare of his eyes. Sherise tried so hard not to look at him, afraid that everyone in the room would notice the tension between them, but he was an impossible man to ignore. Everyone stopped talking when he opened his mouth and Sherise couldn't help but give him her full attention, which he soaked up.

Sherise was grateful when Jenna popped her head into the

room and told Jonah he had to wrap it up and head off to the Capitol to meet with the Armed Forces Committee. As everyone stood up, Sherise darted straight for Elena to exchange cards.

"I'll be terribly busy the next few months," Sherise said, "but I hope to be able to help you with the event."

"I'm a pro at this, hon," Elena said. "I was so sorry to hear about Toni. I met her at the Kennedy awards last year and she seemed . . ."

"Such a sad thing," Sherise said, eager to change the topic. "I'm sure she'll bounce back. I'll tell her you said hello. Now, about the fund . . ."

"I'll be sure to call you." Elena was nodding at Jenna, who was waving to her from the door. "That means my car is waiting. You should be my co-emcee."

"Sounds like something to consider," Sherise said, although she was screaming inside. She imagined all the people who would be there and by the end of that night, they would all know who she was.

Sherise decided to head out after Elena and Derrick, who had already left, but just as she reached the door, Walter called her back. Reluctantly, she turned around and began to fume as she saw the look on Jonah's face. Standing in front of his desk, next to Walter, he had a smug look of complete satisfaction and knowledge that he had occupied her mind the entire meeting.

She wanted to smack that look off his face. Little did he know, he no longer meant anything to her. She was done with him. That would be quite a burst to his enormous ego.

"Planning to leave without me?" Walter asked, laughing.

Sherise smiled generously. "I'm sorry. I'd thought you'd already left. I was just . . ."

"The meeting wasn't that bad," Jonah said. "Why are you so eager to go?"

"You're the one who has to leave," Sherise said with just

enough of a hint of sarcasm for Jonah to notice and Walter to not.

"That meeting isn't for another hour," Jonah said.

"But it's all the way in the district," she said. "You'd better get started."

"Not just yet." Walter held up a reminding finger. "Keep Jonah company while I use the men's room. I'll be back in a second and we'll go."

"I can wait for you at the car," Sherise offered as Walter passed her by.

"Don't be silly," Jonah said. "You can wait here."

"I'll only be a moment," Walter said as he left.

Unable to trust herself, and especially Jonah, Sherise decided to wait outside anyway, but before she reached the door, Jonah, with what she assumed was some superhuman stealth, managed to make his way to the door and shut it behind him. She gasped, stopping just inches from him. She hated to admit it but the aggressiveness of his move excited her. The intensity of his eyes as they bore into her excited her even more.

"What are you doing?" she asked.

"Walter asked you to wait here, didn't he?"

"Kind of sad," she said with a tilt of her head. "So desperate for attention you have to trap women in your office."

"You've been avoiding me," he said. "I haven't heard from you since you refused my breakfast invitation last week."

"I'm a busy girl," she said nonchalantly. "And our relationship is strictly professional, so unless we have business to discuss, a breakfast isn't necessary."

"I've been thinking about you nonstop," he said.

Sherise felt her knees weaken a bit from the sensuous tone of his voice. "You're too busy a man to spend time thinking about a woman who isn't your wife."

Sherise inhaled sharply as, unexpectedly, his hand landed on her forearm and stayed. His touch was warm and she felt the heat immediately where he touched her. "Stop," she said, although she didn't move away or try to make him move.

"I'm not a fool," he said in a husky tone, just above a whisper. "You're attracted to me."

"I'm sure you think every woman is." Sherise didn't add that she was sure that almost every woman *was* attracted to him. His power was palpable. "But I—"

"I also know that your flirtation with me was a means to an end. You see, Sherise, I could spot you a mile away. You're an opportunist, the worst kind."

"What is the worst kind?" she asked, ready to defend herself and never apologize for doing what she had to in order to get what she wanted.

"The beautiful kind," he answered. "You think you don't need me anymore. You've gotten rid of Toni, and Walter has basically stenciled your name on his office door."

"So you can see," she said, relieved that she could be honest with him. "This little game between you and me is over."

"You got what you wanted," he said. "But I haven't."

"And you won't," she retorted defiantly.

Without warning he swung her around to face him and pulled her body to his. Sherise felt her body ignite as he closed in against her and when his lips came to hers, she didn't resist at all. His mouth held a mastery as it moved against hers, plying her with its power to open and respond. She felt the sensitive parts of her body begin to tingle as his mouth explored deeper and deeper.

Sherise was alarmed at how fast the pull in her belly enflamed her entire body and she felt her mind begin to escape her. Panicking, the fighter in her urged her to push away and she did. When she was finally free, she didn't hesitate to make him pay for the humiliation she fully participated in, slapping him hard against the left cheek.

Jonah, still engulfed in desire, didn't seem to care that she slapped him. His voice was breathless as he spoke to her. "You should know, I can do so much more for you. The people you met today are nothing compared to the people I know. I can open doors for you, Sherise."

Sherise swallowed, trying to pull herself back together despite her body still being on fire. "The price is too high."

Taking advantage of him having changed position in order to kiss her, Sherise reached for the door and opened it. She rushed out, not caring what that might look like to Jenna, who was sitting nearby at her desk. She just had to get away from Jonah and she had to forget the way that kiss made her feel.

8

"You gotta help me out here," Richard said as he leaned against Billie's desk.

Billie looked up. "Are you kidding me? Richard, I'm already behind on this memo. I have to draft it for—"

"Not with work," Richard said. "Ever since you came in this morning, you haven't said a word to me or anyone else. What did I say?"

Billie was about to tell him about the fight she and Erica had gotten into yesterday at the bridal shop. The last thing she needed was for this firm to think she was some kind of ghetto hood rat that got into street fights on the weekend.

"Bad weekend is all," she said. "And I'm very busy."

"If you're overwhelmed, I can understand if you don't want to help me with my pro bono case. I can see—"

"No!" Billie said forcefully. "The little work I'm doing on that case has been the only saving grace in my entire life right now. I will make time for that. Please don't push me off."

"I wasn't," Richard said. "Just thought if you were overwhelmed I could—"

"What in the hell do you think you're doing?"

Billie was shocked at the actual sight of Porter storming into her office like he owned it, but she wasn't so surprised that he was actually there. She just didn't think she had the stomach to deal with his anger right now and this was not the place.

"Hey!" Richard stood up, blocking Porter as he made his way to Billie's desk.

"Get out of my way, Richard." Porter pushed Richard aside. "This is between me and my . . . Billie."

"What are you doing here?" she asked, coming around the desk.

"More important," Richard said, "how did you get in here?"

"None of your damn business." Porter focused all his angry energy at his ex-wife. "I warned you, Billie."

"Callie let him in," Billie said. "This firm is like Fort Knox. No one is getting in without someone inside letting them in."

"Get your boyfriend out of here," Porter warned. "I don't think you want him to hear what I'm about to say."

"That's it," Richard said, going to his desk. "I'm calling Security."

"No," Billie called after him. "Richard, just . . . can you just give me a second?"

"Are you kidding? No way."

"How sweet." Porter smiled condescendingly as he looked from Richard to Billie. "Trying to play the gentleman is fun, isn't it? But I don't think you want any of this, Richard."

"Richard." Billie rushed over to Richard's desk to grab the phone out of his hand. "Please, I can handle this. Just go and don't tell anyone, okay?"

Richard looked at her, disgusted by her choice and seeming unwavering in his refusal to leave.

"Trust me," she added.

"Five minutes." After a reluctant sigh, he gave Porter another threatening glare before leaving the office.

Billie closed the office door behind him and turned to Porter. "You're sleeping with her, aren't you?"

"Why did you tell Claire about us?"

"Claire, me, and Callie." Billie walked grandly by him with a casual attitude. "You're a busy, busy boy. Who else are you fucking?"

"I'm not sleeping with her," Porter said.

"Then what is it?" she asked. "I need to know."

"I don't give a shit what you need to know," Porter said. "Do you know all the pleading and work I had to do to calm Claire down?"

Billie laughed. Even though she wasn't happy at how easily and quickly she lost control, it felt so good to know Claire was getting a taste of her own medicine and Porter was getting heartache. Why should she suffer through this alone?

"This is funny to you?" Porter asked. "We'll see how funny it is when you want to see Tara again."

"Using Tara again?" Billie made a smacking sound with her lips as she shook her head. "You're as bad a father as you were a husband."

"And you're a bitch!"

"It's about time you get that," Billie said. "I'm not going to be the better person this time. Not anymore. I'm not going to be the one who just takes it."

"I haven't bothered you since you threatened to tell her," Porter said. "Why did you do that? I thought we had an understanding."

"It wasn't on purpose," Billie said, "but I don't regret it. How can you marry her? We were just divorced."

"You idiot," Porter snapped. "I'm not marrying Claire. They were there for her friend, Dana. She's the one getting married."

Billie took a deep breath, at first relieved to find out he wasn't marrying Claire, but then feeling like an idiot for assuming he was.

"She was holding the dress to her body," she said. "It's an easy mistake to make and she made no effort to clear it up. She laughed at me."

"Is that all you have to say?"

Billie shrugged. "What else do you want me to say? I did it. I'm sorry. I can't take it back."

"Yes, you can, and you will."

Billie leaned against her desk, her arms crossed over her chest in a defensive gesture. "I'm not taking orders from you anymore, Porter. Just take this as a lesson. You stay away from me and we won't have any more problems."

"You tell Claire that you were lying about us and then we won't have any problems."

"You must be crazy," Billie said. "You think I'm going to try and help you out with your mistress?"

"She's not my mistress anymore, Billie. She's my girlfriend and she—"

"She will always be your mistress to me."

Porter paused for a second, seeming to realize he wasn't getting anywhere with a sympathy plea for his relationship with Claire. "We had a deal and you broke it. I stay away from you and you don't tell Claire anything. You fucking broke it."

"Like I said," she offered, "it wasn't on purpose."

"Time for a new deal," he demanded. "I keep letting you see Tara and I'll promise to stay away from you if you tell Claire you lied about our affair."

Billie couldn't even stomach the idea of doing that, but Porter's offer was more than tempting. Was it too big a price to pay? She could have Tara in her life and finally be free of Porter. And with Porter no longer trying to seduce her, what did she care about whether or not he and Claire worked it out? She would be free, finally free to move on with her life.

"She won't believe me," Billie said. "She's always suspected this and she knows you're a cheater."

"Dammit!" Porter grabbed a book, a legal dictionary, off Billie's desk and tossed it at the wall.

"People will hear you!" Billie rushed to retrieve the book and place it back on her desk. "Will you just leave?"

"Are you going to help me?"

"I'll think about it," she said. "If you leave now, I'll think about it."

"You won, okay?" Porter threw his arms up in defeat. "You can get everything you want if you do this last thing."

Richard didn't bother knocking on the door before returning to the office. He stood in the doorway with an impatient stance as he cleared his throat. Porter ignored him as he passed him on his way out.

Everything. That was what he said. She could get everything. What a joke, she thought. If she had everything she wanted, she would still have her marriage, the daughter she loved, the job she loved, and the future she'd once been promised. Now, it was about being left alone and seeing Tara once a month. How quickly things change.

Erica knocked for the second time, but didn't hear a response. She knew Jonah was in his office, and looking back to glance at Jenna's desk, she could see he wasn't on the phone. It was five minutes after her update meeting with him was supposed to begin, and Erica wasn't sure what to do. She decided to cross her fingers and just go in even though she imagined walking in on Jonah without permission was not the smartest of choices.

When she entered the office, what she found was curious. Jonah was at his desk, sitting in his chair with his back to the door. He was holding something in his hand. He didn't move until she cleared her throat, upon which he swung around in his chair and looked at her a little surprised.

"How long have you been there?"

Erica stuttered through her answer. "I knocked and . . . I'm sorry, I just . . . No one answered, so . . ."

"What do you want, Erica?" He placed the object on his desk.

Erica could see it was a picture of a woman, and as she approached his desk, she could tell it wasn't his wife. She looked like a woman in her thirties, with long blond hair and a very kind and soft face. It wasn't a new picture.

"It's time for my update," she answered, "unless you want to reschedule."

Jonah gestured for her to sit down. "Despite what Jenna told you, Erica, these update meetings are only really necessary if something has gone wrong with the schedule. If everything is on schedule, you don't have to bother."

"I'm sorry," Erica said, sensing that Jonah was not really present. "Everything is fine, so I'll just—"

"My mother would have been seventy years old today," Jonah said, not necessarily to Erica, but just at her.

Erica looked at the picture. "That's your mother?"

Jonah reached out and gently touched the picture. "She's pretty, isn't she?"

"She's beautiful." Erica couldn't help but be touched by seeing such a soft side to such a strong man.

Jonah nodded. "She meant the world to me. She wasn't just my mother. She was my friend and she grounded me. Her death just threw me for such a loop."

"I understand," Erica said. "It's like you just lose the foundation for everything that matters to you and you're like . . . what am I supposed to do now?"

Jonah smiled at her. "Are you like your mother?"

"I think so," she answered. "I feel like everything I am is from her and because of her. She was so strong and soft at the same time. She never felt sorry for herself even when she was the sickest. She just kept reminding me how blessed the years she had were and that she knew something even better was waiting for her." Erica could feel tears welling in her throat.

"It can't have been easy for her raising you and your brother alone, but she seems like a woman who takes those things in stride."

"Adversity creates strength, she always said."

Jonah laughed. "Wow, sounds just like my mother. I think I would have liked her."

"You would have," Erica said. "Everyone did."

"She never married after your father?"

"She never married anyone," Erica said. "My father and her broke up when he found out she was pregnant."

"Did you ever meet him?" Jonah asked curiously.

Erica nodded, uncertain as to how much she wanted to share. "A couple of times. He came back into her life when I was young. I saw her with him and . . . my mother was too forgiving."

"She took him back?"

"For a while," she said. "But when she found out she was pregnant with Nate, she said she knew he wasn't going to be a good father, so she ended it."

"And he never bothered to be a part of your lives?"

"I guess not."

"He has no idea what he's missed out on," Jonah said. "You'd make any father proud. You're a fighter, you're smart, and very beautiful."

Erica smiled with the beautiful candor that she always had when talking about her mother. "Thank you."

Jonah's tender smile turned a little cautious as he changed the subject. "Speaking of very beautiful, I hope you don't hate me for this, but I want to introduce you to someone."

"What do you mean?"

"He's a former navy sailor, a great kid. He's a military consultant now and he works at one of the big firms in Crystal City just a hop, skip and—"

"Wait a second," Erica said, not sure she was really hearing this. "Are you trying to set me up with someone?"

Jonah seemed to try hard to search for the words. "I just want you to meet him. I think you'd really like him. He's really going places and he's got a solid head on his shoulders."

"Jonah." Erica stood up. "You know I'm engaged to Terrell."

Jonah nodded as if he knew his actions were wrong, but he didn't stop. "A simple lunch or dinner can't possibly hurt anybody. I can give him your number if you—"

"I can't believe this," Erica said, completely disappointed. "Here I am thinking that we're getting to understand each other and then you come at me with this disrespect for my fiancé. I love Terrell and I'm marrying him. I don't want to meet this guy and I don't want you interfering in my personal life at all."

She stormed out of the office feeling as if she had just been played. All that soft talk about their mothers was just an attempt to gain her confidence so she would trust his suggestion about dating someone he found more suitable for her. Who was this man? Or better yet, who in the hell did he think he was?

Erica was in her seat all of one minute before Jonah came bursting out of his office yelling instructions for Jenna to reschedule his afternoon. She heard the name Elena, but didn't recognize much else. Jenna called after him, demanding he stick to his original schedule, but Jonah was already out of the office and on his way somewhere.

Jenna threw her hands in the air and said, "Men!" before returning to her desk.

"Men?" Erica asked, even though she probably should have just stayed out of it.

Jenna, as if not realizing that Erica had even heard her, looked agitated. "Oh, nothing. Just . . . just get the schedule up. We have some calls to make."

"Are you sure you don't want a glass of wine?" Elena asked Sherise, holding the bottle up.

Sherise shook her head. "Technically, this is a business meeting, so I don't think so."

Elena seemed unimpressed with Sherise's professionalism. "Who cares? You're taking a cab, but it's all the more for me."

Sherise watched as Elena walked over to the glass bar situated against the wall in her office, located on K Street. As she poured a second glass for herself, Sherise thought it must be nice to be a rich socialite who could down half a bottle of wine surrounded by luxury, while planning a party, and still call it work. She wasn't going to complain. When Elena called her and asked her to come over and help plan the project launch party, Sherise was salivating at the guest list at Elena's disposal. She had to work hard not to get excited at the sound of the names she knew or show her anticipation as Elena explained the names that she didn't recognize.

"I'm so glad you have the time to commit to this," Elena said. "Considering my client is the government this time around, it isn't like I'm getting a big enough paycheck to hire a lot of help. I sometimes hire professional party planners as consultants for my bigger events, but we're going to keep this small."

"Not too small, I hope."

Elena smiled mischievously. "I never go too small and you know any party that Jonah goes too is going to attract bigwigs. They fight so hard to get him to come to their events, but if he turns them down, then they stalk him at any other event they can find."

"He certainly is in demand."

Sherise hadn't been able to think of anything but that kiss. She wasn't sure at what point she decided that she was no longer going to pretend that Jonah had kissed her against her will. She knew that she had kissed him back after being caught up in the moment. She felt completely guilty and couldn't even look at Justin when she'd gotten home that night. He was too busy with work to notice anything and she made certain to bring Cady to their bed that night just in case he wanted something other than sleep.

Two days had gone by and Sherise found herself thinking about Jonah during the day and dreaming about him at night. Last night's dream had gotten particularly erotic, enough so it woke her up in the middle of the night. It wasn't enough to wake Justin, but she couldn't get back to sleep.

Sherise knew she just had to be patient. She would stay away from Jonah and just let the memory of the kiss subside. Jonah wasn't going to be a big part of the hard work of the project, so she only had to deal with Jenna and intended to keep any communications with Jonah as limited and public as possible. She had never in her life let a man get the best of her. Any mistakes she'd made were because she didn't get her shit under control. Everything she wanted was in her grasp, being handed to her. She wasn't about to let some stupid man put a wrench in her master plan.

"Sherise!"

Sherise broke from her trance, realizing that Elena had been calling her name.

"I'm sorry," she said quickly. "I was just thinking of . . . I'm sorry, what is it?"

"Jonah."

Sherise became instantly defensive. What had she given away? "What about him?"

Elena was laughing, but also looked a little concerned. "Did you completely miss my receptionist telling us that he was on his way here?"

"Here?" Sherise couldn't believe this! She didn't want to see him. "Great! But unfortunately, I have to get going so I'll probably miss him."

"He's not on his way over to the building." Elena stood up and rushed to the door. "He's on his way to the office. He's down the hall."

Shit!

Elena opened the door just as Jonah was about to knock and let out an exasperated yip as she opened her arms for a hug. Jonah leaned down and hugged her petite frame, but his eyes were staring at Sherise every second. She felt frozen in place as he looked at her and she couldn't look away. It was wrong and she got that this was the attraction, but she didn't get how it could be so obvious yet so compelling at the same time.

"Sit down anywhere," Elena ordered. "Sherise is just on her way out."

"That isn't what I wanted to hear," he said as he sat on the sofa just inches from Sherise.

Sherise felt cornered on the edge of the sofa, wishing she had gotten up before he came over, but she felt unable to move as his gaze bore down on her. She felt the power of his presence sitting next to her and tried to tell herself she was being a foolish girl for creating in him something more than just a man. It didn't matter. The second he sat next to her, she wanted to kiss him again.

"Can I get you something to drink?" Elena asked as she returned to her bar.

"Scotch," he answered, although he maintained his attention on Sherise. He quietly whispered, "How long do you think you can avoid me?"

Sherise looked nervously at Elena, who was too busy studying her bar to pay attention to either of them.

"Oh, damn," Elena said. "No Scotch. Let me go see if I have any in the meeting room."

"No!" Sherise called after her, but Elena was already gone.

Sherise started to get off the sofa, but Jonah grabbed her arm and pulled her back. She jerked away from him.

"Don't you start with me!" she warned. She had to be strong. Running away from this man only made him more interested. "You lay one hand on me and I'll—"

"What?" he asked, seeming amused. "Scream? Come on, Sherise. You and I both know you won't do that. You won't do it because you're as eager to kiss me again as I am to kiss you."

"Your arrogance is astounding."

"And your lips are enticing."

Sherise could only describe it as slow motion. He didn't grab her and pull her to him like the last time. This time, he was slow and deliberate as his hand gently reached behind her and guided her head toward him. His lips landed softly on hers in a romantic, tender kiss that had anything but a romantic effect on her. Its sweetness was more painful because she had every chance to resist and she didn't.

It was Jonah who pulled away this time and lowered his hand from her. He smiled at her with a sense of satisfaction mixed with desire.

"So I'm attracted to you," she said, noting how quickly her breathing had picked up pace.

"Finally, you admit it," he said.

"But attraction is natural," she countered. "It's chemical. It doesn't control me and you don't have to let it control you."

"Nothing controls me," he said. "Nothing and no one. But I want you, Sherise. I haven't wanted a woman like this in decades."

"Your wife I presume?" she asked, hoping to throw some cold water on the conversation.

Jonah shook his head. "No, this was before I met Juliette. I was very young and . . . I know you feel this. It's like a kinetic energy."

Of course she felt it, but she wasn't so stupid that she would fall for the I've-never-felt-this-way-before line. Or was she? "Why did you marry your wife if you didn't feel that way about her?"

"Why did you marry Justin?"

Sherise was caught off guard by the comparison. "I love my—"

"Stop it," he ordered. "You don't have to pretend with me. You married Justin for the same reason I married Juliette. He doesn't light your fire like other men have in the past, but you love him and he's safe. He's reliable and offers advantages other than passion. He's the type you marry."

"Don't presume to know anything about me and my husband," she said defiantly, even though inside she was trembling at his accuracy. "Regardless of why you marry someone, once you're married, you have to stick to your—"

Sherise's voice caught as she heard her own words, knowing how she hadn't lived up to them herself. She leaned away as Jonah's hand came to her shoulder, but didn't stop him from touching her. She liked his touch.

"It's hard," he said quietly. "We make decisions that effect the decisions available to us later. But you and I, Sherise, we're the kind of people who gravitate toward flames even when we say and truly believe we want to stay safely away from fire."

She looked into his eyes, hating and enjoying the feeling inside her at the same time. "You don't know who I am. You try to convince me that if you want something you can have it, but I'm not stupid. I've fought larger obstacles than you."

"I'm not an obstacle," he said. "I'm a reward. Just like you."

His arrogance gave her the strength to push his hand away from her shoulder. "My reward is my husband and our baby."

"And you won't lose that," he said. "I have a lot at stake too. Sherise, there is no reason for me to do this, but I can't stop it. I can only promise to be discreet so no one gets hurt."

"Someone always gets hurt."

"I can do so much for you, Sherise."

There was a hint of desperation in his voice and, coming from a man like Jonah, the effect was enormous on Sherise. She could see he was pleading and that made her feel powerful. She was bringing this incredible man to this point and it excited her. She was no different than him, she realized. She loved a conquest.

"I can't . . ."

"Here we go!" Elena returned triumphantly with a bottle of Scotch in her hand.

Sherise jumped up from her seat, feeling like a little kid who had gotten caught doing something wrong. She could see from the look on Elena's face that she sensed something had been going on and Sherise realized her sudden action probably made it worse. She didn't care. She just needed to get out of there.

She needed to get away and stay away from Jonah, but even as she established her resolve to do so, there was a voice inside her that told her she was going to end up in his bed.

When Erica returned to the office, she went immediately to Jenna's desk to turn in the documents she had been sent to retrieve.

"Sorry I'm late," she said, "but they weren't ready."

"Everyone is so damn slow around here." Jenna took the papers. "What did Jonah do to upset you?"

"What do you mean?"

Jenna nodded toward Erica's desk. "He must have done something. He came back with that."

Walking over to her desk, Erica saw the large bag that was sitting in her chair with a short note on top of it. She took the note and read the only word that was on it: *SORRY*.

"It wasn't that bad," she said to Jenna. "It was just . . ."

When Erica lifted the bag she realized what it was. It was a medium-sized camel brown leather briefcase with a laptop insert. She knew the brand and was sure this bag had to cost over five hundred dollars.

"Does he buy a gift every time he upsets you?" Erica asked, feeling the soft leather with her hand.

"No," Jenna said in her usual rushed tone. "But he seems to really want you to like him."

That was clear, Erica thought. But why?

"Is this good news?" Emma Bladen asked as she sat quietly in the wooden chair on the other side of the table from Billie.

"Mrs. Bladen, it's better than good news." Billie had found some time to do research for Richard on this pro bono case. She handed the paper in her hand to the elderly woman, who reminded her of the old ladies that used to live on her block, the women her mother trusted and admired because they had seen adversities that Billie would never have to deal with.

This was Billie's first time at the legal aid center and she was happy to finally meet her client, Emma Bladen, a seventy-one-year-old woman who was facing eviction by her landlord because of her grandson's arrest for marijuana possession during the three months he was staying with her.

"It's a letter from the district attorney's office," Billie continued. "They choose not to charge your grandson because the police had no probable cause to even search him that night. They were only aware of drug activity in the park, but there was no evidence that your grandson, who was talking on his cell phone while sitting on a bench, offered any probable cause for them to search him without his consent."

"But he was still in possession of it when they found him."

Billie nodded. "But this evidence shows that he shouldn't have even been searched. When you add that to evidence we have that he was only staying with you for three months, and your impeccable record and reputation during the nine years you've lived there, we have enough to put a scare in the management company."

"I certainly hope so." Emma's brow creased with worry. "He says I have to be out by the end of this month or he'll put my stuff on the street and change my locks."

Billie reached out and placed her hand on Emma's over the table. "He will not do that! Trust me. We have already gotten the judge to put a stay on the eviction. That is why he had to take that sign off your door."

Emma smiled hopefully and it touched Billie's heart. There were so many people like Emma up against odds that were more than they could handle. This is what she should be doing instead of helping major corporations with all the advantages in the world get away with murder.

"You're not going anywhere, Mrs. Bladen."

"Actually she is," Richard said as he approached, interrupting their conversation. "The aid center's last bus is about to leave, so if you're not on it, you'll have to take a city bus or a cab."

"Oh, I certainly don't want to do that." Emma allowed Richard to help her slowly get up. She reached out and placed a hand on Billie's shoulder. "It's so nice to meet you, young lady."

"Nice to finally meet you too," Billie said.

"You make sure she gets home safe tonight as well?" Emma asked Richard.

Richard laughed. "I certainly will. Right after I take care of you."

Billie just enjoyed the moment and felt certain another victory for the little guy was on its way. But it was late, so she began putting the file back together before heading home soon. That was until Porter made his way from the waiting room into the meeting area of the open center.

"What are you doing here?" Billie asked. "Are you stalking me?"

"Don't flatter yourself," he said.

"You followed me here?"

He nodded. "I wanted to know what you were so busy doing instead of what you told me you'd do."

"Then you are stalking me!" Billie noticed Porter was trying to see what her files were, so she quickly slipped them into her briefcase and closed it.

"Why haven't you called Claire yet?"

"I'm a little busy," she said. "Sorry if I don't have a lot of time to make sure your mistress isn't worried we're sleeping together. And by the way, I'm sure you stalking me is not helping ease her concerns."

"You're full of shit," Porter said. "You have no intention of calling her. Or at least you had none until now."

"What's changed now?" Billie asked. "If I don't tell her, you promise to stalk me everywhere I go? I'm sure that will make things much easier at home for you."

"This has changed," he said, looking around. "Your little pro bono stint."

"This is none of your business." Billie wasn't sure where he was going with this but she did her best impression of not giving a damn.

"I wasn't surprised to see you come here," he said. "You've always been a bleeding heart."

"You used to be one a long time ago as well."

"A long time ago being the key phrase there." He dropped into the seat that Emma had been occupying just minutes ago. "But then I saw Richard show up and thought . . . hmmm, what's going on?"

"Richard is a bleeding heart too," she said, nonplussed. "Stop the presses. Two people who care."

"Then it came to me," Porter said. "This isn't volunteering. This is pro bono. I see from the label on your folders, that's official law firm work you're doing there."

Billie suddenly realized what Porter was up to and she got angry. "Just mind your own business, Porter. Don't you have a girlfriend to go convince you're faithful to?"

"You haven't even been at that firm a month," he continued. "You're not allowed to work on the pro bono cases yet."

"I'm not officially working on it," she said. "I'm just helping. . . ."

"I saw you, Billie. I was standing near the window, watching you."

"That is what stalkers do, isn't it?" she asked sarcastically.

"You were advising that woman. You were counseling her and I have a feeling if I did a little investigating, I could prove

that you've been inquiring about her case and requesting discovery from official sources."

"You don't even know what her case is."

"I'll find out. But I already know as much as I need to."
Porter stood up, trying to loom over her. "I can cause a lot of
trouble for you and your boyfriend."

"Richard?" Billie knew he was trying to scare her, but
mentioning Richard did the trick. "He hasn't done anything
wrong."

"He's letting you work on this case," Porter said. "I'll bet
he's logging these hours as his own."

"Now look, Porter. You want to be an asshole to me, I can
handle you, but Richard has nothing to do with what is going
on between us."

Porter leaned in with a heartless smile. "He does now."

Billie mumbled what she wished she could do to Porter
right now as she clenched her small hands into fists, but she
knew she couldn't do anything here. She didn't think she
could do anything at all. Porter could really hurt her and
Richard's position at the firm, and if that happened, what
would happen to Emma's case?

"Whatever you tell Claire," Porter said, "it better be convincing."

After Porter walked away, Billie fell back into the chair.

"What a fool," she said to herself.

She had it. Freedom, it was in her grasp. All she had to do
was suck it up and tell Claire a lie that she knew Claire wouldn't
even believe anyway. She would be free of Porter and beginning once and for all to get on with her life. But no, she didn't
want to face that bitch and now this was the result. Two steps
forward, three steps back. She wanted to smack herself in the
face for being so stupid.

Porter was holding all the cards again and this time he
could hurt more than just Billie.

9

When Erica came out of the bathroom, she hadn't expected to see Terrell on the bed and she especially didn't expect to see him doing what he was doing.

When he turned to look at her, he didn't have time to recover, so thought it best not to try. He'd expected her to be in there a lot longer.

"What are you doing?" she asked, approaching the bed.

"That was a quick shower," he answered, his voice sounding guilty.

"What are you doing with my phone?" She held her hand out and he handed it to her.

"I was just trying to remember the number for that place that books wedding bands because I was thinking maybe I could take some of this wedding planning off your hands."

"Who are you talking to?" Erica asked angrily. "You think I don't know when you're lying?"

Erica looked at her phone and saw that Terrell hadn't been going through her calls. "Why are you looking at my schedule?"

"Erica, why do you have to be so suspicious?" Terrell slid to the end of the bed. "We're getting married, for Christ's sake. I mean damn."

"I need an answer, Terrell, because you know if you needed to know anything about me you could just ask."

"I would," he said, "but you were in the bathroom."

"What couldn't wait until I'm done taking a shower?"

"I didn't want to wait because . . ." Terrell had to think fast to come up with an answer and do it convincingly. It was damn near impossible to lie to this woman now.

"Why do you need to know my schedule?"

Terrell sighed, thinking that maybe telling as much of the truth as possible was the best strategy. He loved Erica and didn't want to lie to her, but knew she wouldn't understand or agree with his plans.

"I wasn't trying to get your schedule," he said. "If you look a little closer, you can see. . . ."

"This is Jonah's schedule," she said, looking at her phone again.

"I don't drive him around, so I needed a way to get some face time with him. I thought if I knew his schedule, I could run into him. You know, accidentally."

"Why?"

"The work I get from him pays me only twenty-five percent more than Destin work, but the tips are fifty percent more. I don't want it to be a side gig anymore. I can really make some money."

Terrell was telling the truth, mostly. He wanted to get Jonah's schedule to make more money, but he wasn't going to make that money by getting more driving gigs. He was going to make himself a big payday from that elitist snob Jonah Dolan.

"Why didn't you just tell me?" Erica asked, glad to know that more money was coming in on both their ends. This was all good news for the wedding. "I can ask him for you."

Terrell rolled his eyes. "How would that look, Erica? You're already the reason I got the job. I gotta look like the man here some way."

"What in the hell does that mean?"

"I think it's obvious your boss doesn't think a lot of me."

"He recommended you in the first place."

"For you," Terrell said. "But not for me. He's a man and I know how a man thinks. If I keep coming to him through you, he won't ever respect me."

Even though she didn't see how her helping him was associated with his manhood, Erica knew not to interfere with Terrell when it came to things like this. Besides, after her last argument with Jonah over him trying to set her up with someone, she wasn't sure how eager he would be to do her a favor. She only hoped that if Terrell asked for more work, Jonah wouldn't hold it against him that he didn't think Terrell was a good choice for her. Or maybe, she thought for a second, Terrell's assertiveness would impress Jonah and he would begin to change his mind about her fiancé.

"I don't want you sneaking on my phone." Erica dropped the phone back on the bed. "It's an invasion of my privacy."

Terrell held his arms out to her and she fell into them. "I know, baby. I'm sorry, but I just wanted you to think I did it all on my own."

Erica had to laugh at herself. Why did she even care whether or not Jonah approved of Terrell? No matter how much she didn't like it, Jonah's approval mattered to her and not just for professional reasons. Having the respect of a man like Jonah meant something to her. Besides, she loved Terrell and was going to marry him whether Jonah liked it or not. While she didn't need her professional and personal lives to mold well together, it would only be a plus if they did.

"Stop it." Erica tried to slap his hands away as he tugged at the towel covering her wet body. She didn't put too much effort into it. "I'm mad at you. Seriously, I feel violated."

"I've been a bad boy." Terrell kissed her chest above the rim of the towel as he pulled it off. He grabbed her at the waist, lifting her up and tossing her onto the bed. "You're going to have to punish me."

Finally having put Cady to bed, Sherise entered her own bedroom, closing the door behind her. Justin didn't look up from the book he was reading as he sat on his side of the bed. When she slid in next to him, he barely acknowledged her. This was unusual, but he'd been cold to her lately and Sherise understood that it was just a vibe she had been giving.

But she needed to be close to him, to remind her heart where it belonged and her body what it really needed. She needed her husband's arms around her and to feel him inside her. She needed to forget about how much she wanted Jonah and get her mind and body back on the right track.

Justin finally looked at her when she took the book he was reading out of his hand and tossed it on the bed. She snuggled up close to him with that teasing, tempting smile that he loved so much.

"Can I do something for you?" he asked.

She leaned into him and kissed him seductively on his lips.

"What do you think? I usually don't have to give hints."

"Well, lately I've been getting a stay away vibe."

Sherise slid her fingers underneath his pajama top and rubbed his chest. "I know I've been stressed out a lot lately and I'm sorry. You're always so patient with me. You know I love you more than anything, right?"

"Yes, but it is still nice to hear."

"Nice to hear and fun to show."

She brought her mouth to his neck and he tilted his head to the side to accommodate her as she kissed him tenderly. After a moment, he turned back to her and kissed her passionately on the lips.

The sound of her phone ringing seemed unusually loud and alarmed Sherise. Something told her instantly it was Jonah. It was as if he had a pair of eyes on her at all times. Ignoring the sound, she reached up and gently took hold of Justin's ears as she returned his face to hers, but when she kissed him, she could tell that nothing was going to overcome the distraction.

"Go ahead," Justin said, leaning away. "Answer it."

"It'll go to voice mail in just—"

"Answer it," Justin said. "It'll be in this bed with us the whole time if you don't."

Sherise wasn't going to argue that point. Rarely had she been caught up enough with Justin not to answer her phone. For her to try to ignore it now would only lead to suspicion. She slid over on the bed and grabbed the phone off the nightstand. As she feared, it was Jonah.

"Hello?" She felt guilty just talking to him, afraid something would be revealed in the tone of her voice.

"I was beginning to think you weren't going to pick up."

"It's late. What can I do for you?" She hoped that sounded cold and unfeeling enough.

"I guess Justin is around," he said. "I understand."

"I'm not sure you do."

"I wanted to invite you to a party this weekend." After she failed to respond, he continued. "I thought of inviting Walter, but since you're going to replace him, I think you might be the best person to meet the power brokers."

"I haven't replaced Walter yet," she answered. "So maybe he is the best person to invite."

"Walter already told me he hates fund-raisers."

"It's a fund-raiser?"

"Didn't I say that?" he asked, laughing. "I've already purchased a full table and there are a few seats left, so I thought I would invite the two of you."

"I don't think so," Sherise said. She wasn't going to spend one more second with Jonah than was completely necessary. "The weekend is family time and . . ."

"The First Lady will be there," Jonah added. "I look forward to the chance to introduce you. That is if you intend to come."

Sherise took a moment even though she knew the second he mentioned the First Lady, she had made her decision. How could she refuse? Yes, Jonah was a problem for her, but she wasn't going to let him keep her from the First Lady. She had to find a way to take advantage of his connections while resisting his advances.

"I look forward to it," she said, pausing only one second before adding, "My husband and I are both looking forward to it."

"Well, I . . ."

"Good-bye, and please tell your wife I said hello and I look forward to seeing her there too."

She hung up before Jonah could respond and was feeling a certain sense of accomplishment until she turned back to Justin, who had a confused, and somewhat angry, look on his face.

"Is there something you want to tell me?"

Sherise took a second. What had she given away? "It was just business. You and I are going to a fund-raiser this weekend, so keep your schedule open."

"That was Jonah, right?"

She nodded. "He and his wife have asked us—"

"What did you mean about Walter's job?" he asked.

"Honey, you know I'm interested in Walter's job."

"I know you, Sherise. You wouldn't say something like that to a man like Jonah unless there was more to it than you just wanting the job. What's going on?"

"Fine." Sherise sighed, sitting up on the bed. "I was going to save this for a better time, but after the whole Toni fiasco . . ."

"Which you orchestrated."

"With your help." She poked him. "Anyway, Walter said he's going to recommend me for his job."

"Officially?"

"Yes."

"When was that better time you were planning to tell me?" Justin asked. "When your promotion was approved?"

"I've had a lot on my mind," Sherise said. "Things are crazy with this new project. I was getting around to it."

"You were going to wait until it was too late for me to say anything about it."

"What would you have said about it?" she asked. "You know this is what I've wanted. There is no news here."

"Maybe I wouldn't want you to take it."

"What do you mean?" she asked, practically in shock. "Why wouldn't I take it?"

"To save our marriage," he answered.

Sherise was completely blown away. Where was this coming from? What did he know? "Justin, you're starting to scare me."

"You've been back to work for a month now and it's just not working."

"It's working perfectly," she said. "I'm heading a huge project that's opening an endless amount of doors for me. I'm on my way to a big position that will add a big lump to my salary and give me more power. I'll be head of communications for the White House Domestic Policy Council!"

"What about Cady?" he asked. "What about me and what about our next baby?"

"I just had a baby seven months ago, Justin. Can we slow down on the family planning a bit?"

"I agreed to let you go back to work because I knew how much you wanted it, but I don't like the way—"

"You *let* me?" Sherise asked, angrily. "You wanna rephrase that, please?"

"Something is wrong," he said. "I can feel it. Ever since you went back, something is wrong and it's hurting our family."

"I've only been back a month," she insisted. "And maybe what's wrong is your inability to accept that I want to be more than just a wife and mother despite the fact that you've known that since we met."

"Then maybe it's Jonah."

She paused, nervously trying to read his face for what he meant. "Is this about your jealousy again? I'm not in the mood for it."

"Are you in the mood to tell me what role Jonah played in you securing Walter's job?"

"That's it!" Sherise mustered all the righteous indignation she could as she jumped off the bed and stormed out of the room. "I'm sleeping in Cady's room."

Despite her own guilt making her angrier, Sherise was resolute; she knew what she wanted and intended to take it. Justin was in for a world of disappointment if he thought for one second she was going to hang it all up to stay at home and wait for him to show up every night so she could live vicariously through stories of his career.

Billie knew she was being childish, but she didn't want to come face to face with Callie, which was why she hung around in the kitchen nook until she saw Callie leave her desk and head toward the bathroom. All she needed to do was sign out a completed document review project, but she was very behind on her work and completely stressed out. She knew that Callie was behind Porter's access to what she was doing and didn't want to get into it.

Once she was confident Callie was off to the bathroom, she went over to her desk. Reaching for the form she needed to complete, Billie got a glimpse of the receipt report on the wall directly behind Callie's desk. Billie started to freak out. Stepping closer, she realized that her list of deliverables was incomplete. She had forgotten to turn in her billing report for the new case she was on, defending a large retailer from insider trading charges.

But she couldn't have. Billie was swamped and falling behind, but she knew she would never forget to do that. Could she have? Knowing now everything she knew about Callie, she just didn't trust the woman anymore. She had to find out. She looked around to make sure no one was around. The other paralegal desks were empty and no one was nearby.

Taking a seat at Callie's desk, she opened up her e-mail and quickly went for her Received folder. She found her name and opened the folder. Just as she thought, the e-mail was sitting right there, but nothing had been done to it. She knew that Callie was supposed to send it to the partner after checking it off as received. She wondered what the wait was? Was she being paranoid or had Porter instructed Callie to delay her work so Billie would look bad?

Billie forwarded the e-mail herself to the partner. What was Callie going to say or do? She reached into the pen cup on Callie's desk for the red pen that she used for the deliverables list, and just as she checked off the memo as received, an idea came to her.

She turned back to the computer and Callie's carefully categorized e-mails. All of that confidential information in Callie's possession. She was, after all, the head paralegal for the department. Billie had to be insane to think what she was thinking, but she was and she blamed Porter for all of it. He was turning her into Sherise.

"Right on time," Terrell said as he drove up to the limo curve at the Pentagon.

He waved to Jonah's driver, Christopher Lindy, and the man waved back. Christopher Lindy was in his early fifties, in good shape for someone who sat behind the wheel all day and night. He had raisin brown skin and a friendly face. He was a former marine. Terrell had done his research on Christopher because he knew from the first time he met him that Christopher was not a man to be fooled. This is why it had taken him this long to come up with a plan that would allow him to get access to Jonah.

Christopher was a proud father of twin boys. Although he was in his fifties, the boys were only thirteen. Asking around the limo company, everyone mentioned how much Christopher loved his boys and wanted to make them happy. Terrell knew enough about teenaged boys to know how to impress Christopher. At least impress him enough to distract him for the five seconds he needed to get access to Christopher's Town Car, which he had already confirmed was the same one that Christopher used to drive Jonah everywhere.

The last two times he'd run into Christopher outside the Pentagon, Terrell made sure to make small talk, creating a thirteen-year-old nephew who he gave the impression to Christopher was very close to him. A couple of questions about what he should get his nephew for his upcoming birthday and Terrell had his hook.

"Can you believe we're working on a Sunday?" Terrell asked as he approached Christopher, who was leaning against the passenger side of his car reading a newspaper.

Christopher shrugged. "I'm used to it. Mr. Dolan works every day. What are you doing here?"

"Oh, I'm picking up Ricky's slack."

Terrell had to beg and plead with another driver to take his assignment. He may have included a little bit of a bribe too. It was worth it. There was no way to get into the Pentagon without an already approved assignment.

"I need the time and a half," Terrell said.

"Who you telling?" Christopher asked. "Time and half pays for my vacation every year."

"Where do you go?"

"This year, we're going to San Diego," he said. "The boys want to hang out at Universal Studios."

"I wanted to thank you," Terrell said. "I got that game Mission Death for my nephew for his—"

"You got Mission Death?" Christopher put the paper down and turned to Terrell with a look of amazement on his face. "How did you get that? It's not even available to order online until next month."

"I know a brother that works at Best Buy. They got a pre-order stock to review the games and stuff. He gave me one."

"How much?" Christopher asked. "Do you think he'd have another? My sons would die for that game."

"Really?"

Christopher let out an excited laugh. "You don't know, man. They talk about Mission Death all the time."

"You get that game for them before all their friends have it," Terrell said. "Man, that would be . . ."

"I'll pay anything."

"Hold on a second." Terrell rushed to his car and grabbed the game out of a bag in the front seat. When he returned, he could see from the look on Christopher's face that he had him.

"Is this the right one?" he asked, handing Christopher the game. " 'Cause I know they have levels and all that. If it's the right one, I can get you one."

"Are you kidding me?" Christopher asked, looking over the box.

"Yeah, I can get another from my buddy. My nephew's birthday is tomorrow, so I can't give you this one, but I can get another one in a couple of days."

"I'm sure this is the right one," Christopher said.

"Maybe you want to check and see." Terrell gestured a phone call with his hand to his ear. "Nothing worse than disappointed teenagers."

"This says level two, so . . ." Christopher looked uncertain. "You know what? I'm gonna call my wife. The kids have a big poster of the game in their room. She can confirm for me without letting them know."

"Good idea." Behind his back, Terrell turned on the device he'd been concealing.

"I'll be back in a second."

Terrell knew that Christopher would have to walk away from the car to make a call on his cell phone. The waiting area for the limousines and driven cars had bad reception. Anything this close to the pickup area of the Pentagon had serious interference. But fifty yards away it was fine.

As soon as Christopher headed out, dialing his phone, Terrell jumped into action. Thankfully, the window to the backseat was rolled down to keep the car aired out in the warm sun. It was all Terrell needed. He quickly placed the miniature voice-activated tape recorder behind the pillowed head cushion of the seat closest to the window. The device was already turned on, so all he had to do was stick it.

It only took a second and Terrell was set. By the time Christopher turned back toward the car, Terrell was looking at the newspaper he had set down earlier.

"This is it!" Christopher said, holding the game's box up. "My wife almost screamed. This is the one."

"Cool, dude." Terrell took the game back. "You gonna be here Tuesday morning?"

"Hell yeah!"

"Good. I'll have it for you by then."

That would be just enough time to retrieve the tape before it filled up and started recording over from the beginning.

Billie watched as her friends reacted to her telling them about her latest drama with Porter while they sat outside a café in Dupont Circle on a warm Saturday afternoon. Their expressions reflected her own feelings.

"Look on the bright side," Erica said. "At least you didn't sleep with him again."

Billie wasn't sure if she was joking or not, but she didn't

laugh. "Did you hear anything I said? He's ruining my life worse now than he ever has."

Sherise was enraged. "That is it, Billie. I've had it with you."

"How is this my fault?" Billie asked.

"You let that boy get away with murder."

"I'm in this position because of you," Billie said. "You're the one who encouraged me to tell Claire about us."

"I said to threaten to tell," Sherise said. "The subject here was Porter, not that ho."

"Can we fast forward through the criticism please?" Billie drank the last of her frappuccino. "I come to my girls for help."

"I'm taking over," Sherise said. "You can't handle this boy. I'm going to do it for you."

"Sherise!" Erica warned.

"You come to us for help," Sherise said. "I'm offering help."

"What are you going to do?" Billie asked, not believing she was actually asking this. She was desperate though.

"I'm going to pull out the big guns," Sherise said, not yet certain what she was going to do, but finding a distracting challenge in it all.

"Oh no," Erica said. "You're gonna make it worse."

"I'm gonna fix it," Sherise said. "Besides, you're not offering her any advice."

"I could use something from you," Billie said.

"All I know," Erica said, "is I'll never talk to you again if you apologize to Claire."

"I'm not going to apologize," Billie said. "I'm gonna tell her Porter and I weren't sleeping together."

"It's the same thing," Erica said. "And I'll never forgive you for it."

"Well, I have to do something," she said, frustrated. "Richard could get in trouble for letting me help on that pro bono case."

"Is this a firing offense?" Erica asked.

"I don't think so." But Billie wasn't willing to risk it. She was too new.

"Don't even worry about it anymore," Sherise said. "You won't say anything to Claire and you and Richard will be fine. I'll take care of it."

From the tone of her voice, Erica feared Porter might go missing any day now. "Billie is a lawyer, remember. You can't get her involved in anything illegal."

"I'm not going to do anything illegal," Sherise said. "But I am going to do something final. This bitch is blackmailing her. He's asking for it."

Erica looked at Billie. "Aren't you going to stop her?"

"Like she could," Sherise said.

"I'm desperate," Billie said. "Honestly, I'm about to pull a little Sherise myself."

Erica laughed. "What is a Sherise?"

"It better be fabulous, whatever it is," Sherise said. "And it better work or you can't name it after me."

"Callie has been Porter's source for my comings and goings since I started there," Billie said. "I think I've figured out a way to get her out of my hair and make her useless to Porter."

"Sounds promising," Sherise said. "Wanna share?"

Billie shook her head. "I've shared enough."

"Are we forgetting someone?" Erica asked. "Whatever it is you do, it could cost you Tara."

Billie didn't want to think of that. "I have to make sure Porter doesn't do any more damage to me or Richard at work first. I'll figure out how to keep Tara in my life after I get Porter under control."

"Give me a week," Sherise said.

"I can't believe this is my life." Billie leaned forward and lowered her head in an exaggerated manner. "A little over a year ago, I was married and thinking about a baby. I had a career I loved. Sherise, never take what you have for granted. A family, a sense of belonging means everything."

"Why would I?" Sherise asked, getting defensive. Both women looked at her, confused by her reaction, and she tried to adjust quickly. "I mean, yeah. I know, but . . ."

"What is it?" Erica asked. "You causing problems for Justin again?"

"Why is it always me?" Sherise asked.

" 'Cause it usually is," Billie said. "Justin is about as perfect a husband as one can get."

"Maybe he used to be," Sherise said. "But he's on some power kick now. Acting like he wants me to be a stay-at-home mom."

"Some women would kill for that life," Billie said. "Staying at home, raising the munchkins while a good husband who makes six figures takes care of things."

Erica raised her hand as she took a bite of her muffin.

"Well, I'm not one of them," Sherise said. "He said he's not talking to me, but he knows which one of us can hold out the longest."

"Is that how you plan to control your marriage?" Erica asked. "Just withhold sex until your husband gives in to your every whim?"

"You'll learn," Sherise said, "soon enough."

"I'm never going to do that to Terrell," Erica protested. "And maybe Justin's mad at you because he has a reason to think your career is taking you away from him."

"What the fuck does that mean?"

"You know what it means," Erica said. "Jonah?"

"You don't know what you're talking about, little girl," Sherise said. "I have no use for Jonah anymore. I've gotten all I want from him."

"And you gave nothing in return?" Erica asked.

"You sound like Justin." Sherise rolled her eyes. "I don't care if I never hear or see Jonah again."

"He's starting to get to you?" Billie asked. This was familiar and dangerous territory for Sherise.

"He's just a relentless flirt." Sherise turned to Erica. "You might want to remind him I'm a married woman and he's a married man. He doesn't seem to care when I say it."

"I'm not talking to Jonah about anything personal anymore," Erica said. "He tried to set me up with someone last week."

"You can't be serious," Billie said, laughing.

"It's not funny," Erica said. "It's disrespectful."

"You might want to take him up on it," Sherise said. "Everyone Jonah knows is connected. You can get that life you just raised your hand to say you wanted. You sure as hell won't get it with Terrell."

"Maybe I will if I withhold sex from him long enough like you do," Erica said sarcastically.

"Fuck you," Sherise spat out.

"Just stop worrying about who I choose to marry," Erica said, "and take care of your own marriage."

"Okay." Billie held her hand up just as Sherise was about to start yelling. "We're all going through some shit right now. We need to rely on each other, not turn on each other. Just remember, no matter what the men in our lives throw at us, we have gotten each other through it all. If we start working against each other, it messes up everything."

"What are you talking about you're not coming?" Sherise snapped into her phone in the lobby of the Mayflower Hotel. "You were supposed to be here ten minutes ago."

"I've changed my mind," Justin said.

"Justin, I need you here," Sherise said.

"You haven't needed me for much recently," Justin said. "So I'm sure you can manage for tonight."

His cold tone was hurtful to her, but she was too angry to acknowledge it. "Don't do this to me tonight. You're a professional and you know how good an opportunity tonight would be for your career as well as mine."

"It doesn't matter because I already sent the babysitter away. No one is here to watch Cady."

"Call her back!" Sherise found a secluded corner in the lobby where no one could see her arguing with her husband over the phone. "I don't want to do this alone."

"You'll have Jonah," he said flatly.

"I want you," she answered. Jonah was the problem. Justin was going to be her shield; his presence was going to keep her mind focused on making an impression on the room, not giving in to her attraction to Jonah.

"I'm not interested in putting on the Washington face tonight," he said flatly. "When you're ready to talk about our family and our future maybe things will change."

Sherise was fuming. "So this is punishment? I don't want to be a Stepford wife and mom, so you pull all your support for my career."

"I'm not doing this with you over the phone, Sherise."

"Fine." She sighed, trying to calm down. "I'll come home. Thanks to you I'll miss meeting the First Lady, but if you're going to be this way, then—"

"Don't."

"Don't what?" she asked.

"Don't come home," he answered. "The party is where you want to be and I think we could use a break for one night. I've got Cady and I'm fine. Why don't you just stay at the party? I'd rather you not come home and huff and puff, blaming me for missing another opportunity."

She cleared her throat, asking quietly, "You don't want me to come home?"

She was completely unprepared to deal with Justin's rejection. Even when he was angriest with her, he didn't want to be away from her. She was the one who always pulled away. What was happening?

"I just . . . I just want a break for a few hours," Justin said. "Things are so tense around here right now I think we could both use a night off from each other."

After he hung up, Sherise kept the phone to her ear for a few seconds more. She wasn't sure what just happened and she was both too angry and too hurt to really figure it out. Did he even want her coming home at all tonight?

"There you are."

Despite how good he looked in the uniquely tailored tuxedo, the expression on Sherise's face as soon as she saw Jonah must have been a dead giveaway because he looked offended. This was not the time.

"What have I done now?" he asked.

"What do you want, Jonah?" Sherise finally put the phone in her purse.

"I got concerned. I was told you were here about fifteen minutes ago."

"You have someone watching out for me?" she asked. "Your wife, maybe?"

He looked her over, observing her fire-truck red Suzi Chin silk chiffon dress with an empire waist cinch. "You look incredible."

"Avoiding my question?" she asked, ignoring how pleased she was at his visual approval.

"My wife couldn't make it tonight," he said. "So I brought along one of my staff members and his girlfriend. He's eager to meet the powerful just like you."

"I'm not as eager as you think." Sherise offered him a bleak, tight-lipped smile.

"What's wrong?" he asked. "Why haven't you come inside?"

Sherise removed his hand the second he placed it on her shoulder. "Don't start with me."

"I was just trying to comfort you, Sherise. You're obviously upset."

"What do you care?" she asked. "I'm not going to sleep with you."

Jonah laughed. "I wasn't asking you to. At least not tonight. Where is your husband and why are you in the lobby?"

"I'm not going in," she said. "Justin isn't coming."

"Is something wrong with Cady?"

"No," she answered flatly. She didn't appreciate him pretending to care about her baby.

"So," he said, "then why are you letting Justin's disinterest stop you? You need your husband to meet the rich and powerful in DC? Maybe in the beginning you did, but if you haven't noticed, Sherise, you're doing fine on your own."

"I don't need him here," she said. "I want him here."

"I'm here," he said definitively.

She couldn't tear her eyes away from his gaze and this time, when he placed his hand on her arm, she didn't move away.

"Tonight could be a life-changing moment for you," he continued. "Are you going to let him hold you back? Are you going to let him prevent you from putting your unforgettable mark on that crowd?"

Sherise was trying to breathe slowly to avoid hyperventilating. This was all too much. Had she just spent the last five minutes, five entire minutes, talking to the First Lady of the United States?

"Are you okay?" Jonah asked.

Sherise looked at him with a gleam in her eyes. "I'm trying to breathe. Did I give it away?"

"Give what away?"

"How incredibly awestruck I was."

"Not really." He laughed. "You seemed happy, but she's used to that. You got five minutes of her time, Sherise. That is saying something."

"I remembered to say good-bye, didn't I?" Sherise wasn't sure. It was all a blur.

He nodded. "Your etiquette was perfect."

"She won't even remember me," Sherise said.

"Oh, she'll remember you," Jonah said. "You're ridiculously unforgettable."

She looked at him, still feeling her heart jumping in her chest. She could see he was excited by her excitement and it turned her on more than she expected. Jonah had kept a reasonable distance all night long with the exception of a few inappropriate glances and stares. At first, Sherise was uncomfortable, but three senators, a couple of House members, and the deputy director of communications for the White House later, she was in euphoria. Many of them had already heard about the party Elena was planning and said they would consider attending.

Sherise impressed them all as she usually did, always getting compliments for being so composed and mature for someone her age. Jonah was by her side off and on, introducing her to the biggest names and sometimes attracting them to her by just being near her. It was incredible and Sherise had to admit, watching the way powerful people gravitated toward Jonah made him intensely attractive.

"You're always beautiful," he said, "but when you're on fire, you're like . . . you're just amazing. You're shining. It's like I could see you right now even if I was a mile away."

She felt on fire and full of adrenaline. She wasn't sure how long they were staring at each other, but she didn't need any words spoken to know to follow him when he started walking away. She was being reckless, she knew. People could be looking at them now. She knew she was catching eyes and, of course, Jonah always had eyes on him. But she didn't care, and the second they left the main ballroom, Jonah found a corner behind a line of telephone and laptop centers.

When she joined him, there was no hesitation, no words as he grabbed her at her waist and pulled her body to his. She reached up and pulled his face down to hers and their lips met in a mad frenzy. His lips were warm and moist and tasted like the strawberries they'd had for dessert. The taste of them sent spirals of desire through every inch of her body. As she opened her mouth, the kiss deepened and Sherise felt a heightened sense of desire. Her body was moving against his as her fingers played with his hair.

She felt his hands grip her butt hard, pulling her pelvis to his and gently stroking her cheeks. She wanted him so bad right now she could already taste him. His mouth was hot and sweet against her neck as he left searing kisses everywhere.

"I want you," he whispered into her ear. "I have to have you, Sherise."

"Just kiss me," she ordered breathlessly, and her mouth sought his again.

"Tonight," he ordered, leaning away. "Let's go upstairs."

The realization of his words scared Sherise to death and gave her the strength to push away. "No. No, I can't. We can't."

"How can you deny this?" he asked. "You know how much I want you and you—"

"Jonah." She was almost pleading with him. "We wouldn't be able to turn back from this. The consequences are too grave."

"Damn the consequences!"

"You're a man," she said. "Your consequences aren't the same as mine. I have to go."

She pushed away from him and turned to leave, but he grabbed her by the arm. Pulling her back to him, he placed his hand over hers.

"Take this," he said.

She looked down and saw the key card. "Jonah, I'm not . . ."

"I know." He closed her hand over the card. "You aren't ready. You're scared. But I have the luxury suite here."

"Did you anticipate this?" she asked, not sure why she wasn't offended. Shouldn't she be?

"My wife and I weren't intending on driving all the way back to Leesburg tonight, so we got the room." He let her hand go. "I have it until Sunday night. I'll call you tomorrow when I'm free. If you're ready, you'll come. If you're not, you won't."

"I won't," she said, offering him the key back.

Jonah ignored the gesture, refusing to take the key. "I think you will."

He left her there, holding that key, and it felt as if it weighed ten pounds in Sherise's hands. Looking to her left, she saw a garbage can, and her first thought was to throw it in there now. Do it now so even if she changed her mind later, she wouldn't have it.

She couldn't. She just couldn't. She felt the current of excitement rushing through her, a current that she hadn't felt in a long time. It wasn't just about meeting the First Lady and all these important people. Her career ambitions were one thing, but what she was feeling tonight was another. It was Jonah. It was his energy, his power. He was like a magnet and despite the danger and risks involved, Sherise wasn't willing to walk away from it yet. Not just yet.

10

"Where in the hell have you been?" Richard asked the second Billie approached him at the desk.

"I don't want to get into it," she answered. Billie placed her briefcase down on the desk. She wasn't sure she could even begin to explain all the conversations that had been going on in her head on her way to the legal aid center tonight. First and foremost, she wasn't planning to come and she had rehearsed all the excuses she would give Richard over the phone, but none of them was convincing.

Porter scared her. He was an expert at empty threats, but Billie sensed that he wasn't kidding this time. And considering Richard's career could be in jeopardy this time, not just hers, she didn't want to take a chance.

But she was taking a chance. A big chance, and it was all based on Sherise's promise that she would take care of it all. Sherise had her faults, but Billie knew that when Sherise wanted a problem solved, she got it solved. Billie sometimes questioned her tactics, but based on her own plan to deal with Callie, she wasn't in a position to judge.

When all was said and done, this work was the one thing that kept her sane. It meant something and it reminded her of who she was. She didn't want to give it up and even after this case was over, until she was cleared to do pro bono work through her firm, Billie was going to find a way to keep doing this on her own.

"I wasn't going to come," Billie said.

"Why not?"

"I'm not supposed to be doing this," she reminded him. "Isn't it kind of playing with fire?"

"Officially you aren't supposed to be here, but don't worry. No one will find out."

Billie rolled her eyes. "Where is Mrs. Bladen?"

"She's gone," Richard said. "You missed the celebration."

"What celebration?"

Richard handed her a piece of paper as he closed up his briefcase.

Billie read the first few lines and started jumping in joy. "Oh my God! They caved."

"Any attempt at eviction has been terminated," Richard said. "Your suggestion scared them a bit—that we countersue and threaten to expose their continued threats to Emma despite the fact that the court said there will be no eviction during the proceedings to the court."

"She must have been so happy to get this news!" Just then, Richard stood up and Billie wrapped her arms around him.

He hugged her back as he laughed. "You have a strong hug for such a tiny woman," he said.

"It feels great, doesn't it?" she asked, leaning away.

In that moment, Billie and Richard locked eyes and something told her that he was going to kiss her. Scared, she pushed away instantly and could tell from the surprised look on his face she might have thought wrong.

"What?" he asked.

"I'm sorry . . . I . . ." Billie just waved her hand dismissively.

He offered a friendly smile. "I'm not stupid, Billie."

"I'm sorry, Richard. I'm just really off on a lot of things right now and I thought you were . . ."

"I thought I was too."

They shared an awkward glance.

"Look, it's okay," he said. "You're not ready for a relationship. I can tell. You don't have to say it."

What Billie couldn't tell Richard was that it wasn't so much that she didn't want to kiss him. She was more afraid that someone would see and then tell Porter. Porter was always on her mind and she needed it to stop. She only hoped that Sherise would come through.

"You're insane," Sherise whispered to herself.

The key card was just an inch from the slot to the luxury suite at the Mayflower Hotel but she couldn't insert it.

After leaving the party last night, Sherise tried twice to throw away the key, but couldn't bring herself to do it. She was still high from the excitement of the night when she got home, but Justin wasn't interested in hearing anything about it. Sherise hadn't intended to argue with him, but they ended up arguing anyway. She tried to explain to him how for once, she could possibly provide him with some contacts instead of the other way around, as it had been for most of their life together. Nothing mattered to him.

She brought Cady to the bedroom to sleep with her that night with Justin sleeping on the sofa in the living room. She didn't want to be alone because the second she gave in to her thoughts, she was thinking of Jonah and his proposition. She'd woken in the middle of the night after a dream that began as an erotic lovemaking encounter between her and Jonah and ended with heartbreaking abandonment of Justin. Billie hated her and Erica refused to talk to her.

Sunday morning came and after a silent breakfast, Justin left for his office. She knew he was just trying to get away from her, because there was nothing Justin could do on a Sunday at his office that he couldn't get done at home. She was out back soaking up the sun with Cady when she got a text. She knew it was Jonah and she ignored it for a half hour. When she couldn't take it anymore, she thought she would delete it before she could even read it, but the second she went to push the delete button, she couldn't help it. She had to read it.

Till 5

That was all it said, but that was all that it needed to say. Jonah was going to be in the luxury suite at the Mayflower Hotel until 5 P.M. today. She deleted it right after reading it and put the phone away, but it ate at her for an hour. Sherise couldn't describe what was happening to her as she felt the tension rise at the thought of going to the hotel. She wanted Jonah very bad, but she couldn't have him. That fact only made her want him more. She imagined what it would be like to be in his arms, to feel him inside her. She imagined his mastery in everything also applying to the bedroom.

She pretended as if she was in a haze as she called the babysitter who lived down the street. She had just gotten back from church and would be over in a half hour, eager to make time and a half her usual fee for an emergency. Sherise initially told herself she wanted the girl to say no and that would be her excuse. She couldn't meet Jonah because she had Cady. But she knew the second she picked up the phone to dial the babysitter, she was going to go to the hotel one way or another.

But standing outside the hotel room, nothing stopping her, she couldn't do it. She felt lonely and unappreciated, but she knew the risks were too high. It wasn't just hurting Justin, which was enough of a reason to turn back, but it was letting down her girls, Billie and Erica. Like Justin, they accepted Sherise for who she was, faults and all. But if they found out that she had done this, after all their warnings and advice, although they would still love her, they would lose all respect for her. Their opinion meant more than anything to Sherise's sense of worth and she didn't want to let them down.

Sherise grabbed the key card with both hands and tried to break it in two. She bent it as hard as she could. It would bend, enough that it would be unusable, but she couldn't seem to break it.

"Dammit!"

Just then the hotel door swung open. Sherise gasped as she looked up to see Jonah standing inches from her. She was struck by the magnetism of his presence and the unusually eager look on his face.

"You're late," he said.

"I wasn't going to come," she answered.

A slow, sly smiled formed at the edges of his lips. "Yes you were."

His unceasing arrogance angered her. "You conceited bastard. I—"

Jonah grabbed her and pulled her into the room. He pressed her against the door as it slammed shut, and pressed his lips against hers in a possessive, demanding way.

Feeling the weight of his body against hers ignited Sherise's flame. She reached out and grabbed at his polo, pulling it up. He leaned back and let her lift it off, but only for a second before claiming her mouth with his again.

Sherise felt like she was going crazy with every touch. She couldn't get enough of him, wanting more with every little bit she got. Their mouths separated to breathe but only for a moment as they tore at each other's clothes. Sherise was shocked by the carnal desire that erupted inside her as their naked bodies fell onto the sofa in the sitting room of the large suite. She didn't know where the bedroom was, but she wasn't willing to search for it. She wanted him now.

On top of her, Jonah slid his hands up the inside of her

arms as he lifted them above her head. His hands gripped hers as his mouth went to her full breasts and his tongue explored the rest of her body. His fingers then gently caressed the soft belly of her arms, just barely making contact with her skin. Sherise didn't know what he was doing but the touch was driving her crazier than his mouth was. Her body began to move underneath him, out of her control.

He went lower, lifting her legs and opening them wider. His tongue teased the edges of her center, before entering her tenderly and then deeply. Her fingers dug into his hair as his tongue devoured her.

She was moaning and pleading with him and finally he lifted up and came back to her. When he entered her, he was full and hard and Sherise felt as if she was being drenched in fire but the pain was so good, so sweet. Her instinct was to control him, direct him, but Jonah didn't take, nor need, any direction in the bed. He dominated her, making her feel completely ravished from the first thrust to the last when she exploded in orgasm.

He let her take control the second time they made love, with her on top, but Sherise still couldn't manage him completely. He grabbed her at the hips and brought her down on him with force and speed. She came twice the second time, completely entranced in an erotic euphoria.

The third time, he took her from behind and Sherise came again, but found her greatest pleasure in knowing that Jonah finally lost control. She felt powerful and in control and it aroused her more than she imagined.

It was nine o'clock when Sherise finally returned home and when she stepped inside, the first sound she heard was Cady laughing. The guilt that had been plaguing her the entire way home set in massively at this point. Every step into the house was painful as she gingerly closed the door behind her. The sounds were coming from the kitchen and she thought if she just went up the stairs she could avoid it all. She could avoid having to look into the face of her baby, whose happiness she just put in jeopardy.

She had gotten up two steps before she heard her name called, but it wasn't the babysitter. It was Justin, and as she turned around she saw her husband coming out of the kitchen and walking toward her with their baby . . . her baby, in his arms.

"When did you get home?" she asked, coming back down the stairs.

"About an hour ago." He was looking at her cautiously. "Where have you been?"

"I was running some errands and needed—"

"You don't have to lie," Justin said. "I know where you were."

Sherise's heart stopped. "What?"

"You were doing the same thing I was doing," he said, switching Cady from one arm to the other.

"I was?"

He nodded. "I didn't go to work. I had to clear my head. I don't like what's going on between us anymore than you do."

"It's not what I want," Sherise said, feeling her entire body sigh as soon as she realized he didn't have any idea what she'd been doing.

"This is natural," he said. "Transitioning back to work after maternity leave can be a difficult time for a family. Everything is different now that Cady is here and we just aren't dealing with that fact."

"Justin." Part of her wanted to reach out and touch him, but she didn't feel as if she had the right to touch her own husband. "I know we have a lot to deal with but I just can't take it all right now. So much is going on."

"But the longer we wait to deal with this, the harder it will be on someone."

"Me," she said. "You mean on me."

"Or me," he answered. "I'm willing to compromise on this, but I feel like you're not even willing to do that. I feel like I'm losing you or . . . like I can't trust you're thinking about us instead of just yourself."

"I love you and Cady more than anything." Instead of touching him, Sherise placed her hand gently on Cady's cheek. "I just . . . Justin, you know who I am. You know what I need."

"I've always known," he said. "But I always felt like Cady and I were what you needed more than anything else. I don't feel that anymore."

"I'm so sorry." He could never know how much. "I'll never need anything more than I'll need you two, but that doesn't mean I won't need more at all."

"I just need you," he said.

As his hand gently stroked her hair, Sherise felt the tears welling in her throat. She didn't want to upset him by moving away, but she didn't feel worthy of his touch. Instead, she held her hands out to Cady, who jumped into them immediately.

"I'm gonna change her," Sherise said, quickly turning her back to her husband. She was already crying as she headed up the stairs, but she bit her lip to keep quiet.

Inside Cady's room, Sherise closed the door behind her and her crying intensified. She felt horrible. She felt dirty. She felt guilty. She felt all of this not just because she had just cheated on her husband for the second time, but because she knew in her heart, no matter what, she wanted to be with Jonah again.

Billie was ready to panic. She needed one more second but she heard footsteps right outside the paralegal's section. If she was caught, she was in serious trouble and all her work would be for nothing. She didn't have another time she could do this. Reminders to all the associates would go out today, Monday. It was seven in the morning. She knew Callie would be in, but didn't expect any of the other paralegals to start showing up before eight.

Billie finished her last click and hopped up from Callie's desk just as someone walked in. She was both surprised and relieved to see it was Richard, but he seemed to immediately sense something was wrong.

"What are you doing?" he asked.

"Just turning in my draft," she said as she came from behind Callie's desk.

Richard's brow furrowed and his expression made it clear he wasn't buying it. "Seriously, Billie. What the hell are you doing?"

She walked over to him. "I'm not doing anything you need to be concerned about."

"What the fuck kind of answer is that?" Richard placed a document in Callie's in-box.

"I'm not doing anything illegal if that's what you meant." Knowing that Callie should be back from the bathroom soon, Billie headed out of the area and back toward her office. "Just let it go."

He followed her. "I don't want you to do something that's going to get you in trouble."

Billie turned to him, touched by his concern. She had been expecting a different reaction. "Thanks, Richard, but I'm not going to get in trouble as long as you don't say anything."

"You had guilty written all over your face," he said. "You better be glad I was the one who walked in on you."

"You didn't," she said. "You didn't walk in on me. You didn't see anything. Look, you know that Callie is helping Porter spy on me."

"I told you to tell the bosses about that."

"I can't right now." After Billie stepped into the office, she pulled Richard in and closed the door behind him. "I can't be the new girl who whines too."

"That's not whining," he said. "She could get in serious trouble for that."

"Don't worry about it," Billie said. "I've taken care of everything. Callie isn't going to be a problem for us anymore."

"Why would she be a problem for me?"

Billie didn't want Richard to know about Porter's threats over the pro bono work he had given her. Richard was her only friend at the office and she didn't want him mad at her and she didn't want him to worry either, if it wasn't necessary.

"I told you she was making it seem like something was going on between us."

"I'm not afraid of him," Richard said as he went to his desk.

You should be is what Billie wanted to say, but she kept her mouth shut. Right now, she was scared of Porter and what he could do, but Richard didn't need to know any more than he already did. She was going to deal with Callie, and Sherise was going to help her deal with Porter. And maybe after all was taken care of, Billie could focus on other things.

Christopher was waiting anxiously as Terrell drove his car up behind him at the Pentagon. He grabbed the game and jumped out of the car. He could see Christopher trying to walk toward him, so he hurried up. He needed to be at Christopher's car or else it would take too much time to get the recorder back. He had much less time this time around than when he put it there in the first place. Probably one second or two.

"Here it is, man." Terrell handed him the box and started walking toward Christopher's car near the window. He was happy to see the window was rolled down like it was before.

"You don't know how crazy my boys are going to be when they see this." Smiling from ear to ear, Christopher reached into his pocket. "How much did we say, seventy-five?"

"Yeah, that's good." Terrell accepted the money. Only a ten-dollar profit, but he wasn't in this to make money off Christopher.

Terrell watched Christopher gaze at the game, shaking his head. There wasn't a lot of time. He had to get this guy out of his way and make sure no one else was watching, but Christopher seemed too entranced with his prized game to want to move an inch.

"You probably should put that away," Terrell said. "I don't know about you, but my bosses always tell me you don't want the client seeing you do anything other than reading the paper when they come out."

"Yeah," Christopher said with a nonchalant shrug of his shoulders. "Mr. Dolan doesn't care that much, but I should put it away."

"He'll be out any second," Terrell added, even though he didn't know if that was true or not.

Christopher slapped Terrell on the shoulder. "This is a good day, buddy."

Terrell laughed and nodded as Christopher looked at the box again, before turning and heading toward the front of the car. Terrell knew that he had to put something in either the front seat or the trunk and the front seat was better. This was good news.

Without wasting a second, Terrell reached into the car. He felt for the device and the second he didn't find it where he knew he placed it, he began to panic.

"What the fuck," he whispered as his hands searched frantically.

He glanced at Christopher, whose body was halfway in the car as he messed around in the front. Terrell didn't have a choice, so he quickly turned around, leaned into the car through the window and searched harder for the device.

He finally found it beneath the left side of the pillow. It

must have slipped from the top where he placed it. Feeling relieved, he grabbed the device and was about to pull it out
when he heard the front door slam shut.

"Dammit!" he said. There was no way Christopher wouldn't
see him even if he leaned out now. What was he going to do?
He was caught. Caught spying on Jonah Dolan.

"What are you doing?" Christopher asked.

Still leaning into the car, Terrell turned to him and smiled.
Christopher wasn't amused, but Terrell had a plan. This was
different than getting caught in the usual street hustles he had
played. A strong fist and fast feet weren't going to get him out
of this. He had to use his head.

Terrell slowly leaned out of the car, concealing the device
in his hand.

"I'm checking out your leather, man," he said. "And the
trimming on your inside, right there beneath the window.
Your car isn't even in the same class as mine."

Christopher's frown slowly, cautiously evened out as he
seemed to be deciding if he was going to trust Terrell. Terrell
never faltered. He made sure not to seem nervous or too eager,
playing it as casual as he knew how to. It worked.

"Yeah, they have me driving a bigwig," Christopher looked
at the car and touched the trim above the tire. "First class all
the way."

"I'm not knocking my car," Terrell said, almost hearing a
hint of a sigh in his voice. He hoped Christopher hadn't noticed. "It's a tight ride, but nothing like this. I would love to
drive something like this."

"Maybe one day," Christopher said. "You never know.
Lobbyists aren't the top of the food chain. You get a big government assignment, you'll spend your day in this ride."

"Smooth, right?"

Christopher nodded. "Rides like it's gliding on air."

"Sounds nice." Terrell took a moment to seem reflective

before moving on. "Well, you be sure to tell me what your boys say when you show them that game."

"It's gonna be insane, man. Thanks again!"

"No problem!" Terrell waved as he was already walking back to his car.

He was sure to act casual just in case there was an ounce of suspicion still in Christopher, but as he sat down and shut the driver's side door, Christopher no longer seemed to care about him.

Terrell felt that familiar high that came with getting away with a close call. He missed that feeling. He had been doing his best to stay on the straight and narrow for Erica's sake. He loved her and wanted her to be happy, but he missed this. As he rewound the recording device, Terrell thought of Erica and what she might say if she found out what was going on. When they were younger, his explanations worked on her, but he didn't feel like they would anymore. That was why she could never know about this. That would be part of his deal with Jonah. Erica would never know.

The device was voice activated, so it only came on if someone within five feet of it was talking. Jonah must have been sitting right next to it because he could be heard loud and clear as he instructed Christopher to take him to the Mayflower Hotel.

Mayflower Hotel? On a Sunday afternoon?

This was exactly what Terrell was hoping for. He was going to get something on Jonah and bring that man's ego down to size. Blackmail was not Terrell's expertise. His hustles had been more immediate and less complicated most of his life. However, it was time to step it up, and with the wedding coming, he needed more money than a few upscale tips could provide.

After hearing about Jonah's interest in Sherise and then seeing the two of them in the kitchen at Sherise's house, Terrell was on to something. Jonah had to be having an affair. Men like him always were. They were powerful and had the world revolving around them. None of the rules applied to them and women flocked to them in droves. They would try hard to keep their secrets from members of the media or others in their social set, but they ignored people like Terrell. He was invisible to them and he would use that to his advantage.

He listened for a few minutes more as Jonah whistled a bit before speaking some reminders on a personal recorder. His spirits were lifted as he listened to Jonah order flowers and expensive champagne to the luxury suite at the Mayflower Hotel. This was definitely an affair. Terrell could see money signs all around him. He only had a few minutes before his client would show up so he hoped to get something even better.

He did, but he wasn't at all happy.

"Yes, dear," was how Jonah responded to a call.

Terrell assumed it was his wife. He couldn't decipher anything she was saying, but she was yelling loud enough for the recorder to pick up the static and make a pinging sound. All he could hear was Jonah's responses, and the tone of his voice told him that he was not happy to have this conversation.

"What did he tell you?" Jonah asked.

"Juliette, listen. Listen."

Terrell wasn't sure but he thought he remembered Juliette being his wife's name when he met her at Sherise's house.

"I'm not trying to do anything to you," Jonah continued. "Juliette, look, I just wanted to introduce him to Erica."

Terrell sat up straight.

"I wanted her to meet a nice guy her own age. I didn't . . . I know he's your cousin. I wouldn't introduce her to anyone I didn't know."

Terrell couldn't believe what he was hearing. Was he hearing what he thought he was? Had Jonah tried to set Erica up with his wife's cousin?

"What the fuck?" Terrell asked.

Jonah made some exasperated sighs. "I am not trying to bring her into your life. You've made your feelings clear about that. It was just a date. I only wanted her to know there are better . . ."

"Better what?" Terrell asked, as there was a pause in the tape. He wanted to smash his fist through the windshield. What was going on behind his back?

"It doesn't matter," Jonah said. "Juliette, I have a lot more work to do. If you want me home in time for dinner, you've gotta let me finish this."

Out of the corner of his eye, Terrell spotted movement. He turned off the tape and looked up in time to see Jonah exit the building and walk toward the car in front of him. Jonah didn't look up. He was focused on the BlackBerry in his hand and ignored the world as Christopher opened the door for him and he stepped in.

Terrell had two plans and made the decision right there and then that nothing would take priority over them. First, he was going to find out who Jonah was having an affair with and blackmail the hell out of that bastard. Second, he was going to find out why Jonah and his wife were so interested in who Erica was dating.

"Despite the plaintiff's statement to the court, Grady Pharmaceuticals has not been allowed enough time for an appropriate discovery."

"Wait!" Richard held his hand up to stop her.

Billie paused as she sat on the front of her desk facing him as he sat behind his. She was reciting the draft of a reply to the court that was due to the head lawyer on the case in a few hours.

"What's wrong?" she asked.

"Sounds like you're complaining," Richard said.

"I am," she responded.

"No, you should rephrase it as if you are asking the court to clarify a point of confusion that you believe the plaintiff is under."

Billie laughed. "You want me to smart-ass the court in my statement?"

"Do you want my advice or not?"

Just then, a knock came on the office door and both Richard and Billie said, "Come in" in unison.

Alexandra Steele, a paralegal in the White Collar Crime practice, poked her head through the door with a look on her face that told everyone she had something juicy to tell. "Did you hear?" she asked.

"No," Billie answered, but had a feeling she knew exactly what Alexandra was about to say.

Alexandra came fully into the office. "Well, if you check your e-mails, you'll get a message from Alec Allistair. As of today, I'm the head paralegal for the White Collar Crime practice."

Billie could barely contain her joy.

"What happened to Callie?" Richard asked, reaching for his BlackBerry.

"I'm not at liberty to discuss that." Alexandra flipped her strawberry red hair back. "You should just know that while things might be a little slow over the next couple of days while I get situated and clean up this mess, everything should be back on track momentarily."

"Wait!" Richard yelled as he read his e-mail. "You know you want to give us some dirt."

"In my new position as head paralegal, I can't. . . ."

"We'll get it out of you eventually," Billie said as she hopped off her desk. "What did she do?"

"She has been a little lax in her work," Alexandra said.

"In response to recent complaints about assignments within the White Collar Crime practice that have not been received by management . . ." Richard was reading directly from his BlackBerry. "Steps have been taken to locate such assignments and everything that was previously missing has been found. Steps have been taken to acquire extensions within any court applicable. In addition, Callie Brewer is no longer with the firm. Effective immediately, Alexandra Steele . . . blah, blah, blah."

"There have apparently been some . . . mix-ups with work that Callie was responsible for," Alexandra added. "If you want to know more, ask Alec."

"Give it up," Richard said as soon as Alexandra left.

"I found out that Callie was holding on to my work longer than she was supposed to," Billie offered.

"She was trying to make it look like you were late turning in your stuff?" Richard asked.

Billie nodded. "For a few things. It gave me an idea."

"You should have just told Derrick."

"We've been over this, Richard."

"This is different than her telling your ex who you had lunch with. This is work."

"But I need to get her out of my life, period. Besides, I didn't trust they would take my word over both hers and Porter's considering they think he's so amazing and she's been here a long time."

"What did you do?"

Billie explained how she got the idea to take a few deliverables from other associates that were in Callie's in-box and place them in the folders that Callie set aside for e-mails that had been received and forwarded. When those assignments weren't turned in on time, enough people would complain and it would be found out that Callie failed big time.

"You put cases in jeopardy?"

"No," she protested. "I made sure the documents in question were not urgent or any delay wouldn't hurt our client at all."

"Did you read this e-mail?" Richard asked. "Extensions had to be sought in court."

Billie was a little confused by that part. She made a point of making certain that delaying the documents would ruffle some feathers but not have any lasting effect. She may have missed something, but she was under time constraints and couldn't get caught at Callie's desk. "The e-mail also said everything was fine."

Richard's eyes stared at her judgmentally and she didn't like it.

"You don't know what I'm going through," Billie said. "Porter has all the advantages and I had to get something!"

"At what cost?" he asked. "This isn't you, Billie. Being underhanded, deceitful, and all that. What exactly did you get out of this?"

1 1

Sherise watched as a naked Jonah sat up from the bed and admired his physique. He was incredibly fit for a man his age and was extremely confident in being naked. She enjoyed watching him move, his every gesture.

"I can't stay," he said as he knelt down to open the hotel room's minibar. "You can order room service or we can try and raid this fridge here."

"Is that it?" she asked.

Jonah turned to her with a quizzical look on his face. "Is what it? Are you trying to tell me I didn't get the job done?"

"You were better the second time than the first," she said, "but no, that isn't what I'm talking about. You seem eager to leave, so I'm thinking you may be done with me."

Jonah laughed as he returned to the bed, sitting on its edge.

"You find this funny?" Sherise asked.

"I find it hilarious," he said, opening the tiny bottle of wine he'd taken. "Hilarious to think any man could be done with you."

Sherise smiled, sitting up in bed. "Then why are you so eager to leave?"

"One can't keep the president waiting." He motioned for her to come join him on the edge of the bed.

She shook her head.

"Why are you so stubborn?" he asked.

"Would you prefer I come when called?"

He took a sip of the wine. "No, Mrs. Robinson, I am not done with you. Not by a long—"

"Don't call me that," Sherise said, covering herself up with the bed's comforter.

Jonah's smile faded. "I'm sorry. That was wrong of me."

This was all wrong, Sherise knew, but any reminder of who she really was spoiled the mood for her. She enjoyed the fantasy that existed when she was with Jonah.

"Allow me to make it up to you," he said as he reached for something on the side of the bed. He came across the bed with one hand behind his back. He leaned in for a kiss and Sherise obliged.

"What are you up to?" she asked.

He winked at her and revealed what was behind his back. A tiny red velvet box that fit in the palm of his hand.

This was only the second time they'd been together and, not expecting a gift yet, Sherise was a little hesitant to accept it.

Sensing her hesitation, Jonah opened the tiny box and revealed two small flowery white-gold and brilliant diamond earrings.

"Jonah." Sherise finally took the box and looked at the beautiful earrings, so clear and dazzling. "You know I can't take this."

Disappointed, he accepted the box back as she offered it to him. "I want you to have them."

"And do what with them?"

"Wear them the next time we're together."

She was touched by the sentiment and found the idea of wearing these earrings, and nothing else, the next time they made love enticing.

"It's too dangerous," she said. "Justin could find out. Someone could notice."

"Keep them in your purse. No one will—"

"Jonah, I don't want to risk having to answer questions."

He seemed injured, but only for a moment. "You have to let me give you something."

"I'm not your kept woman," she said stubbornly.

Jonah laughed as he returned to finding his clothes and getting dressed. "I'm not a fool, Sherise. I know you wouldn't enter into any relationship if there wasn't something in it for you. Well, besides the obvious."

"I'll have to work on that ego of yours," she said.

"It gets bigger every time I make love to you."

Sherise smiled, knowing he was talking shit just to make her feel special, but it was working.

"You're right," she said. "I do need something from you. Help for a friend of mine."

After buttoning his pants, he opened his arms wide. "I'm at your service."

Sherise smiled at the thought. He was. One of the most powerful men in DC would do anything for her, and she loved it.

"I have a problem and his name is Porter Hass."

"How many of those do you plan on going through in one night?" Terrell asked.

Sitting next to him in bed, Erica looked at her lap full of bridal magazines. She had gone through three so far and had two more left. "As many as I can before I fall asleep," she said. "They all have so many good ideas."

"They all look the same," he said. "Just different titles. *Brides, Weddings, Bridal Guide, Bride Noir.* It's ridiculous."

"They're all different." Erica pointed to individual magazines. "This one is for black brides, this one is a general bride magazine, and this one is for DC-area brides. This one is just for dresses while this one is all about food."

"And a new issue of each of them comes out every month," Terrell said. "It's a scam. Probably cost a ten spot each."

"It's worth it," she said. "I'm getting all kinds of ideas. I'm gonna show them to the girls this weekend."

"Speaking of the girls . . ." he said, "what is the story with Sherise and your boss?"

Erica eyed him curiously. "There is no story."

Terrell smiled. "Come on, baby. You don't have to lie to Daddy to protect your girl. You yourself said that if Jonah was interested in anyone, it was Sherise. Something is going on there."

"How would you even know?" she asked.

Terrell told her about the time he encountered Sherise and Jonah in Sherise's kitchen.

"You misinterpreted," she said, even though she was starting to suspect he hadn't.

"I know what I saw."

"It's a flirtation. Sherise will flirt with anyone she thinks can get her something. She always has. She knows where to draw the line."

"If it ain't her," Terrell said, "it's someone else, 'cause that man has got a jump off."

"He probably does," Erica said. "But it's not Sherise."

"What do you know?"

Erica shrugged. "Jenna gets this look on her face lately. Like whenever he leaves and she has to change his schedule or he requests to keep his schedule open."

"A look?"

"A look like . . . like he's up to no good."

"What else?"

Erica turned to him. "Why are you so interested in Jonah's sex life?"

"So he gets to be the only one who interferes in people's sex lives?"

Erica gave him a suspicious glare. "Boy, what are you up to?"

"He takes an unusual interest in your personal life," Terrell said. "Maybe you should try and take an interest in his so he can see what it feels like."

"It doesn't work that way," she said. "We aren't equals in the workplace."

"What kind of things is he asking you about yourself?"

"Any and everything." She waved a dismissive hand. "It's not important. I hardly see him anyway. Just for a second when he runs in and out of the office."

"What about his wife? What is her deal?"

Erica made a face. "Besides being a cold bitch, how would I know? She doesn't come by the office. As far as I can hear, she doesn't even call him at work. I don't think they're close."

"Why doesn't she like you?"

"Who knows?" Based on the only two times Erica met her, the woman didn't seem to like anyone. "I get the feeling she's jealous of any woman in Jonah's life. She probably knows he's unfaithful."

"That night at Sherise's dinner, she kept staring at you. Didn't you notice? Sherise was flirting with her husband all night, but she kept looking at you."

Erica had noticed, but had forgotten it already. Why would that matter?

"I'm just saying," he said. "There's a story with that dude and it might be in your best interest to try and find out what it is."

"And report back to you what I find?"

"Well, Erica, it would have been nice to know that my girlfriend's boss—"

"Fiancée," she quickly corrected.

He nodded. "That my fiancée's boss is trying to set her up with somebody."

Erica was shocked. "How in God's name did you know that?"

"It doesn't matter how I knew," he said angrily. "It matters that you didn't mention it to me."

"What good would that have done?"

"What did you say to him?"

Erica socked him in the arm. "How could you ask me that?"

"I don't know," he said. "I'm sorry. I just . . . there's something wrong with that guy. He's up to something and I think he wants me out of your life. I just get all crazy if I think about you with someone else."

"Stop," Erica said as she took his face in her hands and turned him to her. She looked intently into his eyes. "He has no say in who is in or out of my life. He's just my boss. He's not my dad and he's not even my friend. I love you. Nothing that goes on in that office will change that."

Terrell hoped it was true, but he wasn't going to rely on hope. He was going to find out what was going on.

While placing dishes in the dishwasher, Billie looked at her ringing phone, intending not to answer it no matter who it was. She'd had a long day. But when she saw Tara's name come up on the Caller ID of her phone, she dropped what she was doing and answered it.

"Hey, baby girl!"

"I have a date!"

Billie wasn't sure she heard her right. "I'm pretty sure you don't, little Ms. Only Fourteen Years Old."

"Okay," Tara conceded. "It's not an official date, but I'm going to a birthday party at a friend's house and that boy Jesse is gonna be there."

"With adult supervision." Billie hopped on her kitchen counter.

"Yeah, yeah, yeah. My point is I need you to come over and help me pick out the right outfit."

Billie sighed. "Oh, sweetie. I wish I could, but you know that's not going to happen."

" 'Cause she's back?"

"Claire? Claire has moved back in?"

"Yesterday. It was nice while it lasted, but at least Daddy isn't sulking around anymore."

This would certainly buy Billie some time. "I have an idea. Why don't you put your outfits on the bed, take a picture and send it to me, and I'll tell you what I think."

"That's lame, but if it's all I can—"

"Hello, Billie."

Billie waited while Porter and Tara argued over yet another interruption of her phone call. Finally, Porter won over and Tara called him a name before storming off.

"Don't start with me," Billie said. "I tried to call Claire but she won't pick up. I'm doing my part."

That wasn't exactly true. Billie made a few calls to Claire to make it seem like she was trying to reach the girl, but she timed them for when she expected a very low chance of Claire answering. She never left a message, but the call would be on her phone in case Porter doubted her. If Claire ever called her back, Billie had no intention of ever picking up the phone.

"I'm not calling about that," Porter said. "I'm calling about Callie. And what the fuck is Sherise up to?"

"I don't know what you're talking about," Billie said.

"You got Callie fired," Porter said. "I know it was you, so no use in denying it."

"You don't know anything," Billie said. "And from what I hear, a lot of people had a bone to pick with Callie because she was slacking off."

"She wasn't slacking," Porter said. "And you know it."

"Unless you're willing to admit that you specifically asked her to hold up my work, then you don't really know shit."

After a short pause. "That was fucking lame of you."

"I keep forgetting," she said. "You're the only one who gets to do underhanded stuff. Don't worry, I'm sure your sympathy fuck made her feel better."

"I'm not fucking her," he said adamantly. "I was never fucking her. I offered her a job at my firm if she . . ."

"If she what?" Billie asked.

"Forget Callie," he said. "You wanna tell me why your slut of a friend is getting all up in my shit?"

"I don't have any sluts for friends," Billie said. "The only slut I know is sharing your bed right now."

"What are you up to, Billie?"

"I'm just trying to live my life," she said. "One without you in it."

"You're not getting rid of me that easy," he said before hanging up.

Billie felt another headache coming on and suddenly was in serious need of a drink. "Whatever you're doing, Sherise," she said as she hopped off the counter and reached for a bottle of Scotch in her cabinet, "you better get it done fast."

Terrell knew he was playing with fire, but he also knew he was about to get paid. It was risky as hell following a man like Jonah, but who would really know? DC on a Wednesday afternoon was a crazy, hectic place and it was full of limos and driven Town Cars.

Jonah had been in the JW Marriott on Pennsylvania Avenue for almost an hour. It was a good choice. It would only take someone who worked near the White House a few seconds to cab to, and anyone at the Pentagon in Virginia only had to cross the Fourteenth Street Bridge and they were there. Of course Jonah didn't take the main entrance. Christopher dropped him off at a side entrance with automatic doors and a glass enclosure.

While Christopher left quickly after dropping Jonah off, Terrell found a convenient spot across the street to park and wait. Forty-five minutes later Christopher returned and parked himself about ten paces from the entrance. It was just a matter of time.

Terrell knew he could be in over his head, but he didn't care. The possible score was too big, and more important, he needed to know what the hell this man was all about. Of course the intention was to blackmail him about an affair and make certain that part of the deal, in addition to money, would be that Erica's job would be safe. But things were different now. Jonah's interest in Erica's personal life was a problem for Terrell and he needed to make part of the deal getting Erica a good job, but one that was far away from Jonah.

Terrell was trying to come up with explanations he would offer Erica if she questioned where all the money he was using to buy her the wedding of her dreams was coming from. Suddenly the exterior glass doors of the hotel opened and Jonah stood just inside them. He stayed in the safety of the enclosed entrance area as he waved to Christopher, who started the car.

"I got you, boy." Terrell grabbed his cell phone from the passenger seat and placed it to his eyes to take a picture.

He pressed, but nothing happened.

"Damn phone." He had thought about getting a real camera, but then figured there was no need since the one in his phone had served him well most times.

Looking at the phone, he quickly pressed the right buttons to make the camera work, but by the time he went to take a picture of Jonah, it was too late. He'd been caught. While Christopher had driven up to the entrance, Jonah hadn't gotten in. He was still standing in the entrance, staring across the street directly at Terrell.

Slowly Terrell lowered the camera, never taking his eyes off Jonah. Even from this distance, he could tell the man's entire body had stiffened like a log. Terrell wasn't sure what to do, but the second Jonah started walking, he knew he wasn't going to the car. He was headed for him.

Terrell turned the car on and stepped on the gas as fast as he could. He wasn't sure how close Jonah had gotten to him and he didn't care. He was too busy trying to figure out how to salvage his mistake.

Sherise had grabbed her purse and was headed out of the hotel room when Jonah called her on the phone. What was he doing? They had agreed no more calls that could be traced back to private phones.

"You just don't like rules, do you?" she asked.

"What have you told your friends about us?" Jonah's voice was clearly angry and agitated.

"What?" Sherise glanced down the hallway to make sure it was clear before stepping out. "I haven't told anyone anything. What's going on?"

"Erica's fucking boyfriend was outside the hotel!"

"Terrell?" Sherise froze in front of the elevator. "What are you talking about?"

"I came out of the hotel and Terrell was in a car across the street. I think he took a picture of me with his fucking phone!"

"It wasn't him," she said. "He doesn't know anything."

"I knew he was trouble the second I met him. Don't come out of the hotel."

"Is he still there?"

"No, but he could come back around. Sherise, this cannot get out! How the fuck did this happen?"

"I don't know!" Sherise felt her stomach tightening. She thought she was going to be dizzy when she stepped into the elevator. "I'm going to find out."

Inside the elevator, Sherise turned off the phone even though she could hear Jonah still yelling into it. She fell against the wall and held the phone to her chest. Her heart was beating rapidly and her head was spinning.

"Oh my God," was all she could say, over and over again.

★   ★   ★

The second Billie stepped out of the building heading to pick up a quick lunch, she was caught in the middle of a crowd of people. Walking around downtown, one was used to getting bumped into, but she was caught off guard when she felt someone grab her arm and pull her away from the sidewalk and against the wall of the building.

Billie, assuming she was being mugged, swung with all the power she had. She was tiny but tough and wouldn't give up her purse without a fight. Unfortunately, after she heard her attacker yell in pain, she knew something was wrong.

"What are you doing?" she asked, turning to face him.

"Jesus fucking Christ!" Porter was holding his chin where her fist connected. "Why did you do that?"

"You grabbed me!"

"So you break my jaw?" He was rubbing the spot now.

Billie felt bad, looking to see if there was damage. "I think you'll be okay."

"I'm gonna need a doctor," he said. "Just more shit to fuck up my day."

"I'm sorry," she said. "You shouldn't go around grabbing people in DC."

"Jesus, Billie."

"Stop whining," she said before realizing that his protests were not about her punch, but just in general. "What is it?"

"You gonna try and act like you don't know?" His pained expression quickly turned to anger.

Billie sighed. "Come on, Porter. I don't have time for this. I'm hungry and I—"

"You ruined my career and you want me to give a shit that you're hungry?"

Billie's eyes widened in shock. "I haven't done anything! Why do you blame me for everything? With the quality of asshole you give off, you've got to have more enemies than just me."

"I was up for partner at the end of the year, Billie. Suddenly I'm being told that my bid for partnership is being deferred . . . indefinitely."

Billie wondered what in the world Sherise could have done. She had connections, but this seemed above even her seemingly endless abilities.

"Maybe you did something," she said. "You're always up to something, Porter."

"I'm serious, Billie. This is my career!"

"Stop yelling at me," she ordered. "I didn't do anything to you."

"Your friend Sherise was nosing around about me last week."

Billie stood there, nonresponsive.

"Don't act like you don't know what I'm talking about," he warned.

"Sherise doesn't give a damn about you," she said. "She was probably just dogging you out to someone because of how you treat me."

"Why do you have to tell her everything?"

"What's the matter, Porter? You were hoping we could keep your blackmail of me just between us?"

Porter frowned. "I'm not blackmailing you."

Billie could only laugh as it was obvious from Porter's expression that he meant exactly what he said.

"Get a dictionary, asshole," she said. "Look up 'blackmail.'"

"So this is revenge?"

"I didn't do anything," Billie insisted. That wasn't really a lie. She didn't.

"I asked my associates for a reason why my bid is being deferred," he said. "They wouldn't tell me."

"Maybe it's discrimination," she said jokingly. "You should sue."

"Stop making light of this," Porter said. "Everything I've done in my career has been to make partner. Billie, you know that. How many nights did I tell you that when we were lying in bed? You know how important this is to me."

Be strong, she told herself. "Nice try, but I don't have time to reminisce with you, Porter."

"Did you ever love me?"

Billie was angry now. "When will you ever stop trying to play me? I don't have a soft side for you anymore, Porter. I . . ."

Before she could think to protest, Porter grabbed her and his mouth came down hard on hers. After a second of shock, Billie began to push away, but she was powerless against him. She felt panic set in as she could sense her desire awakening. She couldn't let this happen again.

"Stop it!" she screamed as she pushed away. "You touch me again and I'll start screaming."

Porter looked around as if trying to determine whether or not it was worth it to try again. Seeming to decide against it, his shoulders fell and his puppy-dog face took over. "Billie." His voice was intentionally pitiful. "I'm pleading with you."

"Don't waste your time," she said, although his pitiful state was compelling. She liked feeling in control of their dynamic.

"What do you want?" he asked. "You can see Tara whenever you want. I promise I won't ever say anything about you or Richard. Do you want money? I can give you—"

"Stop!" She was disgusted that he thought he could pay her to make up for the suffering he had caused her. "I don't know what you think I can do."

"Undo whatever was done."

"I didn't do any—"

"Billie, stop fucking with me." His pitiful tone turned insistent now. "I don't believe in coincidences. Every step that I have made in my career has been to reach this moment. I may make a lot of mistakes in my personal life, but not in this. I find out that Sherise was asking around about me last week and all of a sudden this happens."

"I didn't . . ."

"Well, she did!" he insisted. "I'm telling you, promising you that I will leave you alone. I will stay out of your life. You can see Tara any time you want. Just undo this."

"Your promises mean nothing."

"Do you think I . . ." Porter stopped talking and swallowed hard. He looked around as if he could find what he needed to say somewhere around him.

Billie couldn't believe this shit. Was he really choking up? What in the hell was going on? She should walk away right now. No, she should laugh and walk away right now. Maybe she should punch him in the face again, laugh, and walk away.

"I'll see what I can do," she said tenderly. "That's all I can promise. I'm not lying when I say I don't know what happened, but if I can help you I will."

"Thank you, Billie." He reached out to touch her arm.

She slapped his hand away. "I'm not promising anything, so don't thank me yet."

Billie walked away shaking her head, ashamed at herself for giving in to him . . . again, but also wondering how many ways Sherise was going to kick her ass for doing so.

"Hold on, dammit!" Terrell yelled as he rushed to his front door. Whoever was there was banging on it like there was a fire.

He looked in the peephole before opening the door. So it was her! He could only imagine what was about to go down now.

"Erica isn't here," he said as soon as he opened the door.

"I know that." Sherise practically knocked him over coming into the apartment. "Which is why this has to be quick."

"Look." Terrell closed the door. "I know what you're—"

"You're in over your head, boy." She tossed her purse on the sofa and placed both of her hands on her hips as she eyed him. He had a cocky look on his face that she was gonna smack off.

"Who you calling 'boy'?" he asked. "Look, woman, you need to watch how you talk to me. This is my house."

"Just tell me what you're up to," she ordered.

Terrell nodded and slowly walked over to the sofa. He sat down and crossed his legs.

"Don't fuck with me!" Sherise shrieked.

"You kind of gave yourself away," he said. "I would have figured you to be a little smoother than that."

"What gave it away?"

"I assume you're here about creeping with Jonah."

Sherise felt sick to her stomach at the sound of someone else saying that. "Can you just cut to the chase?"

"The chase is I didn't even know it was you he was creeping with. I mean I suspected, but Erica said—"

Sherise gasped. "What have you told Erica?"

"She doesn't need to know about this," he said seriously.

"No one does," Sherise said. "Did you have any other reason to believe it was me?"

"Besides you practically handing your ass to him in front of everybody? I mean, honestly, I don't know how Justin puts up with your flirting."

"You stay away from my marriage," Sherise warned.

"I don't care about your marriage," Terrell answered back. "It don't look like you do either."

"Then what are you up to?" Sherise asked.

"You ain't got nothing to worry about." He leaned back, placing his hands behind his head. "Your marriage is not the one in trouble."

Sherise couldn't believe what he was thinking. "You always were a good for nothing little hustler."

"Shouldn't you check that attitude toward me?" he asked. "I mean, I could call Justin up and share your secret with him."

"You have no proof and I will deny everything." Sherise kicked the coffee table that separated the two of them out of the way. "And if you try to run your little hustle on me, I will make you wish you were dead."

Terrell stood up, unwilling to let this woman try to punk him. "You think I'm scared of you. I'm from—"

"The streets," she said. "I know. You've said it before. You seem to forget where I'm from. It's that same block where Erica is from. She's my sister. You know the bond we have, the three of us. You wanna fuck with that? Go ahead and try and mess with my life and see how I devote my life to messing with yours."

Terrell knew what she was insinuating and it enraged him. "Erica would never leave me."

"We'll see about that." Sherise tossed her hair back. "But if you don't fuck with my family, I won't fuck with the one you hope you can have one day."

Terrell sneered at her. This wasn't the first time he wanted to put Sherise in her place, but never more than right now. No one was going to take Erica away from him.

"I already told you," he said. "I'm not about you."

"I know. You're about Jonah, but you're making an even bigger mistake."

"I got this," he said. "Now run home to your baby and that husband you cheatin' on."

"I know all you're thinking about is a hustle and dollar signs are flying in front of your eyes, but Jonah Dolan is not a man to fuck with."

"Just stay out of it," he said.

"This is for your benefit," she said.

Terrell laughed. "Yeah, I'm sure you're worried about me."

"I don't give a shit about you," she said. "But Erica, for some reason I can't see, loves you. Jonah is headed for the White House. Anyone who tries to fuck with that is gonna end up a missing person."

Terrell looked her over to see just how much she believed what she was saying. "It ain't that serious."

Sherise shook her head. "You fool, it is just that serious. And don't think that your relationship with Erica will save you because Jonah would love to have you out of her life."

"Tell me what the fuck is up with that. What is his deal with Erica?"

"Are you listening to me, boy?" Sherise was yelling now. "Do you want to get hurt or worse?"

"What?"

Just a second before Sherise let out that last line, Erica opened the door to her apartment. Almost dropping all the files in her arms, she was in a rush because she'd heard Sherise yelling on the other side of the door.

"Baby." Terrell rushed over to her and kissed her on the cheek. "What are you doing home so—"

"What is going on here?" Erica asked. "Sherise, what are you doing here and why are you yelling at him?"

Sherise felt a thud in her chest and intense anxiety creep in on her. She had a deal with Jonah. She had promised to talk to Terrell and he'd promised to keep Erica late at work. She never expected this.

"Erica." Sherise threw her hands in the air. "I don't . . . It's so complicated."

"I'm listening," she said, closing the door shut.

"It ain't nothing," Terrell said. "She's just talking smack. You know how Sherise gets."

" 'Do you want to get hurt or worse,' is what I heard." Erica placed her work on a table and her purse on top. She checked out Terrell, who looked completely guilty, and then Sherise, who looked like she was going to throw up. "Somebody better start talking now."

Sherise nervously paced the room. All the thoughts floating in her head were slamming against each other, but in a second of clarity she realized what she had to do. She had to neutralize Terrell as a threat to her and Jonah, as well as himself. She would have to deal with the consequences between her and Erica.

"Sherise," Terrell said. "Why don't you just leave?"

"I'm not going anywhere." Sherise walked over to one of the stools behind the kitchen counter. "Not until I tell Erica what's going on."

Despite Terrell's immediate protest, Sherise told Erica everything. She told her that she was having an affair with Jonah and after getting past the look of complete disappointment on Erica's face, she went on to tell her that somehow Terrell had found out and was following Jonah with the intent of blackmailing him about the affair.

"I haven't blackmailed anyone," Terrell protested.

Erica looked at him, her expression clearly showing her hurt. "What were you planning to do?"

"You were trying to take a picture of Jonah," Sherise said. "He saw you. You ran off like a little coward when he tried to confront you."

"Shut up," he said. "Look, baby. I can explain this whole thing."

"I just did that for you," Sherise said.

This time Terrell came to within inches of Sherise and pointed his finger in her face. "You shut up!"

"Hey!" Erica grabbed him and pulled him away from Sherise. "You need to calm down."

"This bitch is always trying to get in our business!"

"You made it my business," Sherise said. "You're fucking with my life."

"Well, maybe if you wasn't such a fucking ho that wouldn't be a problem!"

This time, it was Sherise who Erica had to grab and control. She was stronger than Sherise and was able to pull her back.

"You need to go!" Erica told her.

Sherise turned to Erica. "Look, I can explain this."

"What are you gonna explain to me?" Erica asked. "Justin is the one you cheated on."

"I know." Sherise was quickly in tears. "I know, but I also know you're mad at me and . . ."

"Of everyone you had to go and have an affair with, you choose my boss?"

"I didn't choose him," Sherise pleaded. "I swear. It just happened."

"Oh, please." Erica could barely stand to look at her. "You were practically handing your ass to him on a platter. This shit did not 'just happen.'"

"That's what I told her," Terrell said, laughing. "I said—"

Erica's glare in his direction stopped Terrell in his tracks. She turned back to Sherise. "I want you to go," she said.

"Erica." Sherise reached for her.

"Now!" Erica pointed to the door and stepped out of the way. "Terrell and I have to talk."

The second Sherise closed the door behind her, Terrell started his excuses and pleas, but Erica put it to a stop.

"If you lie to me," she said, "you will be sleeping in the street."

Terrell nodded in acquiescence. "Fine, Erica. What do you want me to say?"

"It's my job to make this clear?" she asked. "I don't think so."

"Okay," he said. "Okay, she's right. I was gonna blackmail him. I was gonna make him give me money to keep quiet about his affair."

Erica felt sick to her stomach. She was shaking her head without any idea of what to say.

"Baby," he pleaded. "It was for us. I want to give you the wedding of your dreams and this was—"

"Don't you dare!" she yelled. "Don't you dare try to make this about me."

"It is about you," he said. "It's about us, our future!"

"You never stopped hustling," she accused. "Even when you said you did, you didn't."

"I'm a different man than I used to be. You know that. You wouldn't have agreed to marry me if I was still that man. But I saw an opportunity I couldn't pass up and that damn man just rubbed me the wrong way."

"So you decide to ruin his life and my career?"

"No," he said. "Part of the deal—or at least it was going to be—was that nothing was to happen to you or your job."

"That was part of the blackmail?" Erica shook her head in disgust. "My job security? Oh my God. You were gonna just let me keep working for him after blackmailing him for money?"

"I don't want you working for him at all."

"You are such a fool!"

The accusation was insulting enough to Terrell, but the look of disgust on her face was what really hurt him. "It was a bad idea, I know."

"No, you don't," she fumed. "Sherise is right. Jonah would eat you alive. You think you're a hustler? Please. A man like that?"

"I can hold my own," Terrell said defiantly. "And that man you seem to think is so above everybody else, in addition to cheating on his wife, has got another situation going on that you need to be worried about."

"Go ahead," she said. "Try to focus on what everyone else has done wrong."

"I'm thinking about you," Terrell said. "Jonah is not safe for you. I can feel it."

"How much?" she asked.

"What?"

"How much is jeopardizing our relationship and my career worth?" she asked. "How much were you going to blackmail him for?"

"There is no price worth losing you."

He rushed after her as she headed for the door. Just as she opened it, he slammed it shut and came up behind her. He pressed his body against her and kissed her on the neck. "Don't go, baby," he begged. "I promise. I won't—"

"Your promises don't mean shit to me right now."

When she elbowed him he fell back, and she rushed out of the apartment. She needed some air and she needed someone to tell her what the fuck was going on. Did she even know the man she was planning to marry?

12

"Where has everyone been?" Billie asked the second she answered her phone. "I've been calling and texting you and Sherise all day and night."

After not getting a response, Billie knew something was seriously wrong. "Erica, what's going on? And please don't tell me someone is in the hospital or worse."

Sitting in the café of a bookstore a few blocks from her apartment, Erica was finally ready to talk, but wasn't sure where to start. "All hell has broken loose," she said.

"What?" Billie's anxiety was growing with every second of silence on the other end of the line.

"Where do I start?" Erica asked. "Well, first of all, Sherise is fucking Jonah."

"No she's not," Billie said. She reached for her television remote and turned on the mute. "Why would you think that?"

"She told me." Erica recited the events from earlier that evening describing how angry she was at Sherise for getting involved with Jonah and ending with tears about how betrayed she felt by Terrell.

Billie went through several states of disbelief, but tried to keep it together enough to comfort Erica. "Baby, I am so sorry. I can't believe he'd do this."

"Can't you?" Erica asked. "I can. He's been a hustler his whole life. Everything is a game, no matter what the consequences."

"But he's changed. He changed for you."

"Have you been listening to anything I've been saying?" Erica wiped away the tears on her cheeks. "He hasn't changed at all."

"Just because he's fallen back into some old ways doesn't mean he's that person again."

"It does if he never stopped being that person. I don't know what he's been up to, Billie. I don't even know him."

"You do know him," Billie said reassuringly. "It's just . . . I'm not gonna try and make excuses for him. It's such a dangerous thing to do."

"That's what I told him!" Erica didn't care who was looking at her in the café. "He doesn't know the kind of danger he's dealing with. I'm sitting here thinking I hate him and I never want to see him again and then on the other hand, I don't know what I'd do if something happened to him because he tried to hustle the wrong person."

"We'll figure it out," Billie said. "Come on over. You can stay here until you can stand to look at him again."

Billie hung up the phone floored by what she'd just heard. Sherise was out of her mind. What did that girl think she was doing? She had a child with Justin!

Billie began to call her but decided against it. She didn't want to talk to Sherise right now. She was probably panicking and needed a friend, but with Porter's infidelity so fresh in her mind, Billie didn't think she could be that friend to Sherise. At least not now. Now, she could only focus on Erica and the foolishness Terrell had created.

Sherise felt pure dread as she heard Justin walking up the steps of their house.

"Sherise!" he called out.

"In Cady's room!" she responded.

When he appeared in the doorway, he smiled at the sight of his wife sitting in the window with their baby happily cooing on her lap.

"Sorry I'm late," he said, walking over to them.

Cady jumped at the sight of him, raising her arms in the air. Justin leaned down to pick her up and planted several kisses on her lips.

Sherise couldn't stop the tears that came at the sight of them together. He loved Cady so much. She needed her daddy. And Sherise thought she might have ruined both their lives for a few moments of pleasure. She didn't know what she could do, should do, and it made her feel completely helpless.

"What's wrong?" Justin asked, noticing her tears.

She wiped them away as fast as she could, standing up. "Sorry, just a bad day at work. Things are piling up and . . ."

Suddenly, she was sobbing uncontrollably and Justin wrapping his free arm around her only made it worse. Why did he have to be so kind, so caring?

She leaned her head into his chest and could feel Cady pulling on her hair from behind. She knew there was nowhere in the world she wanted to be but here and no amount of power or connections was worth more than the comfort and love she was feeling now.

"Better?" Justin asked.

She lifted her head and turned to face him and Cady. Cady responded by smacking her on top of her head and laughing. Justin started laughing and Sherise couldn't help but laugh too, even though it was the last thing she felt like doing.

After extracting Sherise's hair from Cady's fingers, Justin went to the crib and placed Cady inside.

"It's a miracle," he said. "No protest."

"She's tired." Sherise came up behind him and wrapped her arms around him. "She'll be out in five seconds."

"Sounds like a good deal to me." Justin turned around and

wrapped his arms around her. He looked tenderly in her eyes. "Want to talk about your day?"

Sherise shook her head. "I just want to have a quiet dinner with my husband."

Justin kissed her on the forehead. "Look, baby. We'll figure this out. I love you and you love me and we both love Cady. I knew who you were when I married you and it's why I married you. You deserve Walter's position and—"

"Stop." She pushed away from him, turning her back to him as she returned to the window. "Stop being so . . . good to me."

Justin was clearly confused. "I . . . I'm sorry. Would you prefer I fight with you and be an asshole?"

"You're not an asshole," she said, turning back to him. "You're a wonderful, incredible man and I love you so much more than any career or position I could ever get."

Justin figured she was probably saying this because she'd had such a bad day at work, but he didn't care. It was what he wanted to hear and the look on her face, the pain she seemed to be feeling, made him believe her. But he loved her. He would believe anything she told him.

"Like I said," he added. "This is our family and we'll work it out."

She ran to him and hugged him as tight as she could this time. She was such a fool, but she wasn't going to go down without a fight. She was going to hold on to the man she loved and make a family for their baby.

Erica was fuming.

Jonah had been in and out of the office all morning and was acting as if nothing was wrong. She could tell from the awkward glance he gave her upon first coming in that he at least suspected she knew what was going on. She wasn't sure what she expected him to do. This was work and they were supposed to be working, but after everything that she'd found out last night, Erica just couldn't pretend nothing had happened.

Jonah had been back from a lunch meeting for a few minutes when Jenna left to attend a head assistant's meeting in the department. Erica decided it was now or never. She knocked on the door but didn't wait for permission before coming in. Sitting at his desk, Jonah was scrolling through his BlackBerry and looked up somewhat amazed at her audacity.

"I'm very busy right now," he said after a moment.

"I'll be quick," Erica said. She sat in the chair across from the desk.

Jonah placed his phone on his desk and took a deep breath as if he knew what was about to come. "Well?"

"I know everything," she said.

"I wish I could say the same," he answered back. "I'm still curious as to the meaning of life in general, but it must be nice to know—"

"You're joking with me?" she asked. "How can you joke about this?"

"Joking tends to lighten the mood and I felt this mood needed some lightening."

"Let me set the mood," she offered. "I know you're sleeping with Sherise and I know Terrell found out and was about to blackmail you."

"That's an inventive young man you've latched yourself onto."

"Is this why you hired me?" she asked. "To get close to Sherise?"

Jonah made a face that showed he didn't appreciate at all what Erica was insinuating. "I promise you my friendship with Sherise is not about you. It was a coincidence that she and I did business around the same time I brought you on."

"And just a coincidence that you started sleeping with her?"

Jonah hesitated a moment before answering. "Erica, this is an office. That is not a proper topic for an office."

Erica let out a lively laugh. "You've gotta be kidding me! You expect me to just shut up and mind my own business about it?"

"When it is none of your business, yes I do."

"I can't do that." Erica hopped up from her chair. "How can you expect me to ignore that you're sleeping with my best friend? My best married friend at that! Justin is my friend too, by the way."

Jonah was beginning to look very irritated, but Erica didn't care.

"You're married," she reminded him. "It's all just too disgusting to ignore. You should be ashamed of yourself. I thought you were someone I could respect. I thought you were someone that everyone admired and looked up to. Turns out you're just a weak man like every other man.

"And even if you're going to cheat on your wife," she continued, "can't you at least have enough respect for me that you would not choose someone who could interfere with our working relationship?"

From the look on his face, Erica felt certain Jonah was just a second from firing her. His expression was stone, his jaw clenched, and his eyes bore into her. Unwavering, she stood with her head held high.

But suddenly something changed and Erica wasn't sure what to make of it. Jonah's stoic expression softened and he began to shake his head. He looked away for a second before turning back to her.

"Sit down, Erica."

She stood where she was.

"Sit down," he ordered.

This time she did as she was told. He had the kind of voice that made you listen to his orders and not want to hear him repeat something a third time.

So, she thought, he must want her to be seated while he fired her.

"I am sorry," he said softly. "Erica, I . . . First of all, this had nothing to do with you. The last thing I wanted was to involve you in something like this."

Erica was caught off guard. "How . . . How could I not be? She's my best friend."

Jonah nodded. "It hurts me so much to see you look at me like this. I would have preferred you never know something like this about me. I want you to look up to me. I want you to admire me. Your opinion of me means so much."

Erica wasn't sure how to react. He seemed incredibly sincere, almost on the verge of getting very emotional, something she never expected to see in a man like Jonah.

"I am very ashamed," he said. "I hope you believe me when I tell you this was not intentional."

"I don't know," Erica said, not just thinking of Jonah, but of Terrell. "I'm not the most trusting person in the world and with everything that has happened, I just don't know who I can trust. Who can I believe? What's the truth and what's just a convenient lie?"

"I know," Jonah said. "You have a hard time trusting men. It's not your fault. It's mine."

Erica blinked. "What? Why would you . . ."

"Because I let you down." He got up from his chair and walked over to the bookcase behind his desk. "You deserved better and I wanted to be better for you."

Erica could tell he was looking at the picture of his mother again. Was she supposed to feel sorry for him? She didn't have it in her.

"Things happen," Jonah said. "You don't always make the best choices, but you just have to do . . ." He trailed off and seemed to be staring into space.

"Jonah?" Erica found his sudden silence eerie.

Clearing his throat, he turned back to her. "Terrell hasn't made it any easier."

"I'm not going to defend anything he's done," Erica said, "but I wasn't aware two married people having an affair was supposed to be easy."

"Did he explain to you what his plan is?"

"We haven't really talked in detail," she said. "But I don't think he plans to do anything now. Whatever happens, I can't say you won't deserve it."

"And you still think you want to marry this man?"

Erica's jaw dropped. "You want to give me advice on marriage?"

"This is not about me," he said. "It's about you and your future."

"Yeah," she said sarcastically. "Maybe I can kick Terrell to the curb and get lucky and marry a man like you."

Jonah walked over to her and sat in the chair to the left of her. "Erica, I don't want this to ruin our personal or professional relationship. I don't know how this is going to turn out, but . . ."

"You don't know? How about ending it?"

Jonah had a regretful expression on his face. "I'm sorry you've been adversely affected by my relationship with Sherise, but I won't let you tell me how to live my life."

"Fine." Erica stood up. "You do whatever you want, but this relationship is purely professional and nothing else. I'm not going to be your friend or whatever else you think you're making me by your little small talk and gifts."

He called her name once as she left the office, but Erica didn't turn back. She closed the door behind her, grabbed her purse from her desk and went to lunch. While she was surprised that she hadn't gotten herself fired, Erica wasn't really sure what that encounter with Jonah meant. It was more personal than she'd expected, but she made it that way by demanding he explain his sex life to her. She shouldn't care what happened to him, but Sherise was supposed to be her friend and Terrell was supposed to be her husband one day.

While she didn't have the stomach to deal with Sherise, who had already left her a dozen texts, e-mails, and messages since she kicked her out of the apartment yesterday, she knew that she couldn't hold off confronting Terrell any longer.

Sherise was trying very hard to focus on her work today. Her mind was all over the place. So much had happened in the past few days that it was difficult for her to even concentrate on what was in front of her face. But she didn't have any time to feel sorry for herself. There was a job, a husband, a baby, and life didn't stop so you can wallow in self-pity over your own mistakes no matter how disastrous those mistakes were.

Jonah didn't bother to knock on her office door at all even though it was partially open. When he stepped inside, he closed it sharply behind him.

"What?" Sherise was not at all expecting to deal with him today. She had been avoiding him as best she could, unable to deal with what she knew she had to do.

"I don't like being ignored," he said.

"You can't do this," she pleaded, rushing around her desk to face him. "You can't be here!"

"This is your fault," he said angrily. "I've been trying to reach you. I'm a very busy man, Sherise. Do you think I have time to chase after you?"

"I thought that was what you liked the most," she said.

Despite it not being her intention, her words seemed to arouse him as he immediately reached for her and pulled her into his arms. When he leaned in to kiss her, Sherise pushed away.

"Stop it," he ordered. "I want you. I miss you."

"It's only been a few days." Sherise freed herself from him and took a few steps back. She couldn't ignore the appeal of a man wanting her so badly that only a few days apart could make him seem ravenous, but she had to fight it.

"You don't miss me?" he asked.

Sherise couldn't believe he was doing this. "You're acting as if everything hasn't fallen apart."

"It hasn't," Jonah said confidently. "A blip in the road, yes, but—"

"A blip in the road?" Sherise was incredulous. "We've been found out. It's all over. We could both lose our marriages."

"We won't," Jonah said.

As he moved toward her, Sherise took a few more steps back. "No, it's too risky. Terrell is an idiot street thug and he found us out. Who else could?"

"We'll be more careful."

"Being more careful isn't going to do anything for me. My friends won't even talk to me. Jonah, this is just too much."

"Isn't that part of the excitement?"

"The risk of losing my husband and tearing my family apart?" she asked. "No, that is not exciting. And losing my friends' respect?"

Jonah got upset. "How many people are you telling?"

"If Erica knows, Billie knows. Besides, neither of them are answering my calls, so they're both mad at me."

"They'll get over it," he said dismissively. "Just make sure they don't tell anyone else."

"You don't understand," Sherise responded. "Those girls mean everything to me. We grew up together. We're sisters. We're closer than sisters."

"And that's why they'll get over it," he said. "Baby, you did exactly the right thing. Your girls are not going to tell Justin anything. They wouldn't do that to you. And I won't let Terrell blackmail you."

"He wasn't going to blackmail me," Sherise said. "He was after you."

"Whatever. That asshole isn't going to hurt me. I won't let him."

Sherise's brow furrowed. "What exactly do you mean by that? Either you're going to pay him whatever he wants or you're planning to do something to him. Are you planning to do something to him?"

Jonah's face was emotionless. "Nothing I don't have to."

Sherise sighed, not believing she was having this conversation. "You can't hurt him, Jonah. He's Erica's fiancé."

"She is not going to marry him," Jonah stated adamantly. "I won't let that happen."

Sherise was confused. "How do you intend to do that and why is who Erica marries any of your business?"

"Erica can do much better than him," Jonah said with a hint of emotion in his voice. "He'll only bring her down. He's a criminal, a thug. You don't want her to marry him, do you?"

"I want Erica to be happy," Sherise said. "Terrell makes her happy. You know what, Jonah? I need to know what the hell is going on with you and Erica."

"Nothing! I told you I'm not interested in her that way."

"I get that, but you *are* interested in her. You're upset over the marriage plans of an assistant you've had for a little over a month."

Jonah slammed his fist on her desk. "I'm upset because the woman I want is ignoring me! I'm upset because a piece of shit thug wants to blackmail me! I'm upset because someone who is in my confidence is supposed to be marrying that piece of shit thug and—"

The sound of the office door opening shut Jonah up, and Sherise felt panic set in as she saw her husband walk through the door.

"What's going on in here?" Justin asked. He came face to face with Jonah. "Why are you yelling at her?"

Refusing to answer Justin and without looking again at Sherise, Jonah turned and walked out of the office.

Son of a bitch! He was going to make her get out of this on her own.

"What's going on?" Justin asked again, approaching his wife. "Are you okay?"

"I'm fine," she answered, even though she was anything but. "It was just . . . He's a very difficult man to please."

Justin held her face in his hands and looked into her eyes. "What aren't you telling me, Sherise?"

She wanted to scream, but she wasn't going to. She wasn't going to give in to her fear. "He's not happy with my work. He's a tantrum thrower."

"I don't care," Justin said. "He can't yell at you like that. You have to tell Walter."

"No. I'm not going to go whining to my boss. I can handle this." Sherise moved away from him and sat down behind her desk. She took a deep breath.

"I'm going to talk to him," Justin said. "I don't care how powerful he is, he can't yell at you."

"What do I look like if my husband does my whining for me?" Sherise said. "Justin, please let me handle it. What are you doing here anyway?"

After not hearing a response, she turned back to him and was terrified by what she saw. It was doubt. Clearly he was doubting everything she just said. It was written all over his face and she felt like she was going to lose it.

"What is it?" she asked, her voice skipping a beat.

After a second, he said, "Men don't yell at you, Sherise. Especially not men who are so clearly attracted to you."

"So clearly?" she asked.

"It was obvious from the first second he laid eyes on you." Justin came and sat at the edge of her desk. "What's really going on here?"

"Isn't it obvious?" she asked, trying desperately hard not to show her panic. "I put on my little show for him, but after I was given the position, I stopped trying to impress him. I'm not as pretty to him as I was before."

"This is the danger of flirting your way to the top," Justin said. "I've warned you."

"I can handle myself," she said. "And I can handle Jonah Dolan."

Sherise was rubbing her temples with her hands when she felt Justin's hand come to her shoulder. She stopped and looked up at him. He loved her, she could see it in his eyes. All she could think was that she would die if she lost him.

Justin hated seeing his wife so upset. Whatever was going on, it was taking a huge emotional toll on her. It was his job to make her pain go away.

"You were right last week when you said what we have is more important than any position. I should have known something was wrong at work."

"I meant that, Justin." Standing up, she leaned into him and kissed him slowly on the lips, savoring the taste of him. "Not just because things are hard here. There are always hard times at work. I meant it because it's true. If it's what our family needs, I can slow down."

She would do that. She would do anything. But first, she had to figure out how to get Jonah out of her life.

When Sherise showed up at the outdoor café a couple of blocks from Billie's apartment, she could tell from the way Billie looked at her that this was going to be an ugly meeting. She was just happy that someone finally returned her call.

"I know what you're going to say," Sherise said as soon as she sat down on the sofa near the front window of the place.

"You don't really," Billie said. "And don't try to sweet talk your way out of this, Sherise. I don't have the patience and I know all your games."

Sherise felt defeated even before starting. "I'm not going

to try and make excuses. I'm just glad you're willing to talk to me. Erica won't."

"Can you blame her?"

"I get that you're both disappointed in me," she said. "Trust me, I'm beyond disappointed in myself."

"You cheated on Justin," Billie said. "After we warned you. We told you to watch out. You've done this before, Sherise. We warned you and you could've gotten in trouble. You didn't learn your lesson?"

Apparently, she didn't. Sherise couldn't believe this. She had cheated on her husband now, twice. Who was she? How could she do this?

"Please don't lecture me," Sherise said. "I know there is nothing but wrong on my part here. I know the signs were there. I was wrong to think that I had the strength to fight my attraction to Jonah. I failed. Okay?"

"It's not okay," Billie said. "Are you going to tell Justin?"

"No!" Sherise exclaimed. "No, Billie. He can't know. It will kill him. You have to promise. . . ."

"Remember who you're talking to," Billie said. "I was Justin not too long ago. Didn't I have a right to know?"

This only made Sherise feel worse. "I'm not Porter."

"Yes you are," Billie answered. She knew she was hurting Sherise's feelings, but she deserved it. "You have no idea how many painful feelings this has brought back to me."

"Porter lost you," Sherise said. "I can't lose Justin. What about Cady?"

"You're thinking about her now? Bad timing, Sherise."

Sherise waved away a barista who came to ask her if she wanted a drink. "Look," she said. "I know I fucked up, but I'm telling you, I am begging you not to tell Justin. This is between you, Erica, and me. We've kept our secrets all our lives. You can't tell me you're going to turn on me now."

Billie rolled her eyes. "I'm not going to tell him anything. I was hoping you would be willing to."

"Well, I'm not," Sherise said. "I've already hurt him enough. I won't let him know how much I failed him and I won't risk tearing Cady's family apart."

"So I guess there is nothing else to say," Billie said. "You're going to keep lying to your husband. Are you going to keep cheating on him too?"

"No," Sherise said. "Of course not. But getting rid of a man like Jonah isn't going to be easy."

"Again, something you should have thought of before."

"What can I do?" Sherise pleaded.

"With Jonah? I don't have any idea."

"No," Sherise said. "With you? How can I get your forgiveness?"

Billie reached out and placed her hand over Sherise's. "You know I love you, girl."

What they'd been through, their lives growing up together meant more than any mistake one of them could make. Billie knew that. She was angry now and would be for a while, but there wasn't a chance in hell she would turn her back on her sister.

"What about Erica?" Sherise asked.

"It will take her a longer time. She's dealing with Jonah every day now. This affects her more."

"I just wish she would agree to talk to me."

"There is something I need from you," Billie said, suddenly remembering her own issues. "But I don't think it's possible anymore."

"Anything!" Sherise was eager for the chance to do something right.

Billie replayed her conversation with Porter from last week and asked Sherise exactly what had been done.

Sherise leaned back on the sofa. "I have no idea. I told Jonah that Porter was making trouble for you and I needed to get him out of your life. He said the best way to get rid of Porter is to give him his own problems to focus on."

"Well, he certainly did that."

"This is good," Sherise said. "He's focused on his job. He won't be bothered with yours."

"Only problem is," Billie said, "he thinks I might have had something to do with it because you'd been asking around about him before this all happened."

"He has no proof."

Billie spoke cautiously, aware of the reaction she would get. "I kind of . . . kind of told him I would . . . try and find a way to . . ."

"Oh my God."

"I just feel like the point has been made," Billie said. "Is it possible to get Jonah to undo whatever he's done?"

"I can try and find out what he's done," Sherise offered, "but I doubt it will be undoable."

"Then never mind," Billie said. "If it means you have to keep him in your life for even a second longer, it isn't worth it."

Sherise wasn't sure if there was anything she could do, but she had a lifetime of making up to do with her friends. She decided this was as good a place as any to try to start making it happen.

13

Terrell was leaning against his car, playing a game on his phone when Christopher drove up. For some reason he just assumed that Christopher was coming to pick up Jonah and hoped that his own client would show up before Jonah came out. It had been more than a week since their last encounter outside the hotel and Terrell was still trying to figure out how to handle it, but with Erica gone, he couldn't get his head straight.

He'd expected to have been fired by now, but day after day he showed up for work and was sent to the Pentagon. He was wondering what Jonah was up to, but knew that there wasn't anything he could do. Erica had not come home yet and Terrell was sick to his stomach over it. As mad as he was at his loss of the obvious money-making opportunity Jonah's infidelity could bring, nothing compared to the empty feeling he had without Erica.

So what was he supposed to do? How was he supposed to play this?

Unfortunately, he wasn't going to get any extra time to figure it out because Christopher wasn't coming to pick up Jonah. He was dropping him off. After a short pause, Christopher came around the car and opened the back door.

"Dammit!" Terrell said under his breath. Placing his phone in his pocket, he stood up straight. He wasn't going to look like a punk next to this asshole even though he had to admit that Sherise's warnings bothered him a bit.

Jonah didn't hesitate. The second he stepped out of the car, he handed his briefcase to Christopher and made his way to Terrell. He had a look of purpose on his face and stood only a few inches from his would-be foe.

"Not going to run away this time?" he asked.

Terrell sneered. "I don't run away."

"So that wasn't you speeding off last week?"

"I don't know what you're talking about." Terrell looked past him as if he wasn't interested in anything Jonah had to say.

"Whatever you were planning isn't going to work," Jonah said. "Now that Erica knows about your little venture, I don't think you want to risk it. Because if you make even an attempt to blackmail me or Sherise, she'll find out."

"Who said anything about blackmail?" Terrell asked. "Maybe I'll just tell your wife or call the news."

Jonah laughed. "With what proof? Please. You need to stick to your street hustles, Terrell. You're not ready for the big time."

"Maybe you win the blackmail game," Terrell said, "but what you don't know about the streets is what a man from them will do for his woman. I don't know what the fuck your deal is with Erica, but I'm gonna find out."

Jonah's smirk faded. "Unlike you, I would never hurt Erica."

"Something is going on," Terrell said. "I don't know what it is, but if you hurt her, I'll bring the streets to your ass."

"It's a dangerous thing," Jonah said. "Threatening a man like me."

"That's my woman," Terrell said. "And I'll kill for her."

Jonah looked him up and down before saying, "I almost believe you." Without another word he walked away.

Terrell didn't feel any better. *Fuck the blackmail,* he decided something else concerned him. The second he mentioned Erica, Terrell noticed a change in Jonah. He got defensive and toward the end there, he wasn't sure, but it looked like Jonah got a little scared.

Was Erica in danger?

Sherise was the last person that Billie expected to see knock on her office door. "What are you doing here?" she asked.

"Wow," Sherise said. "Is it still that bad?"

"I'm sorry." Billie waved her in. "I was just surprised. Come in."

Sherise stepped inside and turned to Richard, who was already up and in front of her, holding his hand out.

"I'm Richard," he said.

"This is my friend Sherise," Billie said.

"I know," Richard said. "You're Justin's wife."

"Have we met?" Sherise asked, thinking he looked a little familiar.

"You saw me at the mall," he said, "but we weren't introduced. I've seen you here before. You're kind of hard to miss."

Sherise laughed, but fought the urge to flirt. It was like instinct to her, done without a thought, but she felt Billie staring her down. "Nice to meet you," she said flatly.

"Do you two need some privacy?" he asked.

"No," Sherise said. "I'm actually here to see my husband. I just thought I would stop by and see my girl's digs."

"Shared digs," Billie said. "Not as impressive as it may seem."

"I like it," Richard said.

"Walk me," Sherise requested.

Once in the hallway, Sherise told Billie what she had come here to tell Justin, and Billie couldn't believe it.

"Are you sure?" she asked as they arrived at Justin's department.

"No, not at all, but I have to do this. I have to save my marriage and get my focus back on what's important."

They stopped outside Justin's office and Billie could see the look of fear in Sherise's eyes. "You didn't want to do this," she said.

"I know," Sherise responded. "But I have to in order to fix things."

"I love you," Billie said, opening her arms wide.

Sherise hugged her and felt like she was going to cry.

There was a reason she stopped by Billie's office before going to Justin. For as long as she could remember, her strength was found in her girls. It was their support and their love that helped her make the good decisions and get over the bad ones.

"Hey, baby!" Justin waved her into his office while still on the phone.

Sherise met him halfway and gave him a big kiss before walking over to the sofa next to his desk. Her stomach was hurting and her chest felt tight, but she had to do this. She couldn't even have waited until they got home tonight. That was too much time for her to change her mind.

Justin quickly got off the phone and came over to his wife. He jumped on the sofa next to her with a wide smile on his face. He was always happy to see her on her rare visits to his office, but the look on her face told him this was not a visit for a quickie.

He gently ran his fingers through her hair, cupping her face with his hands. "What's wrong, baby? Jonah again?"

"No." She took his hand and placed it against her lips. She kissed his palm softly before placing it on her lap. "This is actually good news."

"Doesn't look like it."

She smiled. "Hard news, but good news."

He slid as close to her as he could get. "I can take it."

"I'm going to quit my job at the Domestic Policy Council."

She could see Justin begin to protest. "Before you say anything," she urged, "please listen. I've lost my way. I got so obsessed with winning everything that I didn't care about what I lost. You'll never have any idea how much I regret what has happened to us because of my greed."

"I knew who you were when I married you," he said. "You'll never be happy without a career."

"I didn't say I was giving up a career. I'm not crazy."

"But you're leaving?" he asked, unable to deny how happy he was to hear this. There was something about that job that told him it was a threat to their family. "Are you sure, baby? I told you we can work this out."

"That's what I'm doing," she said. "I'm working it out. If it's okay with you, I'd like to just focus on you and Cady for a while."

"Is that all right with me?" He leaned in and kissed her on the lips. "My beautiful wife devoting herself to me and our baby? I think I can bear it."

She went to kiss him again, but he leaned back.

"You have to want this," he said. "Because if it's just for me and to break this ice between us, I won't let you do it. You deserve to be happy too."

Sherise couldn't stop the tears that formed in her eyes. How could she have risked losing this man?

"With each second," she said, "I can't believe how much more I really want this."

When Erica walked into her apartment for the first time since walking out on Terrell, she found both him and Nate sitting on the sofa playing SEGA. Some things never changed.

Neither of them realized she was in the apartment until she slammed the door behind her.

Terrell jumped up from the sofa and started around it. He could tell from her cold stance that she wasn't here to make peace so he kept his distance, though he was so happy to see her.

"Hi," he said, sounding awkward.

"So you finally remembered where you live?" Nate asked, only bothering to nod his head in her direction before returning to his game.

"It's nice to see you too, little brother." Erica gave Terrell one last look before heading for the kitchen.

"We've run out of food," Nate said. " 'Cause you haven't bought any."

"I haven't been gone that long." Erica grabbed a can of pop from the refrigerator. When she turned around, Terrell was standing at the counter. He looked pitiful enough, but that wasn't going to move her.

"Are you . . . okay?" Terrell asked.

Erica shrugged, leaning against the refrigerator. Just seeing him made her angry again, but it also made her realize how much she missed him. She didn't know what she was going to do.

"Nate!" Terrell called back even though he kept his eyes on Erica. "Why don't you go hang in your room for a while?"

"What am I, twelve?" Nate got up from the sofa. "And when is anyone going to tell me what is going on?"

"No one is going to tell you anything," Terrell said, "because this is between me and Erica. We're dealing with something, but that's okay. We love each other more than anything and we're gonna work it out."

Erica couldn't divert her eyes from his as he spoke.

"Your sister knows I would give my life for her and I know I can't live without her, so no matter what the problem, even the big ones, we always figure out how to work it out. We've been doing it since the beginning and neither of us has put four years into this relationship to give up on it just because we hit a speed bump."

"This is more than a speed bump," she finally said, despite being touched by his declaration.

"Do you really need me to leave?" Nate asked. " 'Cause I'm feeling kind of invisible right now."

"Leave," both Terrell and Erica said in unison.

"You can't possibly think that would be enough," she said after Nate had left them alone.

"I know I have a lot of work to do," he said, "but I wanted to get that out before we talk. You did come home to talk, right?"

"I came here to talk, but I don't know what to say."

"Say anything," he said. "Yell, scream. Anything is better than silence. I missed you so much, baby."

After a short pause, Erica admitted, "I missed you too. But dammit, Terrell, how could you do this?"

He started walking toward her. "Baby, I just got caught up. You know how it is."

"Stop." She held up her hand to stop him. "And no, I don't know how it is. What I know is what you promised me."

"I made a mistake, but I've made them before and we got past them. You've made mistakes and we got past them."

"So you're trying to compare anything that has happened between us before to this?" Angry at the audacity, she slammed her pop on the counter. "You used me to get access to my new boss, one of the most powerful men in DC, to blackmail him and my best friend for money?"

"I had a relapse," Terrell confessed.

"Relapse my ass," she said. "This is more than a hustle. This is full-fledged criminal behavior. What the fuck?"

Terrell sighed, unable to come up with anything he could say. There was no defending what he had been planning to do even though he had the best of intentions.

"How can I trust you?" she asked. "You jeopardized my job, and—"

"Jonah didn't fire you, did he?"

"No," she said. "As a matter of fact, he . . . It was weird. He apologized to me . . . excessively. I went off on him and I was sure he was gonna fire me, but he ended up apologizing profusely and almost getting emotional. It was strange."

"He's always been that way around you," Terrell said.

Erica didn't know what exactly Terrell meant by that, but she was too preoccupied with how disappointed she was in him to even begin to deal with Jonah's odd behavior.

"So you finally decided you miss me," Jonah said when he answered his phone.

"You love to gloat." Sherise managed as sexy a voice as she could, even though she was very nervous.

"I've missed you," he said quietly into the phone. "I need to touch you, to feel you."

Sherise was surprised that she didn't have the same reaction to those words that she would have had a couple of weeks ago. Everything had changed. If only she could have felt this way before, none of this might have happened. But she knew she couldn't look back now. She had to focus on making amends.

"When can I see you?" Jonah asked.

"I don't know," she replied. "It's just really too risky, Jonah."

"I know it's more complicated now and we'll have to be even more careful. But it's not impossible. I'll do anything, Sherise. I have to see you."

"I do need something from you," she said.

"Anything," he repeated.

"Whatever it was you did about Porter Hass worked. I can't thank you enough."

"You can."

"What was it you did, exactly?"

"One of the partners at his law firm owed me a favor. I called it in and asked that he spread rumors about Porter's professionalism and possibly some personal dalliances that, if they were to come to light, could embarrass the firm."

Sherise spoke in the most seductive tone she could muster. "You're amazing, how you just get things done like that."

"I can get anything done," he said.

"Can you undo it?" she asked.

"Why the hell would you want me to do that?"

"I'm trying to make amends to my best friend, who is mad at me because of . . . us."

"To hell with her," he said. "You don't need her."

At first Sherise was angry, but hearing him say such a thing only confirmed for her that he was a big mistake, so she was grateful for it.

"I may not need her," Sherise said. "But I owe her. Can you do it?"

"It's impossible to undo," Jonah answered. "The rumors are out there."

"So you aren't willing to do anything," she said. "Then I guess I don't have time to see you."

"Wait." His tone was desperate and angry. "I don't appreciate you doing this to me, but I know I can fix this for you. When can I see you?"

"When you've fixed it." She hung up without another word.

Jonah was more famous than Terrell ever thought. After starting his research of the man, he realized there was an endless amount of information about him. He was a war hero, married into money, and impressed a lot of powerful people. He was no innocent, having made some enemies along the way, but most everything was a positive picture of a powerful man who was tailor made for a future in politics.

Terrell was frustrated. Nothing gave him anything he could work with to help find out why Jonah had such an interest in Erica. Sitting at the kitchen counter, he was just about to close the laptop when he decided to relive every conversation he had with Erica about Jonah. In the kitchen, in the bedroom, at the dinner table, and sitting on the sofa, she had given him little snippets into the man. Every little bit added up—the gifts, the stories about his family, the interest in her personal life.

He wasn't sure why but one conversation in particular kept coming back to him. It was the conversation he and Erica had about Jonah trying to set her up with someone who turned out to be his wife's cousin. Terrell picked up the recording device on the counter and played the part he had been playing over and over again, when Jonah was talking to his wife on the phone. What did he mean? Why was she so angry about Erica?

"What does it all mean?" he asked himself.

He went back online and looked for information on Jonah's life before he became the famous military hero. There wasn't much to see except that his mother was very important in the community when she died. Jonah was only seventeen. Terrell remembered how often Jonah spoke to Erica about his mother, about how her death changed him. Erica mentioned that Jonah decided to go into the military to get away from his father because they didn't get along after his mother died.

Terrell decided the best way to find out about a very young Jonah was to search for information on his mother. He searched for a moment and found something interesting at a Web site that devoted a page to her work with a charity feeding the homeless. There was a short description of her family, including:

Amelie Dolan's children have followed in her footsteps. Her twelve-year-old daughter, Heather, is an active member of Best Buddies, a group that works with disabled children. Her seventeen-year-old son, Jonah, spends weekends volunteering at Metzer Medical Center.

"What the fuck?"

Metzer Medical Center was where Nate worked!

Although it could clearly be a coincidence, Terrell refused to believe it was. He grabbed his phone and dialed Nate's number. He picked up after a few rings.

"What's up, man?"

"How did you get your job?" Terrell asked immediately.

"What?" Nate sounded confused. "What are you . . ."

"I'll explain later!" Terrell was yelling now. "How did you get a job at that hospital?"

When Nate told him the answer to his question, Terrell almost dropped the phone.

"For the love of Christ!" Billie yelled out the second she reached her apartment.

Standing in front of the door was Porter, leaning against the wall swinging his keys around his fingers.

"Will you ever go away?" she asked.

Porter smiled, offering his arms for the grocery bags that were in her hands.

She handed him one of the bags just so she could have a free hand to open her front door. Once inside, she grabbed the bag back and pressed her hand against his chest, pushing him back.

"You're not welcome inside," she said.

"I want to talk to you," he said. "Also thank you."

"What for?" she asked, still blocking the entry.

"My boss told me that they may have gotten some bad information and the managing partners are willing to consider me for a partnership again."

"Good for you." Billie knew Sherise would come through. Even with all she was going through, she would always do what Billie needed.

"One problem," he added. "He said they'll consider me next year, not this year as originally promised."

"It's still good news."

"Are you gonna let me in or what?"

Billie rolled her eyes, stepping aside. She didn't want to be alone with him. She knew what her weakness was and she wasn't going to take another step backward.

"So what did you do?" he asked.

"I helped you." Billie placed the bags on the kitchen counter. "Just like I said I would."

"Billie, no offense, but you don't have the pull for this."

Billie looked at him. "You don't know everything about me."

"I'm gonna find out," he said. "I'll talk to Sherise."

"No you won't." Billie laughed. "You're scared to death of her."

Porter frowned as if upset that this truth was clear. "Are you gonna help me or what?"

"I did help you," she said.

"I want to be reviewed this year like originally planned, not next. Whatever you did, you need to do it harder so I get back to where I was."

Billie took a deep breath and exhaled before turning to Porter. She saw the expectation and self-centered expression on his face.

"No."

Porter blinked, seeming surprised at her reaction. "But you have to."

"No, I don't. I didn't have to do what I did."

"It was your fault they—"

"It was your fault!" Billie knew she stumped him with the force of her voice. She pointed her finger at him. "This is all your fault. If you hadn't used Tara against me, thrown your mistress in my face, tried to seduce me every chance you weren't trying to blackmail me, none of this would have happened."

Porter scowled, but didn't have a response.

"So no," she continued. "I won't help you get your review for partner this year instead of next. I'm not going to help you with anything anymore."

Porter laughed. "You don't hold all the cards in this, Billie. I still . . ."

"Try it," she warned. "I dare you. You saw what I can do. In just a matter of days of asking I destroyed your career and in just a couple of days after asking, I revived it."

"By spreading lies," Porter said.

"That's just the thing." Billie was waving her finger at him with a playful smile on her lips. "I was thinking about what your firm must have heard about you to make such a drastic change. It got my mind going. I've seen a lot and heard a lot. The years we dated, the years we were married, and since."

"Bullshit."

She ignored him. "I was thinking of all the things you've done to bend the rules to win a case, to get a client, or other things like blackmail and getting a paralegal to give you information about lawyers in a rival firm."

She could see the expression on Porter's face flattening. She didn't expect to hear "bullshit" come out of his mouth again.

"And I realized," she continued, "how much ammunition I have against you. Before, I wouldn't use it because I just wasn't that kind of person. But you saw how easily I got rid of Callie. I'm different now, Porter, thanks to you. I have a lot of ways I can deal with you now, and I'm no longer afraid to use them."

"Look, Billie. I just want—"

"Aren't you listening to me?" she asked. "I don't care what you want anymore. I don't care what you need. I don't care about your whore of a girlfriend or you. And if you think for one second you're going to use Tara to hurt me, I will make you pay."

Porter was shaking his head as if disbelieving everything. "You wouldn't do that."

"A few days ago you might have been right, but I now realize a friend did something very difficult, something I know will make her problems worse, just to make me happy. She did it even though she didn't want to. That friend asked only one thing of me. It's to be strong enough to fight for a chance to get on with my life."

"By ruining mine?" Porter asked.

"If you bring it to that," she said decisively.

"Billie." His voice was low and soft as he took a step toward her. "It doesn't have to be like this."

"You're right." She walked right past him and went to her front door. "And it won't be as long you don't make me take it there. Our relationship, every single aspect of it, is over. I want you out of my apartment and my life. For the last time."

Porter acted as if he was still unconvinced, but he walked toward the door anyway. "You won't be able to stay away from me, Billie."

"You just watch me," she said before slamming the door in his face.

Billie stood at the door for a few minutes trying to come to terms with what she just did. She wasn't happy about being the kind of person who threatened to ruin someone's life, but she couldn't deny that it was also empowering. Maybe Sherise was onto something. For the first time in a long time, Billie felt like she was in control.

She felt like she was free of Porter for good.

★   ★   ★

Terrell stayed out of Christopher's view as he waited for Jonah to come out of the Capitol Hill Club. Christopher had been waiting in front of the restaurant for about fifteen minutes and Terrell knew if he saw him, he'd know something was wrong.

It would have been easier for Terrell to wait until he had to pick up a client whose schedule coincided with Jonah's, but that wasn't going to be for two more days and Terrell couldn't wait for this. So he checked Erica's phone for Jonah's schedule and found out he was having lunch at the club.

He was standing across the street near the Metro entrance, waiting for the right time, and finally, he saw it. As Jonah exited the building with two men, both in military uniform, Terrell started across the street. He got across the street without Christopher noticing him.

Jonah was shaking the hands of both men when he saw Terrell walk toward them. Terrell could tell from the look on his face that he wasn't at all happy, but he smiled long enough to send the two men on their way before Terrell reached him.

"What in the world do you think you're doing?" Jonah asked.

"Terrell!" Christopher came up behind him and grabbed him by the arm. "What are you doing here?"

Terrell jerked his hand away. "I need to talk to Jonah. You can stay if you'd like, but I think he'd prefer you give us some space."

Jonah eyed Terrell for a few seconds with a look of disgust on his face before telling Christopher to go wait at the car. He led Terrell away from the front of the club toward a tree on the corner.

Jonah started in on him right away. "I don't know what the fuck you think—"

"I know," Terrell said. "I know."

"You know what?" he asked. "And this better not be about Sherise because that—"

"About Erica." Terrell could see the expression on his face change. He had his attention now. "I told you I'd find out. It wasn't that hard. I just had to pay attention."

"You don't want to do this," Jonah warned.

"You sought her out," Terrell said. "Erica was confused about why she was hired and you convinced her that it was word of mouth. But it wasn't. You wanted her near you. You wanted to get close to her and learn about her. You brought her gifts and tried to get her to like you, to open up to you."

"I'm warning you."

Terrell ignored his warning. "Your wife gave you away. She knows too and she didn't want Erica anywhere near you. She didn't want you bringing Erica closer to her family. That's why she didn't want you setting her up with her cousin."

Jonah seemed genuinely surprised. "How the fuck do you know that?"

Terrell could see that he got one in there and had the advantage now.

"Erica's brother works at Metzer Medical Center," he said. "He reminded me how he got that job. They loved his mom there. She'd been working there, in the children's ward, as a receptionist, for most of her life."

Jonah was looking around now, as if nervous someone else could hear.

"She was working there twenty-six years ago," Terrell went on. "The same time you volunteered there. So tell me, Jonah. Did you run off to the marines when you found out you got the black girl pregnant? And why did you decide now you wanted to play secret daddy to—"

"Enough!"

"Are you Nate's dad too?"

Jonah brought his fist just inches from Terrell's face before realizing where he was and regaining his composure. He straightened his tie and stood up tall.

"No," he said. "I'm not. And as far as anyone will ever be concerned, I'm not Erica's father either."

"But I know the truth," Terrell said.

"And you can disappear," Jonah said. "Do you doubt that I can destroy this pitiful thing you call a life in a second?"

Terrell stood tall. "I'm not afraid of you."

"You should be," Jonah said. "Since you're such a good researcher, look up the name Riley Alterson. I'll give you a hint. He's never actually committed a crime, but he's in a prison in Michigan for the next twenty-five years because he crossed me. Try Mena Wilkerson. I'll give you another hint. No one has seen her since she tried to blackmail me after we had a one-night stand."

Terrell noticed the look that came over Jonah's face was one of a man who felt like he was beyond the law, had limitless power. He was just like Sherise said he would be.

"Alex Carter," Jonah added. "He flirted with my wife and I gave him an IRS nightmare that ended up making him put a gun in his mouth. Paul Richards screwed me over in a deal and he still can't figure out how he got on Homeland Security's watch list. He can't even fly on a plane to visit his Mommy only three states away."

Jonah tilted his head to the side a bit with a sly smile that made it seem like he was thoroughly enjoying this.

"Now you," he said. "Your background is shady enough to make this fun for me. If you've taken a blood test in the last ten years anywhere, I can get my hands on your DNA. Maybe I'll make you a rapist or just a murderer. Or maybe I'll save myself the time and just make you disappear."

Terrell swallowed hard, unable to hide his fear. "You're crazy."

"No," he corrected. "Not crazy, but I am powerful. I am a man with plans and I will get rid of anybody who tries to put obstacles in my way. I like my relationship with Erica just the way it is and you're not going to do anything to change it."

Jonah placed a hand on Terrell's shoulder, but Terrell quickly jerked it away.

"I hope we're clear," Jonah said. "Erica has been through enough in her life. I'd hate to make things worse for her and I'm sure you wouldn't want to either."

14

Sitting on a lawn chair in the backyard while Cady played on a blanket on the grass, Sherise was very relieved to get the text from Billie saying **Thank you!** She knew that Jonah had come through. Now all that was left was to get Jonah out of her life. She was under no impression that this would be easy, but she had to go into it without any hesitation or compromise. Accepting that this would take time would only assure that it would take forever.

"Where have you been?" Jonah said as soon as he picked up the phone. "You were supposed to call me yesterday. I have to see you."

She wasn't happy to hear the tone of his voice. He seemed already anxious and upset, but there wasn't anything she could do about that.

"I'm calling you now," she said. "Look, Jonah, I'm not going to meet you tonight or any other night."

There was an annoyed sigh on the other end of the phone. "We've been through this before, Sherise. I know you're scared, but . . ."

"I'm not scared," she said, "I'm married. And I'm not going to see you again. This is over. I'm sorry. I know this—"

"This is not over." Jonah's voice was deep and threatening. "It just started, Sherise, and you know how good it's been."

"It should have never started." She made certain to erase any hint of doubt in her voice. "There's a strong attraction between us, based partly on a physical chemistry and partly on ambition and greed. Neither are excuses to cheat on our spouses."

"I've done everything you wanted," Jonah said. "What more do you want?"

"Nothing more." Sherise couldn't play around with this. She knew the longer this took, the more likely she'd be to change her mind and she couldn't do that. She couldn't afford to. She was moving in the right direction.

"We're both adults," she said. "And the situation is complicated enough, so let's not make it more so."

"You don't want to stop seeing me," Jonah said. "I know it. I feel it. What's making you do this?"

"You need to put your ego in check for a few seconds and listen to what I'm saying. This relationship is over."

"After I did one last fucking favor for you?" he asked sharply and bitterly.

"I think we both got what we wanted out of this," she said. "We went into it from the beginning knowing what this was and wasn't."

"You got what you wanted," he said. "And now you think you can just walk away?"

"Jonah," she sighed. "Let's not make this worse. I came very close to having my husband find out everything about us. I have a baby."

"God dammit!" There was a short silence. "Sherise, just meet with me. We'll talk about this. We shouldn't do this over the phone."

"No," she said. "This is going to be our last conversation, Jonah. Ever."

"You forget the project," he said. "We work together."

"No we don't," she said. "I'm off the project. It's going to be put on hold."

"I decide what gets put on hold," he said. "Sherise, you're not going to call all the shots here."

"I don't need to call all of them," she answered back. "I just need to call the ones that involve me. This is over. We're not going to speak again after this."

"We will if you expect to keep your job," he threatened.

"You're threatening me?"

"Sherise, I don't want it to come to that, but I want to see you and I'm not taking no for an answer."

"Thank you," she said. "Thank you for making this even easier. And you can't fuck up my career because I'm quitting."

"Bullshit!"

"You'll find out soon," she said. "You're going to leave me alone and you're not going to lay a hand on Terrell."

"Is that what this is about?" he asked before his voice began to sound like that of a man unhinged. "He told you? Listen to me, Sherise. If any of you tell Erica or anyone else about this, I will make life a living hell for you. I'll make you wish you'd never met me. Terrell will fucking disappear."

Sherise was too shocked to respond. She wasn't even sure what just happened. She opened her mouth but no words came out. She wouldn't dare tell him she didn't know what he was talking about. She was too scared.

"Are you there?" Jonah finally asked in a calm tone, as if he hadn't made his last statement.

"You want me to keep quiet about Erica," she said, trying not to sound as uncertain as she felt. "Then just stay away from me."

"You don't make the rules," Jonah said. "You and Terrell think you can tell me how it's going to be? I'm gonna decide how this goes. You better warn him."

"Erica . . ." she said cautiously, "if she found out . . ."

"She won't," he said. "Dammit, Sherise. Why did you have to go and mess this up? It was so good."

"It was wrong," she said. "And it's over."

She hung up quickly, feeling a quiver of fear in her stomach. She should be grateful to get a view of this side of Jonah because it made it easier to end things with him, but she wasn't grateful. She was scared for herself and especially scared for Erica. She had to find out what the hell was going on.

Her hands were shaking as she dialed quickly.

"What do you want?" Terrell said with an annoyed tone.

Sherise's tone didn't hide her exasperation. "I just got off the phone with Jonah and he freaked me the fuck out."

"I'm working right now," he said. "I'm not interested in conversations between you and your lover."

"Stop saying that!" she demanded. "That's over. He's not my lover. He threatened me and he threatened you."

Terrell pulled his car over to the side of the road. "What did you do?"

"What did I do? He just went crazy. He seems to think you told me something about Erica and he threatened the both of us."

"You told him you didn't know, right?"

"I didn't feel like that was an option."

"Why not? Dammit, Sherise, that man is fucking crazy."

"Exactly," she said. "I didn't need any more of a disadvantage than I already had."

"Don't fuck with him," Terrell warned. "He's fucking crazy."

"You said that already. Now tell me what's going on."

"The hell I will," Terrell said. "Look, just stay away from him and don't bother him about it."

"You don't have to tell me to stay away from him, but you will tell me what the hell is going on. I always knew there was something weird about his interest in Erica. What is it?"

"I'm handling this," Terrell said.

"I'll call her right now!"

"Don't!" Terrell yelled. "Fuck, Sherise. Why did you have to get into this?"

"You started all of this with your snooping around. It's my fault that I'm in this too, but Erica didn't do anything and I'm not going to have my girl vulnerable to a crazy, powerful, and vindictive man."

"He's not going to hurt her," Terrell said. "Just let me—"

"Terrell! It may not seem like it, but the more people who know, the safer we are."

Terrell laughed. "You don't know some of the shit he's done to people who crossed him."

Sherise had no patience left. "Boy, I'm about to reach through this phone and choke you to death. What is going on?"

After a moment, Terrell reluctantly told Sherise the truth about discovering Jonah was Erica's father. It took longer than it should between Sherise's screaming and questions, but he finally got it all out, including Jonah's threats if Erica or anyone else found out.

"You don't have any exact proof, though." Sherise couldn't believe what she was hearing. It had to be wrong. It had to be.

"I think his reaction was proof enough," Terrell said.

"All this time Erica thought Nate's dad was her dad. Why would Achelle do that to Erica? Keep that from her?"

"I'm thinking she didn't have a choice," Terrell said. "I'm thinking Jonah found out he got her pregnant and abandoned her. He joined the marines and never looked back. It was easier to just make Erica think that Nate's dad was hers. Only one set of questions to answer."

"Poor baby." Sherise still wanted to doubt it but it made everything else make sense. His intentions toward Erica had never been sexual, but they had been personal. "I have to call Billie."

"No!" Terrell yelled. "Have you not heard anything I've said? What are you, crazy?"

"I know what I'm doing," Sherise said. "She won't tell anyone, but I have to let her know so we can figure out what to do."

Terrell wanted to strangle her. She was going to fuck up everything. This was not a child's game and her silly flirtations weren't going to get anyone out of anything this time. "I know that Erica is your best friend and all that shit," he said, "but she is my woman. She's my fiancée. We're getting married. I have priority when it comes to issues like this."

"She's more than my best friend," Sherise said, but didn't bother saying more. If Terrell didn't understand what existed between them by now, he never would.

"I will handle this!" Terrell yelled.

But Sherise had already hung up.

"What is going on?" Billie said as she rushed to Sherise's table at Pizza Paradiso, a restaurant in the Georgetown area. When a frantic Sherise had called her, Billie could barely understand anything she was saying. She knew she needed to meet Sherise at this restaurant immediately and not tell Erica.

"You sounded crazy on the phone," Billie said. She could see from the look on Sherise's face that she was very upset. "It's Jonah, isn't it? Oh my God! Did Justin find out?"

"No." Sherise was biting her nails. "Sit down."

Billie knelt down to Cady in her stroller to give her a kiss. Cady reached out to her and Billie picked her up before sitting down.

"So what's up?" Billie asked as she bounced Cady on her knee. "And why can't I call Erica?"

"I need to talk to you first," Sherise said. "Besides, she still isn't talking to me."

"She's just mad," Billie said. "It never lasts that long. When was the last time you tried to talk to—"

"Jonah is Erica's father." Sherise didn't have the mind to explain things in a logical manner, so she just let it go.

For a second, Billie thought maybe the pressure of her life right now must be driving Sherise crazy. She grabbed the glass of water Sherise was drinking and sniffed it. It was just water.

"I'm not drunk," Sherise said. "I'm telling you, Terrell did some investigating and he found out why Jonah is so obsessed with Erica."

"Obsessed?" Billie asked. Had she missed something? "You're not making any sense."

"He confronted Jonah and Jonah threatened him and then he threatened me."

Billie was confused. "Why did he threaten you? What did . . . Wait, what are you saying?"

Sherise tried her best to coherently relay what she'd learned only a couple of hours ago herself. Although clearly shocked, Billie was taking the news better than she expected. When she was done, Billie looked away as if trying to work something through in her mind.

"My instinct says to ask for proof," she finally said, "but I think we're beyond that. There are too many unanswered questions, though."

"I'm scared," Sherise said. "What if what he told Terrell was true about what he's done to people?"

"We can assume it is, to be safe," Billie said. "But we have to tell Erica."

"No." Sherise grabbed Billie's phone away from her as she started to dial. "He said not to tell Erica. He doesn't want her to—"

"That's why we have to tell her." Billie snatched the phone back. "If everything you're saying is true, then he cares about her. It's a fucked up way to show it, but he won't hurt her. Her knowing that you and Terrell know will keep you safe."

Sherise was shaking her head. "You didn't hear his voice, Billie. He was . . ."

Billie held up a hand to silence her while she called Erica and told her, in a convincingly frantic voice, that there was an emergency and she had to come to the restaurant immediately. After she hung up, her voice returned to normal.

"It's going to be okay," she said. "Jonah is just worried about his future plans. He wants to run for president some day, but he also doesn't want Erica out of his life. This is the best plan. Trust me."

Sherise thought she was making some sense, but wasn't sure this was the best way to go about it. Trusting someone had always been a problem for Erica. After knowing what Jonah had been up to, she would certainly cut him out of her life. He would blame them and then what?

Erica saw Billie first, but the second she saw Sherise sitting behind her, she stopped. What were they up to? A forced makeup? She approached them and slapped her purse on the table.

"Did you fake an emergency to get me over here to talk to her?" she asked Billie.

"It *is* an emergency," Sherise said.

"Sit down," Billie ordered. "And before we get started, you have to bury this thing between you and Sherise."

"Don't tell me what I—"

"She made a mistake," Billie said. "Yeah, it kind of messed with your life a bit, but she didn't try and hurt you, and she's hurting more than either of us can imagine now. She's trying to fix it."

"I am," Sherise offered.

Billie placed her hand over Erica's on the table. "We're sisters and shit is about to go down, so it's over. You understand?"

Erica rolled her eyes a bit before nodding. She turned to Sherise. "I'm not really mad at you anymore anyway. I was just mad at the whole situation and you were a part of it."

"I know," Sherise said. "I fucked up, but I can't lose you, Erica."

"No one is losing anyone," Billie said. She would usually

love to see these makeup sessions between Erica and Sherise, who were always fighting, but there was no time for that.

"Is this your emergency?" Erica asked.

"We found something out," Billie said. "It's about Jonah . . . and you."

"What?" she asked with trepidation.

"Terrell was doing a little snooping around," Sherise started.

"Oh, shit!" Erica couldn't believe this. "What is he up to now?"

"He was just looking out for you," Billie said. "No hustle."

"Fine." She sat back in the seat, already pissed before even knowing what was going on. "Tell me."

"He was concerned about Jonah's . . . personal attachment to you," Billie said. "He wanted to know what that man was about."

"I told Terrell," Erica said. "Jonah just likes to know his team. He's—"

"No," Sherise said. "The gifts, all that talk about your personal life, your family. What about trying to set you up with someone?"

Erica didn't like where this was going. "Just tell me what's going on."

"Don't ask me how," Billie said, "but he found some evidence that . . . Baby, your mother wasn't telling you the truth about your father."

"What does this have to do with my mother?"

"When Achelle was working at Metzer Medical Center," Sherise said, "Jonah was a volunteer there."

"Are you kidding?" Erica was getting an eerie feeling. "Why? How does he know that?"

"Jonah left for the marines right after Achelle got pregnant," Sherise said.

Erica swallowed hard, trying to pretend like her mind wasn't going where it actually was. "What? Are you suggesting . . . Oh my god. You're both crazy. I know who my father is."

Sherise was shaking her head. "That's Nate's father. Your mother just thought it would be easier for you to think you had the same deadbeat dad."

"Think about it," Billie said. "Look in a mirror, girl. You're about eight shades lighter than your mother or Nate."

"That doesn't mean anything," Erica said. "My mother said I'm the same color as her relatives in—"

"In the few times you've ever seen your dad," Sherise said, "did he show any interest in you at all?"

"That's because he's a deadbeat, but . . ." Erica felt her chest tightening. "You have no evidence that Jonah even knew my mother!"

"We don't need it," Sherise said. "Terrell confronted him about it and he threatened him."

Erica was speechless. She couldn't believe what she was hearing.

"He thought I knew," Sherise said, "and he threatened me. He's your father, Erica. He sought you out. He's trying to connect with you. He's trying to take over your life by getting Terrell out of it."

"No," she said. "No. No. He's not . . . Why wouldn't he tell me?"

"Probably for the same reason he ran off and joined the marines when he found out Achelle was pregnant," Billie said. "Maybe because it's a little too messy for someone of his stature seeking political office."

"Maybe his cold fish of a wife," Sherise said, "who bankrolls him won't let him. All his money is from her and her family."

"But—but why wouldn't Mama tell me?" Erica remembered the awkward times she asked for more information about her father. Her mother would clam up and look upset, so she just stopped asking. They were figuring out how to survive without him anyway.

"Maybe she was afraid to," Sherise said. "Maybe she was paid not to tell you. Fuck, maybe he threatened her too."

Billie squeezed Erica's hand as she felt it shaking underneath hers. "I know you're in shock, but you have to try and think clearly about this."

Erica was thinking clearly, and as much as she didn't want to believe it, it made too much sense for her to ignore. She felt panic settling in on her. "What is going on?" she asked, feeling herself begin to choke up. "Why are you doing this to me? Why are you telling me this?"

"Because we need you," Sherise said.

"For what?" Erica shot up from her seat, unsure of what to do with herself.

"To control Jonah," Billie said. "Despite his desire to keep you a secret, he clearly wants a relationship with you."

"Control him? Shit, I don't even know him."

"Whether you want anything to do with him after this is your choice," Billie said. "But you have to let him know that you know. That's the only way to make sure that Terrell, Sherise, and I won't get hurt because we know his secret."

Erica looked at Sherise. "Did he really threaten you and Terrell?"

Sherise nodded. "Terrell got it worse, but yeah . . . I'm scared of him now. Now that you know, you might be able to keep us safe because he knows you care about us. He knows he'll lose you if something happens to us."

"Why would he give a shit?" Erica asked. "He was fine with me being nothing to him for twenty-five years. So I tell him I'm not going to accept his stupid presents anymore if he hurts my friends? He won't care."

"He will," Sherise said. "Trust me. I can't explain how I know, but now that he's got you back in his life, he's not going to want to lose you."

"So I gotta just get over this shit and go to work for you?" Erica asked. She didn't know what she was saying really. She was just so upset.

Billie stood up and grabbed Erica by the shoulders. She could see the girl was losing it. "You don't have to get over it," Billie said. "But we need your help. Remember this. We're sisters. We help each other survive and deal with all our shit even when it's painful. This is how we got to where we are and this is how we keep going. Being there for each other."

"This is just too much," Erica said. "It's just too much. I gotta go."

When Erica ran out of the restaurant, Sherise stood up. "We have to go after her."

"No," Billie said. "She just needs time. She'll take care of it. Erica always comes through for us."

Sherise didn't doubt that. She just wasn't sure, despite what she'd said, that Erica was enough.

Erica heard voices behind the door to Jonah's Leesburg, Virginia, home. They knew it was her at the door, but no one was coming out. Instead of pressing the doorbell again, this time she banged on the front door.

Within a second, Jonah opened the door with a confused look on his face. "What are you doing here?" he asked. "It's Sunday night."

It had taken Erica a little while to get out there. Despite her aversion to driving, she rented a car from Zipcar, a local company that placed cars throughout the city that people could rent to drive locally for a short while and return at various spots. She had Jonah's address because she had ordered items for him to be delivered to his home. With traffic it took an hour and a half to make it to his exclusive neighborhood in Leesburg. Plenty of time for her anger and resentment to build up.

To no surprise, his home was the best on the block. It had

to be at least eight thousand square feet with a traditional white column and red brick colonial look. The finely mani-cured front lawn included a small Belgian sculpture fountain.

"What's the matter?" Erica asked. "Don't want anyone in your neighborhood seeing me here?"

Jonah looked into her angry eyes and sighed. "Who was it who told you? Sherise or Terrell?"

"It should have been you."

Jonah nodded. "Yes, but that wasn't really an option."

"I thought you were a man with endless options?"

Jonah looked over his shoulder as he took a step outside onto his porch. He closed the door behind him.

"She knows, doesn't she?" Erica asked, pointing to the house. "That's why she looked at me with those cold eyes. She knows I'm your daughter."

"Yes, she does." Jonah reached out to Erica, but she slapped his hand away. "Erica, you have to understand, this is not the way I planned—"

"Save it," she said. "I know this is not the way you planned on telling me because you weren't planning on telling me at all. You just wanted me to think you were some great guy who was amazingly nice to a nobody like me."

"You're not a nobody," he said sternly. "You're a remark-able woman just like your mother and—"

"Don't you dare!" Erica pointed a warning finger at him. "Don't you dare mention her."

"I cared very deeply for Achelle," Jonah said. "I know you must be thinking I didn't, but I did. We only spent one night together, but it was after an entire summer of connecting and closeness."

"Are you trying to romanticize this?" she asked. "You must think I'm a fool or you just plan to skip over how you deserted her when she was pregnant."

"I didn't desert her," he insisted. "At that time, I didn't ex-pect much from the relationship. We were from different worlds and we found a common place at that hospital and it led to genuine affection. That night . . . just happened and before we could talk about it or deal with it, my mother died."

Jonah's expression stilled and grew serious. "I worshipped her and my world fell apart when she died. I was grieving over her and dealing with my father, who caused me nothing but pain. He didn't give a shit about her. She was his wife!"

"You're not really in a position to judge who is a good husband," Erica said.

Jonah nodded. "You're right, but I do care for my wife and I would be devastated if she died. He barely shed a tear when my mother died. It only made me angrier. Achelle tried to help me, but I pushed her away. I pushed everyone away, but I swear to you, Erica. When I left for the military, I was being a coward, but I did not know she was pregnant. I was just trying to get away from the world that I knew."

"You never contacted her or anything? You say you cared about her."

"I just wanted to pretend like my life was starting over. I barely even talked to my sister. By the time I came home, I was moving on with my life. I had met my wife and we were building a life together."

"And that's it?" Erica wasn't so sure she believed him, but he did seem sincere.

"One day about fifteen years ago, I went to the hospital for a charitable event and I saw her. I couldn't believe she was still there. There was a boy there and he was calling her mommy. I realized that she had her life now and I had mine, and trying to reconnect with her wasn't a good idea anymore."

"She didn't fit so neatly into your new life," Erica said.

"You have to understand," he said. "She was an ex-lover to me. I had no idea you even existed. But yes, my career and my wife's connections had opened up a new world for me and a promise of a future that I wanted more than the chance to rekindle a summer romance."

"So where do I come in?" she asked impatiently. "And please, don't try to make this some love story too."

"It was just fate," he said with a smile. "It's actually quite remarkable, Erica, the way I found you. We knew we were going to get rid of our triple A so I told Jenna to look for another one. She had a list of names on her desk and I happened to look at it when I was there, talking to her. I'm not lying, Erica. That's how I found you. Just looking down for a second. Don't you see how prophetic that was?"

"You saw my last name," she said.

"I saw your middle name next to your last name," he said.

That was her mother's name.

"Achelle is an uncommon name," he said, "and one that I immediately remembered. I thought it was just going to be some odd coincidence that I could laugh at, but when I realized who you were . . . and then I saw you."

"You saw me?"

"I had a private investigator to find out who you were," he said. "He took some pictures of you and sent them to me. Didn't you notice?"

"Notice what?" she asked.

"You look just like her," he said.

"My mother?"

He shook his head as his face, his eyes softened. "No, my mother."

"How sweet," she said coldly. "It touched you enough to want me in your life, but not enough to tell anyone who I was."

"I told my wife," he said. "It's complicated, Erica."

"It's not complicated at all," she said. "She doesn't want anyone to know you have a little brown daughter."

"It's not about you being half black," he said. "It's about you being—"

"You can say it," she said. "Illegitimate."

"There are plans being made for me," he said. "Plans that a

lot of people are investing a lot of time and their entire careers into."

She laughed. "You say it like it's out of your control. You want pity? You want me to feel sorry for you that you had to keep me in the dark?"

"I've never asked for pity," he said firmly. "And I never will. I made the choice to keep you a secret and have you close. I want you in my life, but I've fought very hard to get where I am and go where I'm going."

Erica laughed at the words, thinking of what Billie had just said to her earlier that afternoon, but her reaction confused Jonah.

"I know I have a lot to make up for," he said. "But I swear, I didn't know about you until earlier this year. But I can be a father to you. Even though I know you're not a child, I can be a father to you."

"As long as I don't tell anyone," she said. "As long as I stay your shameful little secret, your messy past, we could have a wonderful relationship."

He seemed disappointed. "I know it's not an ideal situation, but I want you in my life. I don't know what kind of relationship we can have, but anything is worth trying."

"Anything but being out in the open, you mean."

He looked at her suspiciously. "Are you planning on letting this out?"

"Will I be in danger like Terrell and Sherise if I do?"

Jonah's expression held regret. "I apologize for the way I reacted to Terrell, but he came at me like a threat and he'd already almost blackmailed me. When I'm cornered I fight."

She placed her hands on her hips. "Are you feeling cornered now? Because if not, you're about to be."

"I don't expect you to be happy considering what you've found out and the way you found it out, but you need to think before you act."

"If you want me to keep your little shame a secret—"

"I am not ashamed of you, Erica. I am very proud of what you've become despite what you've—"

"If you want me to keep your secret," she interrupted, "you leave Sherise and Terrell alone. And when I say alone, I mean completely alone. If anything happens to them, not only will I let your secret out, but you will never see me again."

"Erica!" Jonah called after her as she walked away. "Erica!"

He reached her just as she opened the car door. "Wait," he said. "I'm not going to do anything to them. I . . . I was just . . . This has to stay secret. At least until I can manage some things."

Erica laughed. "And here I was thinking you were the man, you were in charge. You're just a puppet to other people who tell you how you can and can't live your life. Kind of sad."

Jonah was clearly hurt by her words, but he held himself together well. "You'll come around. A father-daughter relationship is a special thing. We were both denied it and I think you'd like to see how it goes as much as I do."

Erica didn't have a sharp comeback for that, but she wasn't going to let Jonah get to her. It was true that she had missed out on that special relationship and had wished so many times she had a father. She'd wanted to be someone's little princess. She envied the stories Billie used to tell about her doting, loving father, and seeing a man spending quality time with his little girl always tugged at her heart.

"Just stay away from Sherise and Terrell," she said, unwilling to reveal anything to this man.

For the first time since getting this news, Erica began to cry out loud as she drove back home. She was sobbing and gripping the steering wheel so hard, her hands started to hurt.

Terrell knew Erica was home when he got there because he could smell her perfume, and he loved the smell of her. Not only that, her being back made their house a home. He rushed to the bedroom and was upset when he saw her sitting in the middle of the bed, crying and surrounded by old pictures of her mother. He knew immediately what had happened and he wanted to strangle Sherise.

"Damn her!" He rushed to the bed and put his arm around her. "Sherise is such a bitch. I told her not to tell you. I wanted to tell you."

"But you didn't," she said, pushing his arm away. "How long have you known?"

"I confronted him Friday and he . . ."

"I didn't ask how how long since you talked to Jonah," she said. "How long did you know?"

"I suspected earlier that week because of stuff you said about him, but I swear I didn't really even believe it until I confronted him on Friday."

"You didn't think for one moment to share that with me?"

"I didn't want to rock the boat yet," he said. "You just got back and you were barely talking to me."

He could see the disbelieving look in her eyes. "No, Erica. I was not going to blackmail him to keep quiet about you. I went there to make sure what I thought was true and to warn him not to hurt you. I will fucking kill him if he hurts you."

"Yeah," she said. "You want to be the only man who gets to do that."

"Ouch," he responded. "Look, baby, I was gonna tell you but considering he threatened to frame me and send me to jail or make me disappear, I had to figure out how to do it. I needed to clear my head. That guy is seriously evil."

"You cornered him."

Terrell leaned back, amazed at what he was hearing. "Are you backing him? It sounds like . . . Wait, did you talk to him?"

"Yes," she said. "That's where I've been."

"Jesus!" Terrell got up from the bed and started pacing around. "Why did you do that?"

"Let me guess," she said, looking up at him. "I should have told you first? Funny how that works."

"What happened?" he asked. "Did he threaten you if you told anyone?"

"I took care of it," she said. "You and Sherise don't have to worry about anything."

"So, what are you gonna do about him?"

Erica shrugged. "I'll figure that out tomorrow."

"We'll work it out." He sat back on the bed, next to her. "We'll work it out together."

Erica reached across the bed and grabbed her engagement ring off the nightstand. She handed it to Terrell. "Take this," she said.

Terrell didn't move. "No way. We can work this out, baby. I love you and I know you love me."

"I do love you," she said. "But I don't trust you and there is no way we're getting married with our relationship in the state it is. Take it."

Terrell still wouldn't take the ring, so she placed it gently on his lap. "I'm sorry," she said, "but I got too much to deal with."

"But, baby." Terrell couldn't believe she was going to turn him away. She needed him now more than ever. "I'm sorry. I was just trying to look out for you. I can't lose you, Erica."

"Please!" She looked at him showing all the pain she was feeling. He had to see and understand. "I'm not leaving you but, Terrell, if you care about me then you need to accept that the marriage is off the table right now."

"For how long?"

Terrell wasn't a fool. Erica had been wanting to get married for a long time, so for her to give him back this ring meant that there was a big problem between them. And he was scared to death it was a problem he couldn't fix.

"I don't know," was all Erica said in response before getting up and heading to the bathroom.

She shut the door behind her and went to the sink to blast her face with some cold water. When she lifted her head, she looked in the mirror. She loved Terrell, but she didn't need him right now. The pain of a missing father and Jonah's words of promise were haunting her. They reached into the part of her that was a little girl in Southeast DC. Her girls were going to be the only people who could get her through this.

Justin opened the front door to their home just as Sherise was about to insert her key. He could see from the look on her face the day hadn't gone well. He opened his arms to her and she fell into him, hugging him tight.

"I take it you gave your notice." he said as he guided her inside. "How is Walter dealing with it?"

"Certainly wasn't how he expected this Monday morning to go," she said. "Especially considering his last day is this Friday."

"You stood firm, right?" He took her purse and placed it on the sofa as they continued toward the dining room.

She nodded. "I gave the whole family emergency excuse and all, but he made me promise to stay for a month."

"Is that okay?"

"I can handle it."

For Sherise, the best part of it all was that since she would only be there for a month, the project for Jonah would be put on hold and picked up when Walter's and her replacements were found. She would spend her last month just helping find those replacements. And after learning late last night that Erica had given Jonah her warning, Sherise felt like she could finally breathe.

"Where's my little munchkin?" she asked, looking around for Cady.

"She's at the babysitter's," Justin said. "This is for you and me."

The second Sherise entered the dining room she saw the

setup. A romantic dinner for two with candles, silk napkins, and roses was set before her. A large glass of red South African wine and a plate of chilled oysters sat between the place settings.

She turned to him and grabbed his face, kissing him slow and soft. She felt a flutter in her belly and kissed him harder.

"All your favorites," he said as their lips separated. "Anything you want."

"I have everything I want," she said. "Except maybe . . . another baby?"

She saw Justin's eyes light up with joy and she smiled while saying a little prayer in her heart for everything to be all right.

Billie was almost finished making dinner when she got a call on her cell. It was Tara, and that bothered her because Tara was supposed to have been there a half hour ago.

"Where are you, sweetie?" she asked.

"Billie, Billie, Billie." Tara's high-pitched voice had an apologetic edge. "You have to forgive me. Please! Please!"

"What is it?"

"I can't come tonight," she said. "Don't be mad, please?"

"You're telling me now?" she asked. "You were supposed to be here already."

"I know, but Mara Lee called me like an hour ago and told me that Jesse is hanging out at Gallery Place, so I got all excited and forgot about our dinner."

"I'm making your favorites," Billie said.

"I know, but . . . maybe this weekend?"

"Okay," Billie said after a sigh. She was disappointed, but she knew there was no use in arguing the point. Even a nice Italian dinner of Tara's favorites couldn't compete with a cute boy.

"Go have fun, but call me tomorrow so we can make plans. I want to see you."

"I love you, bye!"

Billie strained her pasta before returning to her phone and dialing Sherise's number, but she only got a voice mail. She called Erica and got the same, although she imagined that the last thing Erica wanted tonight was a gabfest over pasta.

"I guess it's just you and me," she said to the pasta, hanging in the strainer.

So this was what it felt like to be free? Felt very lonely to Billie.

Discussion Questions

1. Should Erica have been more understanding and forgiving of Terrell? Does their relationship have a chance?

2. Why do you think Billie still allowed Porter to use her the way he did until the very end?

3. Do you think Billie has gotten rid of Porter for good or will she fall for his games again?

4. Do you think Sherise really loves Justin? If so, how could she fall for Jonah so easily?

5. There seems to be constant tension between Sherise and Erica with Billie playing the peacemaker. What is behind it and is it always Sherise's fault?

6. Billie abandoned her principles toward the end of the book in order to finally get Porter under control. Do you think she can go back to being a "good girl" or has Sherise finally worn off on her for good?

7. Sherise always seems to genuinely regret her marital transgressions. Does she deserve to keep Justin and her family together?

8. Erica has a lot of trust issues. Is she justified in them or should she learn to trust more?

9. Sherise is taking a temporary break from her career ambitions. Will it last? Do you think she could ever be happy as just a wife and mother?

10. Do you think the girls' decision has worked or will Jonah continue to be a problem for all of them?

Turn the page for a peek of Niobia Bryant's sizzling latest,
Mistress No More

Available now wherever books are sold.

PROLOGUE

"HELLO, JESSA BELL"

I *have played the fool, but no more. I swear it this time.*

I made a choice. A scandalous choice. To have my friends or my man: the husband of a friend.

I chose to have my man.

I made a move. A bold move. I sent a message to three friends taunting them all that one of their husbands now belonged to me and only me. Only one truly had reason to worry.

And I made a mistake. An unforgivable mistake. The man I loved—or thought I loved—didn't love me. He didn't need me. He didn't keep his promises. He didn't leave his wife. He didn't come home to me.

And now? And now I have no choice. I lost so much going for the gold only to be left with nothing but the bitter dust of fool's gold in my hands. I risked it all for him. To have him, love him, fuck him on my terms . . . and I lost.

I put my house in Richmond Hills up for sale and leased a home that we were supposed to share. I sent a message that cut all ties with the three women who considered me a friend. My lover and I went from making plans to spend forever together to him telling me we had to slow things down because of my message. Bullshit. If he had stuck to our plan, my message shouldn't have mattered one damn bit.

My celebration and triumph have been replaced by bitter disappointment from his bullshit.

Now I have to make him pay.

I cut my eyes up to the rearview mirror and I could see the fat and flushed face of Lucky, the tubby security guard of the subdivision where I lived along with my three friends and their husbands. I had no doubts that the message I sent yesterday had shaken everyone to the rafters of their stately homes. Not my concern. Not one bit.

I revved the motor of my Jaguar, anxious as hell to get to the home of my lover. It was time for his wife to know the truth. No more guessing. No more games. I was putting his lying ass on blast. I was finally revealing which of the three husbands I had foolishly claimed as my own.

My silver BlackBerry rang inside my purse on the leather passenger seat. Steering with one hand, I dug in my purse and pulled it out. It was him. I pulled my car off the road onto the grass as I looked down at the PDA.

After ending things with a sorry-ass phone call this morning, I had threatened him before giving him the "click." His calls had been nonstop ever since. But was he calling to take back the words that ended things for us or was he just worried that his cover was blown?

I knew if I answered his calls, if I gave him half the chance to sweet-talk me . . .

Taking a deep breath, unable to fight the urge or deny my love, I answered the call and held my BlackBerry to my face. "What?" I snapped, not hiding the anger I still had for him.

I hated that I so badly wanted him to still want me. I couldn't resist him. Deny him. Leave him. I just . . . I just couldn't. Love never fades that quickly. And hope? Hope is eternal.

Yesterday I thought I had everything made. Today? Hmph. What a difference a day makes.

1

One month later

Jaime Hall relished the feel of the cool cotton sheets against her naked skin. She stretched her long limbs before rolling over onto her side to clutch the pillow close to her body. With a soft moan that was filled with anticipation, she pressed her face into the softness and inhaled deeply of the lasting scent of her lover's cologne.

Just the thought of him in her bed and deep inside her walls made her wet as her heart raced.

She wouldn't have ever guessed she would spend her days and her nights lying nude in a bed waiting for a man to come sex her. Never.

All her life she'd played the role of being perfect. The perfect daughter, wife, parishioner, soror, and friend. All roles, as if her life wasn't shit but an ongoing play. None of it really gave her a chance to be herself or even know herself, for that matter.

Until Pleasure.

Jaime squeezed her thighs tightly, putting pressure on her throbbing clit as she craved that man. He was a stripper by night, her lover by day.

The things that man knew how to do were scandalously sinful and she couldn't get enough of him. It felt damn good, for once, to want something and to go for it. To get it. To have it. Damn good.

So good that Jaime could care less that a faux friend had sent a text to her and two other friends boasting about her affair with one of their husbands. Jaime's life did not revolve around figuring out the mystery or deciphering the puzzle of which of the men had betrayed their marriage with Jessa Bell. She'd left her husband and the months of verbal abuse and degrading sex behind. She was sure Aria and Renee gave way more of a fuck than she did about the guilty man. All she wanted that night was her freedom. That message had been just the right damn key to unlock the door to the prison of her marriage.

The old Jaime had spent the day pretending not to care on the outside but filled with fright on the inside that the bullshit in her marriage would be exposed for all to see. The old Jaime cared more about what other people thought, cared, or wanted.

"Not no more," she said aloud, closing her eyes as she tried not to count down the minutes until her lover would walk through the door and into her bed.

The new Jaime was ready to be fucked and fucked well. To hell with her marriage. Jessa. That stupid message. And Eric.

Brrrnnnggg.

Her heart raced as she rolled over to the other side of the bed and scooped up her cell phone. Disappointment flooded her like drowning waves. Flipping the phone open, she rolled her eyes. "What, Eric?" she sighed, sounding as bored as she truly was with his constant attempts at reconciliation. She reached for her monogrammed Louis Vuitton cigarette case and lighter.

"We need to talk, Jaime."

"Talk about what?" she asked, lighting a cigarette. She had given up cigarettes, but the day they'd received that message from Jessa, her fears over a flaw in her marriage being exposed had sent her back to her habit.

"I want my life back. I want my wife back. You know that."
Click.

Her eyes shifted at the sound of the bedroom door closing and a smile spread across her face as Pleasure took his hand from the closed bedroom door and reached for the hem of his T-shirt to pull it over his dreadlock-covered head. Tall. Muscled. Skin deeply bronzed caramel. Black tattoos scattered over his frame emphasized just how built to please.

Pleasure.

"I think we need to consider counseling, Jaime. We both have a lot to forgive . . . and forget."

Jaime barely heard her husband's pleas as she watched Pleasure unbuckle his belt and ease his denims and boxers over his narrow hips. She bit her bottom lip as each delicious inch of his long and thick curving dick was exposed to her hungry eyes. She was ad"dick"ted.

"Jaime . . . Jaime, you there?" Eric said into his phone.

As Pleasure walked the short distance to the bed with his dick swinging across his muscled thighs, Jaime licked her lips in anticipation. "Yeah, listen, I'll call you back," she said, her voice a whisper filled with nervous excitement.

She had to admit she got an extra thrill from having her soon-to-be-ex-husband on the phone begging her to reconcile while her new lover was flinging the covers away from her naked body.

"Jaime, Pastor Richardson still wants us to meet with him tomorrow before church."

Jaime shivered as Pleasure roughly pulled her by her ankles to the edge of the bed. "I'm not Catholic. You are. He's your priest. Not mine," she reminded him, spreading her legs wide as Pleasure dropped to his knees and buried his dreadlock-covered head between her thighs to lick the lips of her pussy.

"Aaah," Jaime cried out, arching her back and circling her hips as she pushed her free hands deep between the thin locks to grab the back of his head.

"Jaime, are you all right?" Eric asked.

Her eyes popped open as she pressed her lips closed. She remembered that her cell phone accidentally dialing Eric while Pleasure fucked her on the floor of the back room of the strip club was how her husband discovered her affair. Even though she and Eric were done as far as she was concerned, she snapped the phone closed, not wanting to give him a repeat of hearing another man give his wife the pleasure he *never* did.

Brrrnnnggg.

Jaime ignored the ringing phone, using her hand to push it off the bed to the floor to land with a soft thud. "I missed you," she whispered, her words floating up to the ceiling as Pleasure kissed a hot and moist trail up her thighs to her flat belly and then to the valley of her breasts. Her body shivered with each kiss. Her pussy ached. Her heart raced. A fine sheen of sweat coated her body.

Brrrnnnggg.

"I love your nipples," Pleasure moaned against the sides of her breasts before his tongue circled a brown peak twice.

Jaime cried out hoarsely, her hands coming up his strong back to dig her fingers into his broad shoulders. "Suck 'em," she begged.

Her wish, just like always, was his command.

"You like that?" he asked thickly, cutting his deep-set coal black eyes up at her as he dragged the tip of his tongue around her nipple before sucking it into his mouth.

Brrrnnnggg.

"Yes," she cried out, arching her back and not giving a damn that her expensive, bone-straight, jet black weave would be well sweated out by the end of the night.

Back and forth he went from one hard nipple to the other until she was dizzy and high off his skills. Before Pleasure her husband had been her one and only lover—and even then she'd waited like a good girl for her wedding night—only to discover that they lacked chemistry. Fire. Passion.

She found more of it with Pleasure's dick inside of her for one hour than she had for many years of marriage. It wasn't just that Pleasure had one of those tree trunk kinda dicks while Eric was average. Ever since she first laid eyes on Pleasure at that bachelorette party all those years ago the man made her sizzle just from looking at him.

"What do you want from me, Jaime?" he whispered in the back of his throat, the faint sounds of a wrapper tearing in the background.

Jaime locked eyes with him as she brought her hands up to ball his thin dreads within her fist. "I want you to fuck me," she admitted, spreading her legs wide as he settled his muscled frame atop hers.

"Right now?" he asked, his breath breezing against her mouth before he licked her quivering bottom lip.

"Please."

He smiled and it was filled with his confidence. His sexiness. His boldness.

Pleasure growled a little as he used nothing but his strong hips to ease the tip of his dick inside her. Her pussy lips closed around him. Her juices caused her flesh to smack lightly in the air.

"No massage tonight?" he asked before nibbling the side of her mouth.

"No."

He gave her another delicious inch, her body spreading to accommodate the width of his dick.

"No edible body paint?"

Jaime tugged his dreads, bringing his head down closer to hers. She sucked his mouth. "No," she stressed.

Pleasure offered her his tongue to suck as he slid another inch of dick inside her.

"Just dick?" he asked.

Jaime sucked his tongue deeply with a purr, still amazed

that this man could make her feel so free. So wild. So freaky. "Just. Dick."

"What's my name?"

"Pleasure."

"And what do I give?"

"Pleasure," Jaime sighed in anticipation.

He growled as he pushed the rest of his dick deeply inside of her until the soft and curly hairs of his dick tickled the clean-shaven mound of her pussy.

"Fuck back, Jaime. Shit, give me that pussy, girl."

Just like he'd taught her, Jaime worked her hips, meeting him stroke for stroke until he took over again and worked her body and her walls until she was exhausted and excited all at once.

Pleasure fucked her like there was nothing else in the world he'd rather do. He stroked her pussy with his dick and spoiled her body with his hands and lips and tongue.

Lord, this man was made for sex, she thought, crying out roughly as he made her come again . . . and again . . . and again.

Hmph. He was worth every red cent.

7-12